I0598435

A Family Affair

by

Jennifer Wenn

The Royal Family, Book One

A Family Affair

Cover Art by *Debbie Taylor*

The Wild Rose Press, Inc.
PO Box 708
Adams Basin, NY 14410-0708
Visit us at www.thewildrosepress.com

Publishing History
First English Tea Rose Edition, 2013
Print ISBN 978-1-61217-824-0
Digital ISBN 978-1-61217-825-7

The Royal Family, Book One
Published in the United States of America

"I'm not fond of balls. I find them rather boring. But I have been abroad for a couple of years and thought it would be a perfect way to announce I've returned for good. But most importantly I hoped I would meet up with some old acquaintances."

"I will give you some advice," Fanny said, giving him her most innocent smile. "It is really hard to meet good friends when one is hiding in the shadows of the balcony."

His laughter filled the air, and she could see heads turning their way. Some people were slowly moving closer to them, and she guessed they wouldn't be alone more than a short while longer.

There were just too many eager mamas out there, ready to throw their daughters at his feet, and they wouldn't let something like a quiet chat between two acquaintances stop them.

"Well, I wouldn't really call it hiding. It's more like trying to remember why I thought it was such a good idea to be here in the first place."

"So what do you think now, when you have actually entered the ballroom, although from the wrong entrance. Was it such a bad idea?"

He leaned closer to her, and the warmth of his arm pressed against hers.

"Now I think it was the best idea I ever had."

Dedication

To Stefan for being humble

Prologue

August, 1801

"I would be an excellent wife."

Fanny could tell she had surprised him with her daring boast. Devlin Ross closed his book and stared at her with disbelief.

"Excuse me?"

No time to waste. Not now when she finally had his full attention. When Uncle Rake dashed out the front door alone, she knew his friend would be somewhere by himself. He'd mentioned the book from school, the one he had to read before their summer holiday was over, so she'd started her search in the library.

And luck was with her. She found her hero by himself, lounging in a comfortable armchair surrounded by shelves containing thousands of books.

"I would, you know," she continued, not acknowledging his confusion. "You couldn't do better. Everybody says so."

"They do?" he uttered, baffled, and she nodded, satisfied with his input to the conversation.

"All the time."

She tried to look as innocent as possible as she told the lie, but just like her parents he saw straight through her.

"Are they now?" His golden eyes twinkled as he gave her one of his breathtaking smiles.

"Maybe," she admitted, and giggled when he rolled his eyes, without words telling her he knew she was lying to him again. She thought no one could love him more than she did. With her head to one side, she sighed in awe, pretending not to see his amused grin.

"So, Devlin, will you?"

"Will I what, Pup?"

She sighed again, but this time with some slight irritation. How would she get the answer she wanted from him if he didn't listen to her?

"Marry me?"

"Oh."

Again she had managed to surprise him, and as he seemed quite out of words, she decided he needed a little push.

"I would be an excellent wife," she repeated seriously, with a grave voice. His eyes twinkled again, blinding her with the bright beauty of him.

"I'm sure you would be."

She liked his polite reply and bestowed her most radiant smile upon him before she moved to sit on his lap, forcing him to put away his book. He sat stiffly, unused to having someone in his lap, so she took his hands and put them around her waist.

"That's good," she praised him.

"Thank you," he said courteously, and she bowed her head gracefully in response.

They sat silent for a while, and she closed her eyes and enjoyed his breath as it caressed her hair. She put her arms around his torso, planted her cheek tightly against his shirt, and listened to his heart beating steadily.

"So will you?"

He used mild force to make her sit up straight so he could look into her face.

"Will I what?"

"Marry me?"

"Oh, I don't know, Pup. I haven't really thought about marriage yet. I'm rather young, you know."

"But so am I, and I know what I want."

He gave her the same kind of fatherly smile her brothers gave her when they thought her silly but didn't want to hurt her feelings by telling her so.

"And you want me?" He sounded serious and interested, but she could tell by the way he was pursing his lips that he was trying hard not to laugh.

"Yup." She nodded.

"Are you sure?"

"I know what I want." Her voice was stern this time.

"Okay." He gave in with a tender smile. "I will marry you, Pup."

She clapped her hands and laughed with joy.

"Now you can always stay here," she cried out, and jumped down from his lap to do a twirling dance in front of him, in sheer happiness.

"I can't stay here. I have to finish school, just as your Uncle Rake does."

Her dancing stopped, and she stared at him with tears in her eyes. For a moment she had lived her dream, but after giving her what she wanted, he'd now destroyed everything.

"You must!"

"I'll come back when school is finished. Then we

can marry."

She pondered his words for a minute. Wait for school to finish? What a horrible idea. In her mind, it would be forever.

"How many days must I wait?" she asked, frantically thinking on how to solve this situation.

"Days?" He laughed. "I'm talking years."

"No!" Her foot stomped angrily. "I won't have it."

"But Fanny," he soothed. "I still can't marry you until you're at least eighteen."

"You can't?"

"No. Only adults can marry."

"Oh."

She hadn't known her tender age was a problem. Eighteen sounded like a very long time away. She would talk to Grand-Papa Hannibal about this. He always knew what to do when she came to him with her problems. He could solve this for her.

Devlin gave her another beautiful smile, and again she sighed with awe. So what if she had to wait? She still wanted him.

"Will you wait for me?"

He stood up and made a cross over his chest.

"I promise."

The door opened and Uncle Rake barged in, calling for his friend. Their holiday from school was nearly over. It saddened her that the two young men soon would leave her again.

She would miss Devlin, her pretty husband-to-be, but she would miss her favorite uncle just as much. He had always been special to her, and she knew she was special to him, too.

"Shall we?" Rake asked Devlin, and gave his niece

a smile full of love as he put a hand on her brown hair and fondled one of the curls.

She looked into his loving eyes, eyes the same smoky-gray shade as hers, and patted his hand.

"Devlin has promised me we shall marry when I turn eighteen."

"How nice, Fanny," Rake said, and she caught him rolling his eyes to his friend over her head.

"How many years is it until then?"

"You are five now, so it's thirteen."

"Oh."

Rake and Devlin grinned at her obvious disappointment before they headed out through the door, leaving her standing there alone but filled with joy over what he had promised her.

She would marry her hero.

Chapter 1

April, 1814

"I can't believe you dragged me here."

Lady Francesca Darling hid a smile as her brother Sinclair—Sin, as he was called among friends and family—growled. Their mother had demanded his presence at the annual Easton Ball, and it had been impossible for him to deny her, thanks to certain of his recent indiscretions.

"I know you are well aware of the importance of this ball," Fanny enlightened him mischievously though unnecessarily, as he was the veteran at these parties, not she. But anything she could do to vex him a little was worthwhile. "If you want to be a part of the social life this season, you have to attend, and look your best. Lady Easton might not be our parents' favorite person, but as her ball is the first, it is here where it is decided who is the height of fashion and who is not. And you do want to be fashionable, don't you?" Sin shot her a look of brotherly disdain, and she hid another cheeky grin. She knew exactly how to tease him enough to irritate him, a great pleasure to her during their childhood days. He was such a dear man, and had more patience with her than she sometimes deserved.

"I prefer being unfashionable."

"Really?"

"Yes, really." He snorted. "Being fashionable would mean having to pretend interest in what all the debutante dimwits are saying as they chat away about fashion and horses and, heaven forbid, how perfectly suitable they find me."

"Sounds awful indeed."

He growled at her again but chose wisely enough not to answer her. She would have loved to discuss with him the importance of getting married. It was one of their mother's most adored subjects of conversation, one Fanny knew Sin detested, so she wasn't surprised when he changed the subject.

"What do you think of your first ball so far?"

"Most interesting, I assure you." She made a wave with her hand, almost hitting a poor elderly lady in the face. When the lady's upset feelings were soothed, Fanny continued as if nothing out of the ordinary had happened. "I have never seen so many people in a ballroom before. There must be thousands upon thousands of socialites here tonight, and everyone in their finest garments."

"A couple of hundred, maybe, not thousands." Sin smiled tenderly toward her, and all the surrounding ladies sighed in awe over the handsome Sinclair Darling, the most eligible Earl of Chilton. She would have, too, if he weren't her brother. Instead, she giggled.

"Still, there are people everywhere, and they all look so utterly glamorous. I can't help but wish I could wear something other than this dull debutante dress."

She looked down at her white dress, beautiful but unbecoming for her complexion. She believed its paleness made her even more homely.

If only she had inherited some of her parents' good looks, as her brothers had. In the right light she might be called somewhat pretty; otherwise there was nothing special about her brown hair and gray eyes.

"I think you look lovely," Sinclair assured her with an adoring smile, and she put away the disappointment over her looks. *No point to sulking over something impossible.*

She put her hand on his elegantly dressed arm. "You are the kindest of brothers. I know how much you loathe these assemblies, and yet you stand here by my side at one of the worst."

"Well, I could hardly refuse. This is your debut season, after all. Furthermore, I want to make sure you find someone to marry as soon as possible, so I can have my life back. Meantime, I'll just stand here, bored to my teeth, ignoring all the desperate mothers, and count the hours until I can get out of here."

"What a fate for a confirmed bachelor."

"Indeed." He grinned, and again the surrounding ladies seemed close to fainting.

Several of Sin's acquaintances came up just then, and after the proper introductions Fanny stayed quiet, looking here and there around the ballroom, enjoying all she saw.

It had been an adventure from the start. At the front door of Easton House she and her mother, father, and two older brothers were met by footmen in the Easton livery who relieved them of their coats.

Then, after her mother made sure everything about Fanny's appearance was perfect, the family had followed others into the ballroom. She had been warned about the matrons' good eyesight and how they didn't miss a thing, not even the smallest strand of hair being out of its place. Too many nervous young debutantes had managed to spoil their whole season, she had been told, because of doing something wrong in that first short minute.

More nervous during her entrance than ever in her life before, she nevertheless, according to her mother, succeeded. Officially, she was now accepted as a part of the *ton*. Fanny wasn't sure what she had done rightly, but if her mother said she had done well, so be it. She had learnt the hard way never to disagree with her mother. Caroline Darling was a loving yet unyielding mother to her three children.

"You look disgruntled." Sin interrupted her thoughts, and she woke from her stupor to find they were by themselves again.

"I was thinking about Mama."

"Ah."

She didn't have to say more. Caroline Darling could drive anyone crazy with her loving parenting.

"Looks like Lord and Lady Easton are about to climb down from their thrones," Sin said, as the crowd started to move toward the walls, leaving a space in the middle of the room empty.

"Do they always sit so pompously on a platform when receiving guests?"

Sin nodded. "It's the same procedure every year. Everyone must be announced to them by their butler and walk past them as we did. Father says it's as though they want to be treated like royalty and not merely the hosts of this ball."

"Not very friendly of them," Fanny mused, and Sin chuckled.

"Indeed. They prefer to patronize their guests instead of welcoming them heartily."

Fanny looked at their hosts, now descending from the platform, and she couldn't help but pity them.

"What small lives they must lead."

Sin shrugged indifferently. "Lord Easton is a jolly enough chap. He is mostly quite amusing, although not the cleverest of men."

"So it's the wife?"

"Isn't it always?" Sin grinned again, and once more a choir of sighs was heard around them.

It was starting to get a bit annoying, Fanny thought, as she glared ineffectively at the admirers. Not one of them saw her. They were all too caught up in gawking at her brother.

"Well, look at that."

The awe in Sin's voice was unmistakable, and Fanny gave his admirers one last frowning look before following his gaze.

In the middle of the ballroom, surrounded by dozens of beaus, stood Lady Charmaine de Vere in all her glory. Thick blonde curls tumbled over her shoulders and down her back, shimmering all over with small diamonds. Her lovely blue dress matched her beautiful eyes, and a faint smile curled her pink lips as she let her group of beaus compete over filling her dance card.

"Oh, I do so hate her," Fanny mumbled between her teeth.

"Come on." Sin sent an appreciative glance across the ballroom. "You have to admit, my dear sister, the chit knows how to make an appearance."

"She does not," Fanny snarled, giving her brother a

murderous glare. He merely grinned in reply.

"She does too. You're just jealous."

Fanny gasped. "I'm not!"

Sin chuckled affectionately. "You are so easy to bait, Fanny. Especially regarding your precious archenemy, Charmaine."

"I can't help it," Fanny admitted and a telling blush crept over her soft cheeks. "We have never liked each other, not even when we were children. There is something between us that just don't match."

"Could it be you're simply jealous of her beauty? She is an astounding young woman, after all, and you wouldn't be the first to want to scratch her pretty eyes out."

"Maybe." Fanny giggled. "Especially as I should be grateful for my dowry, considering how homely I am."

Sin arched an amused eyebrow, and Fanny sent him a sunny smile in response.

"Charmaine's words, not mine. I think she meant to be nice."

"It is unfortunate she has such a bad inside beneath the splendor. Her parents have done a very good job of spoiling her rotten, and now they have to live with her wanting everything her way."

Fanny nodded in silent agreement. Charmaine would sell her own mother if she could gain something by it. She had been adored since the day she was born, thanks to her unusual beauty.

Her sister Penelope, only a year younger, wasn't as beautiful, hence tragically ignored by her parents. Charmaine and Penelope were different as night and day, and as much as Fanny loathed the older sister she loved the younger, who was her best friend.

"What I can't understand is why she isn't taken."

Sin ripped his gaze from the delicious Charmaine and looked down at his sister.

"What do you mean?"

"Most debutantes get married, or at least engaged, during their first season, even the ones who don't look as good as Charmaine. So why is she back for a second season, and this time with Penelope in tow?"

"All debutantes don't marry their first season."

Fanny snorted, knowing her brother wasn't the best source when it came to the unwritten rules of the *ton*. All debutantes wanted to land themselves a husband during their first year. It was harder for a young woman to find an interested eligible bachelor the second year and beyond, with new debutantes introduced every year.

This year Penelope had joined her family for her first season, but unfortunately for her, Charmaine was too exquisite for anyone to notice the not-as-beautiful younger de Vere daughter.

Penelope wasn't ugly. In fact, she was prettier than most of the other unmarried young ladies in the *ton*, prettier than most of the married ladies, too. She was simply not as overwhelming as her older sister.

"I think I have an idea of why she remains unmarried, though." Sin caught his sister's attention.

"You do?"

"It's not so hard to figure out. She is of course aiming as high as she possibly can. With no unmarried royalty available, she wants to become a duchess. And the richest and most sought after unmarried duke is Devlin Ross, the new Duke of Hereford."

Fanny couldn't stop the warmth of a blush that crept over her cheeks, and she cursed silently to herself. Why, after all these years, couldn't she hear his name without turning red as a beet?

Sin, bless his heart, didn't notice his sister's change of color; instead he continued to ponder the mystery of the unmarried Charmaine.

"When Devlin returned from France at the end of last year's social season, he quickly became the darling of the *ton*, with all the loving mamas fighting to have him at their little soirées, to introduce their daughters to him. Unfortunately for them, Devlin isn't at all interested in marriage."

"How can you be so sure of his disinterest?" Fanny tried not to sound too interested.

"He told Uncle Rake, who told me. Devlin is a true libertine. He prefers mistresses rather than a wife. He did notice Charmaine, though, as she is rather hard to miss, but anything more than an occasional flirt on the dance floor wasn't in his mind."

"Of course, Charmaine thinks a little too much of herself to have any notion he might not want her for a wife." Fanny giggled, and Sin chuckled along with her.

As if she knew they were talking about her, Charmaine looked their way, and her eyes narrowed to vivid blue almonds. Fanny gave her archenemy a bright smile, which Charmaine answered with a sneer before she turned her back to them.

"Devlin never plays with unmarried ladies," Sin said as an afterthought. "And I have a feeling the poor fellow will be trapped into an engagement before the end of this season, one way or another. We all know Charmaine has no conscience, and I'm afraid she will probably make something up if he doesn't propose to her. Many marriages have started with an innocent meeting on a balcony or in some other lonely place. All she has to do is make sure someone finds them alone, unchaperoned."

"I guess her parents gladly would volunteer," Fanny mused, knowing most families in the *ton* would do even worse things if it meant they could have the Duke of Hereford as a son-in-law.

It would put them on top of all lists, and put any creditors at ease, as the Ross family was one of the richest families in England and could cover any family's debts with pocket money.

Sin's chuckle interrupted his sister's thoughts. "You know, Uncle Rake told me Devlin didn't find her attractive at all, when he met Charmaine for the first time last season. Apparently Devlin thought there was something cold and dead about her."

"Like a fish," Fanny squealed, not able to hide how amusing she found Sin's words. "We can call her Fishy!"

"You should try to be more subtle," Sin said.

His sister ignored him, losing her mirth as she continued, "I feel bad for poor Penelope, though. Her awful parents have decided to spend all the money on Charmaine this year again, so Penelope has to wear her sister's old gowns. One would think they should put their money on Penelope this year, since it's her first season, but no, Charmaine must have all new dresses, because she can't wear her old ones."

"I can't imagine any lady doing something so dreadful as to wear the same dress twice." Sin winked, but his sister didn't take his bait this time. She was too occupied with thinking about her best friend's situation.

"How can you give one child everything and the other child nothing? It's so unfair. Penelope is just as beautiful. And more importantly, she is a wonderfully nice person."

"I really don't know," Sin replied thoughtfully. "There is certainly nothing wrong with Penelope."

Just then Sebastian, the younger of Fanny's two brothers, brought his little sister a refreshing glass of lemonade. He patted her shoulder in a brotherly way, to show affection, and succeeded in jostling her enough to spill some of the drink on the front of her dress.

The look she gave him was nearly as sour as the lemonade.

Almost.

"Don't you worry, my dear," Sebastian announced cheerfully. "When Charmaine gets older, all her sins, selfishness, and evil thoughts will turn her hair gray and her face all wrinkly and spotty."

"Spotty?" Sin said, arching an eyebrow in a very Darling way.

Sebastian gave his older brother a smile worthy of a saint. Not an easy task for him.

"Why, yes!"

"Spotty?" Fanny had a hard time staying angry at her silly brother, even though he'd just ruined her white debutante dress. She could never stay angry with Sebastian; he was such a happy, loveable clown. And now, thanks to him, she wouldn't have to wear this horrid dress again.

"It is common knowledge among those who know things; old age catches everybody, and no one can escape, not even celebrated young ladies. Especially the mean-hearted ones."

"Like Charmaine," Fanny laughed.

"That's right, sweet pea. Especially ogres like Charmaine."

The three siblings smiled wickedly at each other, unaware of their parents' approach until their father's voice cut through their snickering.

"What on earth are you three up to now?"

"Papa." Fanny threw herself into her father's waiting arms, ignoring outraged gasps from bystanders. With her father, Fanny was always a little girl. She loved the way he made her feel secure and cherished.

"Fanny, for goodness' sake," Caroline Sinclair Darling, Marchioness of Newbury, murmured between her teeth, and Fanny reluctantly brought her arms down from around her father's neck. Her father gave her a little peck on her faintly freckled nose before he put his wife's hand in the crook of his arm again.

"Are you enjoying yourself, my dear?" Caroline inquired, and Fanny nodded with a delighted smile.

"I love it," she declared passionately. "It is more than I ever could have imagined. The people are so fashionable, and everyone looks quite elegant. Thank you so much for bringing me to London."

"It's all your grandmother's doing," the marquess told his daughter. "I still can hardly believe your Grand-Papa let you leave Chester Park, especially since he kept ranting about the loss of common sense among the *ton*. My father has a somewhat hostile opinion of the Season."

"If it weren't for Francesca being the first girl to be born in the Berkeley family for centuries and he's unable to say no to her, Hannibal probably would have locked her in one of the towers and thrown away the key."

"True, true," George agreed with his wife. "But he is too proud of her not to let her attend."

They were the best parents imaginable, Fanny thought as she watched them chat away. The love and respect they bestowed on her was endless, lifting her high. They were the solid foundation of her life.

She had not been an easy child, all curiosity and adventurousness and with no common sense at all. But her parents had managed to find a wobbly path for leading her, one that in the end had worked. Their patience and undeniable love for her and for each other had formed her, until she had become the much calmer person she was today. She liked to think she had gained a little common sense, too, even though her brothers kept telling her she hadn't.

"Fanny." Caroline interrupted her thoughts. "Do you want me to go with you and see if we could remove some of that lemonade your brother so nicely poured over your dress?"

"It was an accident…" A glare from his mother silenced Sebastian.

Fanny bit back a smile as her brother gave their mother a sad look worthy of a puppy. But their mother had a heart of stone when it came to her children and puppy-faces. She had seen too many to even consider changing her mind.

"I can go by myself, if it's all right with you. I do need to sit down for a little while, as I am feeling quite warm. As I understand, the dancing is about to begin, and I need to cool down a little first."

"You go ahead, my dear." Caroline patted her

daughter's curly hair, and with a last loving look Fanny went eagerly away.

She tried to walk in a ladylike manner through the ballroom and not skip or run as the hellion her mother accused her of being, but her heart sang with joy. Finally she was here, taking part in the social life her family had attended without her every year during her childhood.

Her grandparents had always made sure she had a wonderful time during those short months of the Season while the rest of the family danced in London, but she had still missed them immensely.

Listening to her family's colorful stories about life among the *ton,* she had been desperate to see it for herself, and now she finally was here.

And even though she didn't want to admit it, not even to herself, she couldn't help feeling a little extra excited over Devlin being in town during her first season. She knew his promise to her thirteen years ago wasn't something he was about to keep, as it had been made to a small child out of kindness.

But still.

He was in town. She was eighteen. Something was bound to happen. And even if it didn't, she was just the person to stir the pot a little.

Chapter 2

She could hardly believe such rotten luck.

When Fanny arrived at the plush ladies' restroom, she had to her relief found it empty. With a deep sigh, she sank down into one of the red chairs and rescued her aching feet from their temporary prisons.

But the chatter of voices approaching disrupted her solitude, and Fanny groaned aloud as she realized she knew one of those voices too well.

Just the thought of having to spend time listening to Charmaine and her evil drivel seemed a fate worse than death to Fanny, and without hesitation she grabbed her shoes and dashed out through the open balcony door. Hidden behind one of the Roman pillars gracing the terrace, she watched as Charmaine floated into the restroom, closely followed by her two worshipers, Lady Victoria Knightley and Miss Emma Archer.

The two friends fussed about Charmaine, helping her with her hair, giving her cool wet towels, and acting more as maids than as best friends.

Fanny cursed as she stood there in the darkness of the terrace. What stroke of bad luck had hit her? The threesome in the restroom showed no need of hurrying with their business. Instead they sat down and sipped the lemonade they'd brought with them.

She didn't know what to do. She was in a really awkward position. Young ladies didn't go out on the terrace alone; it was against all good etiquette. She knew her mother would be vexed if she ever heard of her daughter's outrageous behavior.

But the other scenario was even worse: joining the threesome in the restroom.

To face Charmaine and her worshipers, to be forced to answer their questions about what she had been doing out on the terrace, of all places, wasn't the best idea. Fanny knew the threesome wouldn't rest until they had dragged the truth out of her, and although she knew she hadn't done anything wrong, it would be too easy for Charmaine to sow a little seed of doubt about Fanny's actions in any conversation thereafter.

In the end, her choice wasn't too difficult. She decided to stay put behind the pillar, trying not to breathe too loudly.

There were others strolling slowly on the terrace, and some even went down into the darkness of the lawn. But they were all outside the ballroom, where lights were lit. No one seemed to notice her standing in the shadows farther along, and she could only hope she would be safe.

At first, being occupied with her thoughts, she didn't listen to the conversation inside the restroom. It wasn't until she heard her own name mentioned that her interest was caught.

"Lady Francesca's dress was so beautiful," Emma said with honest awe in her voice. "I never would have come up with such a lovely idea as putting lilies in my hair as she did, but it was surprisingly fetching."

Victoria agreed. "It was pretty, indeed. I wonder if I should go to our orangery and steal some of Mama's prize-winning roses. I think they would look really good against my complexion."

Emma started to agree with Victoria but was rudely interrupted by Charmaine.

"I found it vulgar," she snapped, and Fanny had to bite her lip hard so she wouldn't propel herself onto the minx and rearrange her.

Unaware of the indignant audience on the balcony, Charmaine continued, "Fanny should think about how easily she looks cheap before she goes out and ransacks her family's greenhouse. One would think a family known for their vast fortune would be able to spend quite a large sum to make sure she looks as good as possible. It all makes one wonder why they don't. They are practically forcing poor Fanny to go clad in greenery. In my opinion, they probably think of her as a lost cause."

Emma and Victoria glanced insecurely at each other, but obviously neither had the spine to contradict the envious words. They had both found her outfit fresh and stylish, apparently, yet neither dared to contradict Charmaine.

"Vulgar, indeed," Victoria echoed lamely, in an effort to break the uncomfortable silence.

"Money can't buy beauty, and Lady Francesca Darling is a perfect example of that adage."

And yet I've gotten plenty of suitors on my dance card this evening, Fanny wanted to holler, but she managed to stay quiet. The mendacious minx! she thought, full of resentment over Charmaine's harsh words.

So what if she wasn't a beauty of the first or even the second water? It didn't mean she wasn't attractive at all. She knew she was somewhat pleasing to look upon, even pretty, in the right light.

She would never stun a man with her beauty alone, but she wouldn't want a husband who was that shallow anyway. She much preferred a man who wanted her for her wit and her heart than for her beauty or her dowry.

Charmaine must have shared the same thought. "It must be so hard for her, being the richest heiress of all time and still outdone by the sheer beauty of others."

The two worshippers looked like two parrots, as they bobbed their heads in agreement.

"I even saw freckles on the bridge of her nose." Victoria shared her piece of horrid gossip with malicious pleasure.

"Oh, my," Emma breathed with horror. "How awful for her poor mama."

"I heard Fanny galloped down Rotten Row the other day, in competition with her brothers, and she actually won!"

Emma nodded. She too was aware of Fanny's outrageous behavior. "Mama almost fainted when she heard about it. She immediately made me promise I would never do something so unladylike as competing with horses."

Charmaine, who never could hold a grudge against anyone who told her exactly what she wanted to hear, shook her head.

"It is common knowledge how unhealthy it is for a lady to ride a horse," she pontificated. "Everyone knows a well-bred lady travels only by carriage, not on horseback, and certainly not without an umbrella protecting her from the sun."

Fanny, outside on the terrace, was outraged; she could hardly believe her ears. Was this how the talk went regarding her?

What was wrong with riding horses, or having freckles, for goodness' sake? She happened to like her freckles, and so did her mother. Again, she couldn't help but feel sorry for these small-minded people who lived only for what others would say about them.

But mostly she pitied Charmaine. *What a sad life she must lead, when she can't find satisfaction in her own good looks without slandering others.*

Fanny had never been envious of Charmaine. She couldn't stand her, but that was because of the way Charmaine treated everyone, especially her younger sister. She really couldn't see anything beautiful about Charmaine; all she saw was the ugliness beneath the shiny exterior.

"Did you see Hereford, by any chance?" Charmaine asked her worshipers. Her voice sounded a little too carefully uncaring.

"Why, now you mention it, I didn't." Victoria clapped her hands excitedly. "Where on earth could he be? He should be here, making sure everyone knows you are taken."

Emma giggled happily. "Oh, it's so exciting; I can't believe you are being courted by *the* bachelor. It's like a fairytale come true. The most beautiful maiden meets the most handsome knight."

"I have to agree with you; we would be a match made in heaven," Charmaine admitted. "But then, I am born to be society's leading lady, and so it's not a surprise he wants to court me."

"I do hope you have saved a couple of dances for him?"

"Of course not." Charmaine laughed as if Victoria

had said something highly amusing. "As long as I don't have his ring on my finger, I am not holding a dance for him." She stood up and walked over to the large mirror beside the door and looked at her image with a satisfied smile. She gently tugged at the edge of her décolletage, forcing her dress down to reveal more of her breasts.

"You do remember I told you not to talk loudly about the courtship?" She frowned as she faced her friends again.

"Oh, yes," both worshipers promised.

"Although I can't understand why not." Victoria pouted. "In my mind, he is an ignorant man if he wants to keep this a secret. You are too beautiful for any man to wait to claim for his own."

"I know," Charmaine agreed. "But there is no logic when it comes to men, believe me."

Without another word, she turned and left the restroom, shadowed by her two friends.

As the door closed behind the three young ladies, Fanny gave a sigh of relief. At last she could re-enter the restroom without being caught in an inappropriate situation.

But just as she left the safety of the pillar, the restroom door opened again, and a new gaggle of ladies came in.

Among them was the hostess. Fanny sighed. Lady Easton was, according to her mother, the worst gossip of the *ton*, other than Fanny's own Aunt Diana. Being found on the balcony by her ladyship would undoubtedly give Fanny's loving parents a great deal of grief. As for Fanny herself, she could kiss a good marriage goodbye.

Not that Fanny actually had done anything. What

mattered in the eyes of Lady Easton and her entourage was what she *could* have done while beyond the window, something like meeting some young man alone in the darkness.

The ladies showed no signs of hurrying; instead, they sat down, chatting, while their maids straightened their appearances.

Fanny groaned, knowing she was running out of time. Soon her mother would wonder where she was and come in search. Caroline would be most distressed if she didn't find Fanny where she was supposed to be, and a distressed Caroline was not what Fanny needed.

There was no way she could stay out on the balcony waiting for the ladies to return to the ballroom. But being found out here by Lady Easton and the other hyenas was not an option, so Fanny looked at the terrace doors farther down the building, the ones that led into the ballroom.

They were not too far away—thirty paces, maybe forty. If she was really quick, she would be inside the ballroom in a minute.

But she would have to pass the darkest section of the balcony, and it made her hesitate. Young ladies of the *ton* and secluded darkness were not a good match.

But then, neither were young ladies and balconies.

She put her shoes back on her aching feet and took a deep and uneven breath before she quietly walked toward the other set of doors.

Music strayed from the ballroom, and the soft tones whirled out into the dark garden, filling it with its seductive message. She could hear voices coming from the darker parts of the garden: men mumbling, women laughing softly.

When she reached the terrace doors leading to the ballroom, she realized she hadn't been breathing at all during her short, brisk walk. That wasn't surprising; she was such a baby when it came to darkness.

Some deep breaths helped to regain her tranquility and made her heart beat slower.

It was the deep breathing that prevented her from a scream when a hand suddenly emerged from the darkest shadows and grabbed hold of her arm. She was pulled sharply away from the doorway and into the darkness of the balcony, her body slamming against something hard and lean.

Her knees went weak, and if the hand hadn't still been holding her arm in a firm grip she would have crumpled to the floor.

"Be quiet," a manly voice whispered, when the air went out of her with a rather loud "ouf."

His words sliced through her dazed mind, and as soon as she regained some of her wit, she tried to pull her arm loose from his hand.

She was on the point of calling for help when a couple emerged from the shadows of the garden—and she promptly closed her mouth again.

The lady was straightening her dress as she walked briskly toward the doors. She looked ready to kill, and it wasn't hard to figure out it was the young man trying to catch up with her who was the target of her anger.

Fanny recognized him as one of her most attentive fortune hunters, Nicholas Pembroke. Maybe he wasn't as attentive as she'd first thought.

As Nicholas disappeared into the ballroom after the woman, Fanny wrenched herself loose from the hands holding her bare arms and turned angrily to face her attacker—and froze.

Her eyes, now adjusted to the darkness of the shadows, had no problem recognizing the man leaning against the cold stone wall, even though she hadn't seen him for many years.

Devlin Ross.

Chapter 3

"You scared me half to death, Your Grace!" She hissed with more anger than she felt, in an attempt to cover up the way her heart skipped a beat.

She could sense the tension going through him and could have slapped herself for so lightly giving up how aware she was of his identity while he, as she could tell from his probing gaze, didn't recognize her at all.

She couldn't help staring at him. He had been such a beautiful boy, perfect in every way. Like one of the Roman statues Grand-Papa Hannibal had placed in Chester Park's garden.

Now, thirteen years later, he was even more beautiful. He oozed manliness, his tall, broad frame suggesting a muscular body hidden in the dark evening clothes. His black hair, combed in a windblown style, was the height of fashion.

His eyes were just the same, light brown, almost golden yellow, as they had been all those years ago. But all the warmth and laughter were gone, all emotions well hidden behind a cold, bored mask.

Or perhaps all emotions weren't gone, as he was actually frowning at her. She knew she should be very upset that he did not remember her, but she had been merely five years old the last time they met, so if he had forgotten her it wasn't so surprising, after all.

"I'm sorry I scared you," he murmured in a low,

smooth tone that sent tremors through her body.

Lord, she had no idea a voice could be so affective. Her whole body was fluttering, and she had to brace herself so she wouldn't lean toward him, begging him to hold her, kiss her, thrill her…

"I didn't think you wanted to be found alone on the balcony, so I did what first came to me," he continued, obviously satisfied with the way she responded to him.

The usual way women responded to him.

It was a pitiful thought, and she realized her reactions were just as pitiful.

"How kind of you, Your Grace. I thank you," she said with all the serenity she could muster, and he gave her a smile that made her toes curl.

He was so beautiful her eyes hurt, looking upon him. His golden eyes burned her like fire and made her all warm, especially in her stomach. It was a strange feeling, something she'd never felt before.

When he made a small movement toward her, her heart flipped, and she felt like she had to drag herself out of a ditch full of quicksand before she could regain her ability to think.

Again.

She made a small curtsy, the sort one gave an elderly person out of respect, before she turned to leave.

He moved impressively fast. One moment he stood leaning against the wall, watching her leave, and the next she bumped into his chest.

Again.

"H-h-how…" she stuttered, losing all her ability to think.

Again.

It was quite frustrating that he had the gift of

turning her into some blubbering idiot, too awed by him to know how to behave. She wasn't used to feeling like this. Usually it was the men, too impressed by her dowry to remember how to woo a woman when they met her; it was never she who didn't know what to say or what to do.

"Maybe," he said, sounding slightly irritated, "I should make sure you are safely returned to your parents."

She was impressed; he actually sounded sincere.

And he *was* irritated with her.

Somehow it felt better knowing she wasn't the only one who was affected.

Having him escort her to her parents' side could not be an option, though. She didn't want to appear in the balcony doorway at his arm. What a scandal that would cause.

Even so, it would certainly put Charmaine's nose out of joint. Fanny lingered at the fantasy for a moment, enjoying the vision of Charmaine in the throes of jealousy.

It would have been delicious to know everyone was talking about Fanny and Devlin and discussing their behavior. *Is there anything between them? Will there be a wedding?*

Poor Charmaine. If she was secretly being courted by Devlin, she would suffer. *O joyous thought.*

"How kind of you, Your Grace. I thank you," Fanny repeated, silently cursing at being unable to think of something astoundingly intelligent and charming to say to him. It would have been so nice to overwhelm him with her wit, but she knew she would never pull it off; he affected her too much; she became a scatterbrained fool.

She swallowed twice and continued, "I can manage by myself, thank you. I can see where my companions are, and I don't think it is such a good idea for you and me to walk through those doors together. Too much talk about nothing, you know."

And, after another insulting curtsy, she put her chin in the air and left him standing there, his mouth wide open.

It was annoying that he should be as beautiful while looking totally dumfounded as he was otherwise.

The warmth of the crowded ballroom hit her, and it was only the thought of otherwise having to face Devlin that made her continue inside. She saw her parents at the other end of the ballroom, talking to some friends of theirs, and love filled her heart as she watched her handsome father give her beautiful mother a smile full of happiness and contentment. It wasn't common for married couples of the *ton* to love each other. Most of the society marriages were more business affairs, arranged to join two noble families or for financial gain.

But her parents were exceptional. George had promised Fanny he would never force her to marry if she didn't find someone she liked. If she wanted to die an old spinster, her parents wouldn't argue with her. They wanted what was best for her, and a loveless marriage was not an option. A rather comforting thought to a mere eighteen-year-old nowhere near the spinster shelf.

As she stood smiling lovingly toward her parents, she suddenly realized the entire ballroom had turned quiet; even the music seemed lower. The dancing couples closest to her stood motionless, staring at her.

The smile slowly faded from her face as she felt a touch at her elbow. She glanced down, and the large manly hand holding her left arm lightly was no surprise.

She groaned, realizing who held onto her, and heard his chuckle in response. His grip became firmer when she tried to yank her arm loose, and she knew she was caught; she was too well-mannered to make her effort obvious.

With a sigh, she turned her head slightly and met his amused golden eyes. He bent his head closer to hers and his breath warmed her skin.

"As I said, I would be delighted to take you back to your parents." His smile broadened at her scowl.

"Thank you, Your Grace, but there is truly no need for you to accompany me."

"Truly?"

Fanny caught herself from rolling her eyes in frustration. "Yes, Your Grace, truly."

"Why not?"

"Why not!"

She hadn't meant to shout, but she was more than a little annoyed. He thought it was hilarious, of course, and laughed loudly. All the ladies in the crowd looked ready to faint, and Fanny probably would have been, too, if she had been less aggravated, as the joy in his face made him look so glorious, so radiant, so utterly magnificent...

"Why, look who the cat dragged in."

The intruder bowed his head in an elegant greeting, and Fanny sighed with relief.

The orchestra started to play more loudly again, forcing the crowd to resume the dance, and Fanny ripped her arm loose to take a step closer to the stylish man before her. Not as perfectly beautiful as Devlin, more of a big and brawny savage, yet he was somehow so elegantly graceful.

"Rake." Devlin smiled toward his friend with pleasure. "How nice to see you. I didn't know you were in town, or else I would have called upon you."

"Well, I normally don't attend the early season. All the mamas, you know. But this little one wanted me to come, and who am I to tell her no."

Devlin looked from Rake to Fanny and back again, and she could easily read his mind as all the laughter left his face and he became cold and rigid. Well, she thought, it probably was an easy mistake when you were a libertine and had no close female relatives to keep you informed.

It vexed her a little that he so easily managed to think of her as a potential mistress, but mostly she found it hilarious, and she couldn't help but tease him a little.

She took another step toward Rake and laid a hand on his arm while batting her eyelashes at him.

"You are so good to me," she said with a husky voice, and one of Rake's eyebrows edged up.

"I am?" he answered, a bit uncertain of what she was up to. That she would play at being his mistress didn't occur to him, as in his world Fanny was a little innocent girl who didn't know anything about things like adultery and kept ladies.

All her uncles thought the same, and her mother had had a hell of a time getting them to allow her departure for London and her debutante season; she was much too young, they said. Like her father, they all thought of her as eight, not eighteen.

Jennifer Wenn

Thank God her Grand-Papa Hannibal had put his foot down and sent her along with her mother, or else she would probably have been at least thirty before they thought her ready for London.

So they all had followed her to London, to keep an eye on her, everyone but Grand-Papa Hannibal and her Uncle Charles, who preferred to spend his time in his church.

Her mother had rolled her eyes so many times her father had told her to stop before she had to live with endlessly rolling eyes.

But Devlin knew what she meant, and she could see how he withdrew. All the warmth that moments earlier had washed over her when he teased her was suddenly nowhere to be seen, and she knew if she didn't tell him the truth now she would never have a chance to come near the real Devlin again.

But the question was, did she want to know him?

Her mind said no, he was everything she didn't want in a husband—too beautiful and too adored, a true libertine from top to toe.

But something in her heart said yes. Maybe it was the little girl who finally had him close again.

Fanny didn't know, and she didn't care.

It was Devlin Ross and, courting Charmaine or not, he made her whole body react, and she wanted to know what it meant. So she hit Rake loosely on the chest, and said loud enough for Devlin to hear, "Uncle Rake, here I am trying to play the part of your latest love, and you so ungracefully spoil it."

She thrust her lower lip out and made a face like a sulking little child, and Rake laughed.

"And you wonder why I didn't understand what

34

you were up to?" He turned to Devlin, who stood staring at Fanny, bewilderment written across his face. "Can you believe the chit? I mean, who would think she could be anything else but a debutante?"

As Rake laughed at his own joke, Fanny could see a small smile return as enlightenment washed through Devlin.

"Pup?" he asked, using the nickname he'd once given her.

"No." She frowned at him. "It's Fanny—or Francesca, if you prefer."

Rake laughed and whacked Devlin in the back with a blow that would have knocked a smaller man off his feet.

"I had forgotten you called her that!"

Fanny rolled her eyes at her uncle, and he laughed even harder.

"Well," he continued, "You were behaving like a puppy, always following poor Devlin around. And there we were, young and eager for a first roll in the hay, but you destroyed all our plans. We had our minds set for Sally Brown, the waitress at the pub, you know, who was known for taking on young men and introducing them into the adult way of life—for a small sum of money, of course."

Devlin laughed, clearly remembering what Rake was talking about, and it itched in Fanny's hand to hit him, just a little, to stun him and take the smug smile off his face.

But before she could decide if it would be worth it, her parents joined them and the moment was gone.

"Devlin, my boy!" George eagerly greeted the younger man, and Fanny bit back a smile as she noticed

Devlin's grimace as he silently endured another of the infamous Darling whacks. "I heard you were back in town and was hoping I would run into you sooner or later."

"Lord Newbury."

Devlin bowed his head politely, showing the Earl much more respect than as a duke he had to before he sent Caroline an appreciative glance. "My lady, you look just as lovely as I remember."

"Thank you, Your Grace," Caroline purred, not hiding how much she enjoyed the younger man's open admiration. "Even though I know you are just being kind to an old woman such as I."

"Oh, do stop begging for more, Caroline," Rake chuckled and was awarded a sour look from his sister-in-law.

"I do *not* beg."

"Oh, yes, you do. And not very subtly at all."

Caroline turned to her husband and gave him a pointed look, ordering him without words to reprimand his younger brother, but George was too busy laughing to care about his wife's silent suggestion.

"As you can see, things haven't changed that much over the years," Rake drawled to his friend, ignoring his misbehaving relatives. "Aside from a wrinkle or two, they all are much the same as they were fifteen years ago."

"Fifteen years," George sighed. "Has it been that long? And here it feels like it was yesterday you two rascals kept making our lives miserable."

"Rascals?" Rake grinned mischievously, and Fanny had no problem imagining just how much misery he and his friend had created. She loved her uncle dearly but was not blind to his not-so-good side. As a grown man he could be a nuisance and had probably been hell to live with as a child.

Just as Lady Newbury opened her mouth, stern determination written all over her beautiful face, the music stopped and a new dance began.

Quickly, before the storm was unleashed, Devlin politely asked if he could take Fanny out on the dance floor, and her parents immediately agreed. Before she could say no, he grabbed her hand and nearly dragged her away from her relatives.

Fanny's heart raced, watching his tall frame in front of her as he led her through the staring crowd. It felt strangely absurd, him being there, and yet so familiar.

This was her childhood hero, the man of her dreams. She had more than once dreamt of him returning to her, and now he was here, and she had not a clue how to handle him. Or herself.

She'd never had a dream come true before.

Chapter 4

"You haven't changed much."

Fanny snorted but kept quiet. Let him try to have a conversation with her. She wouldn't answer him with more than insignificant smiles. She would make him understand she didn't care at all if she never saw him again.

A small part of her knew that was a lie. Well, most parts of her did, but what else could a lady do when interested in a man who was—or was not—courting your archenemy?

The dance parted them briefly, but she could feel his eyes never leaving her.

She knew she dazzled him.

Not with her beauty or wit but by being who she was. He'd had a difficult time keeping up an appearance of indifference with Rake and now, it seemed, an even harder time of it with her. He obviously remembered her all too well. What was it that kept his interest in her? Was it how the child of his memory suddenly had turned into a fully grown woman? That the woman was yet somehow still the little girl who had proposed to him?

The story of my life, she thought as she twirled, men who see me as a little girl.

"I thought you were the most adorable thing I had ever seen," he said as they met again, startling the dancers close enough to overhear. "With all your curly hair, which seemed to have a life of its own, you made me think of you as a little fairy. It was only the dirty dresses you wore that gave you in and told me you were a mere human."

"How nice," Fanny said in her most timid voice, making him laugh at her.

"And you are just as adorable still," he said smiling, and her silly heart fluttered.

"It must be the curls in my hair. You should really give my maid a compliment."

The dance separated them again, but she could see his shoulders shake with laughter. She had a hard time holding on to her own indifference. The truth was she had wished for this day since she was five years old, and now when she finally had her moment, she was throwing it away.

Why pretend to give him the cold shoulder, when he apparently saw right through her? She had to admit she wasn't the best of actresses, and she was a terrible liar. She had long ago realized she was better off sticking to the truth.

The dance took her closer to Devlin again, and this time she met him with a genuine smile.

"I'm not five years old anymore," she said as their hands met.

"I can see that," he said letting his eyes dart downwards for a small second, showing her the meaning of his words.

She laughed, as she was too used to her libertine uncles' constant ranting to be insulted.

As the dance ended, he beckoned toward one of the lemonade tables with a question in his eyes, and she nodded and let him lead her through the dancers.

This part of the ballroom wasn't as crowded as the rest, and Devlin led her to a sofa partially hidden behind a large plant. As they passed a table of refreshments, he took two glasses of lemonade in one hand, keeping the other on the small of her back.

She sat down and thanked him sweetly when he offered her one of the glasses. They sat silently for a while, sipping their lemonade and watching the dancers.

It was a contented silence, the kind you shared with a good friend, someone you were comfortable with.

"I didn't recognize you at first," he said breaking the silence.

"I know."

"I know you knew," he said with a smile, and she laughed at the silliness of their conversation. It was a familiar bantering, one she had had too many times with her brothers, and it made her feel at ease with him.

"Are you always attending the Easton Ball, Your Grace?" Fanny asked.

"Don't call me Your Grace. You know my name."

Fanny blushed and nodded.

"Are you, Devlin?"

He had a strangely distant look on his glorious face as he watched her, and she had to say her question again to make him hear her.

"Am I what?" he asked, apparently not at all listening to her.

"Attending this ball every year?"

"No, heaven help me if I ever will again." He made a terrified face, and she giggled. "I'm not fond of balls. I find them rather boring. But I have been abroad for a couple of years and thought it would be a perfect way to announce I've returned for good. But most importantly I hoped I would meet up with some old acquaintances."

"I will give you some advice," Fanny said, giving him her most innocent smile. "It is really hard to meet good friends when one is hiding in the shadows of the balcony."

His laughter filled the air, and she could see heads turning their way. Some people were slowly moving closer to them, and she guessed they wouldn't be alone more than a short while longer.

There were just too many eager mamas out there, ready to throw their daughters at his feet, and they wouldn't let something like a quiet chat between two acquaintances stop them.

"Well, I wouldn't really call it hiding. It's more like trying to remember why I thought it was such a good idea to be here in the first place."

"So what do you think now, when you have actually entered the ballroom, although from the wrong entrance. Was it such a bad idea?"

He leaned closer to her, and the warmth of his arm pressed against hers.

"Now I think it was the best idea I ever had."

He had completely misunderstood her question, as she was only thinking of him meeting Rake, but his eyes mesmerized her, and she forgot everything they were talking about. The only thing left was him and his smoldering gaze.

She had never been so aware of a man's body, his eyes, and his breath. All she wanted to do was to lean closer to him, to fall into his arms, and then kiss him until they both were too dizzy to think.

A cough interrupted the intimacy, and Devlin moved back, looking up at the person who wanted to catch their attention.

Nicholas Pembroke stood there, his back straight, obviously very nervous and not at all comfortable with having to interrupt them. He bowed his head toward Devlin and murmured, "Your Grace," before his attention went to Fanny, and he gave her a warm smile.

"Mr. Pembroke," Fanny said, acknowledging him.

He held out his hand toward her, and she looked at it a little confused.

"I believe this is my dance," he said, and she could sense he was starting to get a little unsure.

Fanny cursed silently, as she had all but forgotten she had promised him a dance earlier. She couldn't back out of it now. She gave Devlin an apologetic smile before she rose and let Nicholas lead her onto the dance floor, where they merged with the other dancers.

In seconds Devlin was surrounded by his peers, greeting him. The last thing Fanny saw before he went out of sight was Charmaine hanging on his arm, offering him a peek at her generous décolletage.

"You are looking as enchanting as ever," Nicholas told her, and gave her his warm and genuine smile. His compliment was for real, not something he said to impress her.

"You are so kind." She smiled back. "But I do feel very pretty today, as this is my first opportunity ever to wear a ball gown."

"Are you enjoying your first ball?"

"Oh, yes, indeed," she replied cheerfully. "It's more heavenly than I ever could have imagined, and you should know my imagination is ever so colorful."

The dance routine separated them, and Fanny sent Nicholas a friendly smile as he moved away. Unfortunately, he misunderstood the meaning of the smile and couldn't hide his satisfaction.

She closed her eyes, and cursed under her breath.

It was hazardous to walk the thin line between marriage and friendship, and she was bound to fail now and then. It made her a little sad that it was Nicholas with whom she had failed this time, as she really liked him and didn't want to lose his friendship.

Nicholas Pembroke, a younger son to a resource-less viscount, had no other option than to marry an heiress. And to Fanny's frustration, he had set his cap for her.

She liked him a lot, as he was too genuinely good for her not to. But she could never marry him. Her parents wouldn't stop her if marrying him was her wish, but she knew she would never love him the way he should be loved and cared for. To love him as a brother was all she could offer him. There was no excitement in their friendship.

She knew he would come around and ask for her hand in the near future, and she dreaded the moment, because she didn't want to hurt him. He was her friend, and she had no desire to deliberately puncture his hopefulness, but she had no wish to marry him.

Ah, but she knew someone who seemed very eager to become this man's wife, and she couldn't stop herself from probing a little.

"Earlier, when I was outside taking some air, I noticed you and Miss March taking a walk in the garden."

She felt the muscles in his arm twist under her fingers, and she knew she had hit a chord. When he didn't answer, she continued lightly, as if she wasn't really interested in the subject.

"I have always liked Jane. She is one of the kindest persons of my acquaintance, and you know how hard it is to find someone among the *ton* who is interested in someone other than themselves."

Nicholas laughed politely at her joke, but she could tell he didn't find it funny at all, as he did it through his teeth.

"I didn't know you and Jane were acquaintances." Fanny tried to sound indifferent, but this time it was Nicholas who gave her a probing look. She hadn't succeeded.

"We grew up in the same parish but haven't met for a couple of years, as she has been living with relatives," Nicholas said before he moved away from her gracefully, following the steps of the dance.

She had to wait until they were reunited to continue with her probing. She could feel there was a story here, and if it was love, no one could be happier for the couple than she.

Unfortunately, Nicholas too had questions, and as they were brought together again he changed the subject before she had a chance to open her mouth.

"I didn't know you knew Hereford."

This time it was he who tried to sound indifferent, but she could easily tell the importance of the question to him, and she had no doubts about why. Nicholas must have observed the attraction between her and Devlin, and he wanted to know more about this possible competitor for her hand.

"He's a close friend of my Uncle Rake's."

"Oh," Nicholas breathed, obviously pleased with Devlin having another reason for knowing her than being a suitor. "Have you known him for long?"

"I've only met him once before, when I was a small child, so I can't say I have."

"Oh." This time Nicholas sounded less pleased, and she could tell he wanted to ask her more questions about her assumed relationship with Devlin, but etiquette stopped him.

They continued dancing silently, and when the dance was over, he led her in the opposite direction from where Devlin held court. She couldn't stop a smile, as his action amused her.

As she settled on another sofa, the orchestra announced its last dance. It was only minutes until this year's Easton Ball would be over. She could see her parents making their way slowly toward the entrance, and Caroline gave Fanny her you-better-meet-us-at-the-door look.

Fanny nodded in reply and stood again. Nicholas too had seen Caroline's beckoning and was already on his feet, ready to take her to her parents.

Fanny guessed he was ready to do anything he could in his pursuit of becoming her husband, even fawn over her parents. His eagerness was honest, but she couldn't forget seeing him come from the dark with Jane March.

It had been another Nicholas, an angrier and more dangerous-looking man than the polite and well-behaved man she knew. The other Nicholas reminded her more of Devlin, and maybe this was the reason she found him more attractive and interesting than before.

She looked around and found Jane March sitting in a corner, trying very hard not to look their way. When Fanny met Jane's gaze, the other girl blushed and seemed very interested in a plant that stood beside her chair.

Nicholas was certainly not looking at Jane, but somehow Fanny had a feeling he was very much aware of the other girl. There was a story here, and she was almost curious enough to ask him for it.

However, she knew he wouldn't tell her anything, since she was, in his mind, his wife-to-be and not someone with whom he should discuss secret meetings in the dark with other ladies.

When they came to the doorway leading to the hall, Devlin emerged, making all thoughts of the other couple vanish like butter in the sun.

Lord, he is magnificent.

He gave her a grin that made her knees wobble. It was amazing, this power he had over her; just a grin made her want to hurl herself into his—hopefully— waiting arms.

It's not fair for a man to be this gorgeous. He was just too splendid looking. His dark evening clothes made him look so elegant and aristocratic, and it wasn't hard to see he was a man with power, someone who was used to having things his way.

But underneath the glossy outside, danger lurked, just waiting for the right moment to attack. In her eyes it made him even more attractive.

He was a prize for any woman, and if the gossip was true, he'd had affairs with more women than one could count on two hands.

She wasn't stupid; she knew there was more between a man and a woman than an overprotected virgin ever could imagine in her most colorful fantasies, but she had a distinct feeling she really didn't want a husband who was known to too many women. She couldn't help but dislike the notion of him having kissed a large number of the women in this very ballroom. It made her feel jealous and unsure, two emotions she usually never experienced.

Her brothers had both been verbally introduced to this special part of adult life by her uncles, so she guessed it was only young unmarried women like herself who weren't supposed to know it even existed.

She had asked her mother about it, and Caroline had, after a lot of blushing and stuttering, told her she had to wait for the night of her wedding.

Her brothers had blushed just as much as their mother, so they were no help at all with enlightening her, and her best friends were just as ignorant as she was.

So she still remained a virgin, body and mind.

Nicholas, damn his politeness, stopped, forcing her to talk to Devlin instead of just whisking past him at another man's arm. She could have pinched the poor man for being such a ridiculously polite gentleman.

To save her heart from suffering too much, she gave Devlin her most shining, angelic smile.

"It was a pleasure to meet you again, Your Grace." When he made an oh-really face, she continued, "You don't have to believe me, but it's the truth. Now I have to go, as my family awaits me in the hallway, and if I don't get there soon my brothers will probably kill me for leaving them alone at a gathering with our mother and a lot of unmarried young ladies."

"Well," he drawled, as he took a step closer to her, forcing poor Nicholas to step back so she wouldn't be caught between them. "I do want to meet you again, so you'd better hurry."

Fanny didn't know how to respond. She wanted to believe him, to think he actually meant what he said, that he wanted to see her again. But then again, he was used to conversing lightly with ladies of all ages. He could probably flirt in his sleep.

She couldn't tell by looking at him.

He was a picture of a dandy and a libertine, looking handsome and fashionably bored. The warmth she thought she had seen in his eyes was long gone, and the cold, unreadable wall was back.

He was the duke again.

"Goodbye," was all she managed to say before she gave him a curtsy and almost ran toward the entrance, dragging poor Nicholas with her.

When she had slipped through the doorway, she quickly looked back—and caught his eye as he watched her leave. He seemed a little confused, as if he wasn't used to a woman behaving as she did.

Nicholas, the perfect gentleman, fetched her coat and helped her put it on. He gave her a warm smile as he put her hand in the crook of his arm and led her to her family, waiting for her in the large carriage that would take them the short ride to their townhouse at No. 20 Berkeley Square.

His hand held on to hers a little longer than good etiquette might allow, and his beautiful brown eyes looked seriously at her when he lifted her hand to his lips and gave her a slow peck on her hand.

Fanny blushed, as she was feeling awkward and surprisingly unmoved. As gracefully as she could, she removed her hand from his and bade him a polite but deterrent goodbye.

When the carriage drove away, she could still see him standing there, looking a little excited and afraid. She guessed she would have to avoid him as much as possible in the future.

She truly didn't want him to ask for her hand in marriage, and she was thankful he hadn't asked her to join him at the Green Park picnic the next day. She didn't want to hurt him by turning him down.

She sighed and looked out through the window. Love was such a nuisance sometimes.

Chapter 5

Her brothers were as irritated as she had expected.

"I don't want to go to the picnic." Sebastian's surly tone made his unhappiness abundantly clear.

Sin was sitting on the opposite seat, laughing at Sebastian, who made a face at his older brother. Their mother, beside her younger son, patted his knee with so much motherly support Fanny knew her mother was up to something.

She leaned closer to her father and rested her cheek against his warm shoulder while she watched her mother trying not to look too pleased.

"It was you, not I, who invited Miss Archer to the picnic," she said sternly.

When Sebastian snorted, she frowned at him. "Sebastian Darling, this is not the way to address your mother. I thought I had raised you better than that."

Sebastian pushed her hand from his knee. "Oh, come on! You more or less forced me into asking Emma to join us tomorrow."

"I did not," Caroline said severely, while looking too guilty for anyone to believe her.

"Oh, come on," Sebastian repeated. "When she said she wasn't going to the picnic because of her mother's migraine, you told her I was going there without a companion."

Sebastian was starting to look so frustrated Fanny

wanted to calm him down before the discussion turned from skirmish to war.

"In my opinion, I don't think Mother did anything wrong. She merely pointed out how you were going to the picnic by yourself. By no means should that have forced you to anything."

Sebastian was speechless for a second, then threw a pointing finger toward Caroline and accused, "She told Emma—in front of me, mind you—that I am too shy to ask someone to join me, and Emma immediately turned to me and offered me her company, as she didn't want me to go alone to this special occasion."

The marquess, Sin, and Fanny all turned their heads toward Caroline, staring at her in disbelief.

"For heaven's sake, Caroline," George said under his breath.

Sin laughed and winked toward Sebastian, making his brother even angrier, while Caroline twisted her handkerchief between her fingers, not too pleased with the development of this conversation.

"I just wanted to help him a little on the way."

"Help him?" Fanny asked without really wanting an answer. "You more or less threw him at her. You told her he was too shy, and that gave Emma the impression he likes her. How could you, Mama? You put Sebastian in an awfully awkward position with this."

"Do you know what's even worse?" Sin asked with an evil grin. "Now Miss Archer will tell all her friends about Sebastian and his shyness, and before you know it he will be surrounded by young women, all of them wishing to help poor Sebastian Darling out of his misery."

Sebastian groaned and gave Caroline a dark look.

As the carriage stopped in front of their townhouse, George pointed at his wife.

"You will talk to Miss Archer tomorrow, and I don't care what you tell her, but you will make sure she understands that Sebastian isn't, and has never been, in love with her or even slightly interested in her."

"I can't be so harsh," Caroline cried out. "It will hurt the poor girl's heart, and she will be devastated. Emma Archer is a gentle young lady, and deserves to be treated better."

"You should have thought earlier about what she deserves," George said as he climbed out of the carriage. "Or were you too caught up in playing Lady Easton's kind of game?"

Caroline gasped with horror over his rude remark before she made a face to her husband's retiring back.

"I saw that," he shouted over his shoulder as he walked through the front door of the house, followed closely by his two sons.

Caroline sighed and slumped back against the velvet cushions, looking pathetic and regretful.

Fanny smiled lovingly toward her mother.

It wasn't easy being such a caring person and trying to embrace everyone without hurting anyone. Emma Archer was a good person too, even though she obviously lacked common sense, as she let Charmaine walk all over her.

It wasn't a nice thing Caroline had done, giving the poor girl the impression Sebastian had warm feelings for her, as Emma was almost on the shelf and would probably marry the first person who asked her. She was, after all, twenty years old. The clock was ticking.

Fanny put her hand on her mother's.

"I'll talk to her, Mama, and try to make her understand there isn't anything growing between her and Sebastian."

"I never meant this mess," Caroline sobbed.

George's remark had apparently done a good job of instilling a sense of remorse, Fanny thought, as she followed her mother up the steps to the front door. Caroline really didn't like being compared to Lady Easton.

The butler of the Darling family's townhouse, aptly named Butler, waited in the hallway, and in a few minutes he had them relieved of their coats and seated in the airy drawing room with hot cups of tea in their hands. Delicious cucumber sandwiches and scones filled with strawberry jam were placed on a silver tray on the small table between the sofas.

"Night food is really the best thing," Sin said, and stuffed his mouth with a sandwich.

"My regards to Mrs. Lloyd," Caroline told Butler, who stood at the doorway, prepared to bring his employers anything they wished for.

He had been with the family since Fanny's grandfather, Hannibal, was young, and had worked his way up through the servant hierarchy until reaching the pinnacle at the job of butler, when old Jenkins passed away twenty years earlier. He, like a few others of the servants who had been with the Darlings for many years, was more of a family member than an employee, and he was like an uncle for the children of the house rather than a servant. The family had tried for years to get him to join them, especially at family occasions as this one, but he always declined.

When the two youngest of George's brothers joined them, Rake and Jamie, Sebastian immediately snatched the last scone from the tray before either of them had a chance to grab it, and shoved it into his mouth.

"You look like a hamster," Rake told his obnoxious nephew, as he sat down in an unoccupied armchair. "You'd better be careful no one catches you and puts you in a small cage."

"That would be a sight." Sin laughed and poked his brother hard with his elbow.

Sebastian grunted something that sounded like a curse. It was well muffled by his mouthful of scone.

"Did you have a good time?" George asked his younger brothers.

"Indeed we did," Jamie said jovially as he sat down beside Fanny and grabbed a cup of tea with a lemon twist. "But not as good as Fanny had."

"Me?"

"Yes, you, Lady Francesca. You met Hereford again. If my memory serves me right, you were head over heels in love with him the last time you saw him."

Fanny looked at him with scorn.

"I was five years old. I didn't know better."

"But still…"

"What? There is nothing to it. We met and agreed it had been a while, we danced, and then we said goodbye."

"That's it?" Sin let out, aghast. "You mean we had to live with you all that time while you were moping around, mourning the loss of your Prince Charming, and now, when you finally meet him again as an adult, you think of it as nothing?"

"That's right." Fanny met her mother's probing gaze. "It *was* nice to have some kind of closure in meeting him again, but that's it."

"Of course," Caroline said in a very I-don't-believe-a-word-but-to-avoid-war-we'll-let-it-be kind of way. She stood and gave her family a contented smile. "Thank you, my dears, for this evening. It was good of you to accompany us to Fanny's first outing as a debutante. Now I will retire to my chambers, to get some sleep before the picnic tomorrow."

George gave Fanny a kiss on the forehead before he followed his wife out of the room.

The remaining five sipped quietly on their tea for a while, enjoying the silence of the night. Jamie put his arm around Fanny, and she gave him a sleepy smile as she laid her head against his shoulder.

The four men sat silently as they watched her fall asleep. No one said anything until they were sure she was sleeping soundly, and then Rake looked gravely at Sin.

"So what do we know happened?"

Sin shrugged. "I'm not sure. When she went to the restroom, I kind of lost her. Mother more or less forced me to ask Penelope to dance with me, so I had to leave my watch."

When Sebastian gave him an accusing gaze, Sin hissed, "You, better than anyone, should know Mother's not-so-subtle way of taking care of business."

Sebastian winced at the truth of his brother's words, having the Miss Archer situation too fresh in mind, and gave his brother an apologetic shrug.

"Well, I met them just inside the balcony doors," Rake said slowly, "And I can bet my life I caught them only minutes after they entered the ballroom from the balcony."

"What?" the three other Darlings exclaimed, making Fanny stir in her sleep, and they had to wait until she was calm again.

They were all too aware of what could happen with a young girl out on the balcony, as they had all been there, and they had all enjoyed the darkness.

A lot.

"When I think about it," Rake mused. "Fanny was blushing, and Devlin was drooling all over her. I didn't think so much of it then, as I was happy to meet Devlin again after all this time."

"Where has he been?" Jamie asked curiously.

"As far as I know, he's been on the continent for many years now, in the military, and I think it's high time he did return, as I have missed him profoundly."

"A couple of years is an extraordinarily long time for a high-born nobleman to remain as a foot soldier on enemy soil. I can't think the French like our aristocracy more than their own."

"I don't know more than you do, as I only met him for a second or two, and then his attention was on Fanny."

"There is something between them, anyone could tell, and we have to guard Fanny harder, so she won't slip through our net again. We don't want her alone with a womanizer like Devlin," Sin said as he unwrapped his long legs and stood up.

Jamie and Sebastian agreed. Only Rake remained silent, with a strange look on his face.

"You know," he said slowly, "I think I wouldn't mind if Fanny ends up marrying him. Devlin is a really good friend, honest and reliable, and he would never disrespect Fanny or us by mistreating her in any way. And isn't it said a reformed libertine makes the best husband?"

"You might be right about Devlin as a friend," Jamie said sternly, "But it doesn't mean he would be a good husband for her."

Sebastian nodded in full agreement. "I say we watch them closely, but let them have a little room for a possible proposal. If what you say about Devlin is true, Rake, then she couldn't do any better."

"Agreed?" Rake asked, and the other three men nodded silently. They would let Devlin in a bit closer than anyone else, but every last one of them made a silent promise to make sure nothing out of the ordinary ever happened between the two.

Sin lifted Fanny into his arms, and with a short "Night" he walked out of the room and carried her up the stairs to her bedroom, where he gently placed her on her bed and tucked a comforter around her.

"Good night, sweet pea," he whispered as he quietly closed the door behind him.

Chapter 6

The Hereford townhouse at Grosvenor Square stood cold and dark when Devlin entered it at three o'clock in the morning.

Quietly, he closed the door before he went on into the large hallway, where a footman slept in a chair. Devlin took off his heavy coat and laid it on one of the marble benches at the side of the enormous room.

Someone with regrettably bad taste had ordered the townhouse built more than two hundred years before Devlin's birth, and he had many times wished he could rip it apart, the whole house, and build a new one. Something more elegant and sober and not so overwhelmingly large, and especially not stuffed with expensive but tasteless artifacts.

His own father, the fifteenth Duke of Hereford, had made it clear he thought this house was the essence of nobility. Everyone who entered the front door got the message of power and wealth.

To Devlin, the townhouse said more about his father as a person than about the standing of the Ross family.

Conan Ross had been a selfish man, a brutal and unloving father, and an abusive husband, and even though Devlin never spent any time in London as a boy, the house still reminded him too much of all the horrible years under his father's thumb.

The memories of Conan hadn't been the easiest to erase, as his wickedness had spread everywhere, even down to the lowest scullery maid. It had taken Devlin six months merely to get the servants to look at him, as they were too used to crawling in front of Conan, too aware of what he would do to them if he saw something he thought was wrong. Living with Conan had been like living in the darkness under a large, unyielding, smothering blanket.

However, this evening Devlin had seen the light of Lady Francesca Darling.

She had been something special as a child, so filled with energy and so utterly stubborn. Her childish crush on him had embarrassed her relatives, but for him it had been heaven to be adored like that.

No one had ever wanted him the way she had.

He slowly climbed the grand staircase and proceeded to his bedroom, where it was cozier, thanks to the large fire spreading its warmth through the room.

"Had a nice time?"

Devlin looked up as his valet appeared from a dark corner.

Bear was a gigantic man with broad shoulders, limbs like tree trunks, and waist-long brown hair.

Devlin had met him his first day in France when he happened to come upon the cheering group of enemy soldiers who had caught Bear. Without a second thought, he had made an attempt to save the big Englishman.

Due to his inexperience, he had failed miserably.

Instead, he too had been caught and had to listen to Bear repeatedly sighing over his stupidity until they finally were able to escape.

To Devlin's surprise, Bear did not leave his side. Somehow Devlin had won the trust of the beast, and they had been inseparable ever since.

"What do you think?" Devlin rolled his eyes, and Bear chuckled in response.

"That fun, eh?"

"We had more fun the time we were snowed in at the hut in the French Alps. I keep forgetting how philistine the members of the *ton* are."

Devlin took off his clothes and washed quickly before he put on a robe and sat down by the fireplace.

"Want something to wash all the tittle-tattle away?"

"Why, yes," Devlin breathed, and soon he had a glass of brandy in his hand, as did Bear, who seated himself in the other chair.

The giant put his feet on a pallet before he leaned back with a growl that made Devlin shake his head with a chuckle. Sometimes Bear seemed more like a force of nature than the youngest son of an earl, but Devlin didn't mind.

In fact, he embraced Bear's directness and honesty.

There was not a person on this earth he trusted more than the man who sat beside him. Bear would always tell him the truth, no matter what. In war or in peacetime, loyalty and honesty were the best traits.

The only thing Bear didn't share with him was his reason for pretending to be a valet instead of taking his rightful place among the *ton*.

Devlin did wonder, but out of respect to Bear he didn't ask. Some things you needed to keep to yourself, and he knew Bear would tell him when he was ready.

"I met my friend Rake today, a nice surprise. I

haven't seen him since my father's funeral, and then was neither the time nor the place to get reacquainted."

"I guess it wasn't a complete waste, attending the ball?"

"Not completely." Devlin grinned. "However, I will never understand why most of our peers find these functions so important. The same old people gather at the same old places, gossiping about the same old things, and no one finds this strange or boring. The only difference is the latest debutantes, but even they share the same mission as debutantes from earlier years: catch an eligible husband."

"Oh, come on—" Bear laughed—"There is more to the social season than a boring repetition of last year."

"You think?"

"Yes, I do. However, I haven't been around the *ton* for quite some years now, and I guess things might have changed."

"Probably not," Devlin chuckled as he ducked to avoid being hit by the boot Bear threw at him.

"Come to think about it," Bear continued, without acknowledging his boot, which Devlin held a little too close to the fire crackling in the fireplace, "The only good thing about the Season was all the ladies who were more than willing to lift their bedspreads for me."

"Really? I certainly didn't meet any of those today. I was surrounded by desperate mamas and the offspring they kept shoving in my direction. Lord, I felt for the poor girls. They looked just as uncomfortable as I felt."

"Surrounded by mamas with a mission? I must say I owe you an apology. It must have felt like hell, being caught in the middle of all those dimwitted young misses. Debutantes are extremely boring, and I prefer

61

them much more when they have been married for a couple of years, had their heirs, and are free to roam. Then they are interesting indeed."

"Now you're exaggerating," Devlin objected with more force than he had intended. "Some of them happen to be all right."

"Oh," Bear breathed with a knowing smile. "You met a lady."

"No," Devlin growled. "I did not. I only disagree with you when you say they all are the same, because there could be some poor young lady out there among them who happens to be both nice and intelligent."

Bear didn't answer but gave his friend a look that told Devlin exactly how pathetic he sounded.

Oh, for the fires of hell, he thought. Why not share the truth with Bear? The pretend-to-be valet knew everything about him anyway, so why bother to hide something that might affect both their lives in the future?

"I might have."

"Really?"

Devlin sighed. "Yes, really."

"I have to admit I find this hilarious. Here you have been sulking the whole day because you felt you had no choice but to attend this—as you called it—bloody ball. And then you go and meet some little eye-batter who makes it all worth the while."

"The ball still was a bloody nuisance," Devlin snorted. "My opinion about the Season and all its must-go-to assemblies stays the same. What happened tonight is that I might have met someone who puts a little interest into joining my peers and doing the social twirl, just to be able to get to know her better. And maybe—and it's an enormous maybe—she could be the right woman for me to marry."

Bear took a sip of his brandy, but Devlin still could see the faint smile he tried to hide behind the crystal glass.

Oh, bloody hell.

He was the Duke of Hereford, and he was assumed to be a part of the London society. Even though he hated his deceased father, he still didn't want his own future heirs to have less social standing than he had, just because he found the socialites stupid as sheep.

Deep inside, he felt obliged to act like an aristocrat, and dress up in some uncomfortable evening clothes to join the *ton* during these short months until summer. And this was the only reason he had crossed the small park in the middle of Grosvenor Square to enter the Easton townhouse.

The footmen were too occupied with all the shiny carriages arriving to notice him as he slunk past them. Beside the stables, a small gate led into the darkness of the garden, and he arrived unseen and unannounced.

He stood for some time alone, watching the couples sneaking in and out through the balcony doors. He was quite bored and on the verge of sneaking back the same way he'd arrived when Fanny tiptoed past him, and, without thinking, he saved her from disgrace.

He didn't recognize her at first, and he would never have looked at her twice if she hadn't knocked him off his feet with the way she addressed him. She spoke to him as if she knew him well, like a family member, and it vexed him enough to follow her into the ballroom. He knew he was giving the gossipy matrons something to talk about by following her like that, but it turned out to be the best thing he'd ever done.

It had been so nice to meet Rake again.

He hadn't seen his friend since Conan's funeral last year, when the friend came to be there for him in his time of grief. Or, as Rake put it later the same evening when he was too drunk to care about what he said, to celebrate the end of the era of Conan the Black. Rake had always been a better friend to Devlin than Devlin thought he deserved.

They had been roommates during all their years in school and had the grandest of times, playing more pranks than anyone ever found out. They were both suspended a couple of times, and only the high rank of their families caused their re-admittance.

Hannibal even paid a few bribes to keep the two of them in school. He had grunted a lot, but somehow Devlin had a feeling Rake's old man actually was proud of them, which was kind of odd, as his own father was so embarrassed over his son's behavior that he refused to help his son get back into school.

It had been another knife in Devlin's young heart, as he knew how important his father considered education. The headmaster, a caring man with a wicked brain of his own, instead asked Hannibal to donate for Devlin's sake.

And Rake's father had paid without a word.

When school was finished, Rake went into the family businesses, enlarging the already too large Darling riches, while Devlin was sent to the military in order to straighten him out, as his father put it. What Conan didn't know was that, directly after his arrival to the army compounds, Devlin was contacted by the War Ministry.

Basil Sinclair, the high and mighty Earl of Saxton, asked Devlin to join his league of spies and in secrecy go behind enemy lines in search of information.

Devlin immediately agreed.

The following years were spent in France, collecting information for Basil and the ministry. No one knew what he was doing, not even his own father, who got sent notes now and then from the War Ministry about Devlin's general progress in the military.

Last year it all changed when Conan surprisingly died of pneumonia and Devlin had no choice but to return to England.

He'd had a long meeting with Lord Saxton, talking about the future, and they decided Devlin wouldn't continue collecting information now, when he was back in England, as he wasn't as anonymous here in London as he had been in the French countryside. Even so, they both knew he wouldn't hesitate to throw himself into the world of secrets and betrayal he had lived in during the last decade, if he was needed.

Basil didn't have to tell Devlin he was more valuable to them if he engaged in the months of hell—more commonly known among the *ton* as the Season—than if he hid in his townhouse or in his country home. Suddenly he had yet another solid reason to appear open and friendly.

However, now it didn't seem such a pain.

"I thought you had sworn never to marry, so Conan's bloodline wouldn't continue." Bear's quick glance belied the mildly curious, even blasé way he spoke.

"True, but few things in the world stay the same, and now, as I am older and wiser, I have to my own surprise changed my mind."

"Older, yes," Bear joked to take the edge off the serious subject. "Wiser? Not so much."

Devlin didn't catch the joke, being too caught in his thoughts.

"I realized I would only make Conan the winner if I denied myself a wife and children. I told you how my father's greatest pleasure was making me as miserable as possible, and by denying myself marriage, I would die just as sad and lonely as he did."

Bear said nothing, but nodded. He found the decision admirable.

"So, what is your plan now? Marry the chit you met today, and keep her happy and pregnant the next twenty years?"

Devlin shook his head, and laughed.

"Not really, no. I thought I would settle for finding a warm and contented woman who is somewhat pleasant, and who would give me an heir or two."

"Really?" Bear quirked an eyebrow, obviously not as impressed anymore with Devlin's grand plan. "And why on earth do you think it will be enough for you to simply 'settle'? Don't you want a woman who makes your heart beat faster, who makes you smile as you do when you talk about the little one you met this evening? Don't you want someone you can love, and who will love you back?"

"I didn't know you believed in love." Devlin smirked.

"I don't, but you are not me; you are a believer."

"Really?" Devlin mimicked Bear to annoy him, but his friend didn't care, or simply ignored the teasing.

"Please, Devlin, be honest with me. Do you really

want to spend the rest of your life with a woman who from the start you find only 'somewhat pleasant'?"

"If I planned on spending the rest of my life with her, yes, I would want more in the woman I would ask to be my wife."

Bear's confusion was obvious. "Why will you not spend your life together with your wife?"

"So I won't influence the children."

"Influence the children?" Bear's voice trailed off as his chin fell to his chest. For the first time since meeting the giant, Devlin had rendered him speechless.

"I think the best thing for them, my future wife and the child or children she gives me, is to live in peace in the countryside, having a simple life without any of the darkness I grew up with."

"But Conan is dead, so there is nothing left to affect them."

"Yes, there is. Me."

"You?" Bear looked at him in bewilderment, "Have you lost your mind completely?"

Devlin rushed to defend his plans. "My only wish is to erase every last wrong my father ever did to me, to anyone. And by staying away from my children, I know they will grow up without the cloud of darkness that is my constant companion because of my father."

Bear shook his head slowly, as if unable to grasp the deeper meaning of Devlin's words.

"They will have a simple life, without the ghost of my father."

"So to erase the last imprint of your father, you intend to let them grow up without a father of their own?"

"Better to not have a father than to live under the

rule of a rotten one."

"But you are not rotten," Bear yelled as he jumped up from the chair, knocking the small table to the side. He looked down at the brandy fast being absorbed by the thick carpet and cursed loudly as he stomped out.

"It is the right thing to do!" Devlin growled to the now-empty doorway, but Bear didn't reappear.

His friend clearly was upset with him, but he couldn't understand what Bear's problem was. Why did he become so upset with Devlin's plan to stay out of his children's lives? He had told Bear everything about his father, and if there was anyone he thought would understand, it was Bear.

Devlin rang for a servant to clean up the mess Bear had left, and when he was alone again, he lay down on his bed and stared up to the dark ceiling. Could it be he had found the right woman for the job, the very first day of the Season?

Lady Francesca Darling was granddaughter to a duke, used to the life of polite society. She had a loving family who would be there for her, and she would never be left alone as his own mother had been, tucked away at a small faraway estate until she had died when Devlin was just a few years old. No, Fanny would bring his children up with love and laughter and give them a secure start in life.

Maybe she wouldn't understand his decision in the matter of his staying away, but he knew she had a good head, and if he only found the correct words to persuade her, she would come to her senses and admit his path was the right one.

He smiled contentedly.

Life was good.

Chapter 7

It was unusually warm for early April, and the lazy meadows of Green Park were full of thick, healthy green grass. All over the lush carpet, flowers bloomed in every imaginable color.

In the northern corner of the park, near the basin, the *ton* had gathered for the annual picnic, always held the day after the Easton Ball.

As the clock turned three, the otherwise empty park filled with the ladies and gentlemen of the *ton* chatting and socializing while their servants ran around placing tables and chairs.

Everyone was gossiping about yesterday's ball and especially the juiciest bit of all, the return of the Duke of Hereford and his obvious interest in Lady Francesca Darling.

The dandies and the gamblers had rushed over to White's and put their bets about the couple in the infamous Book of Bets. The placed bets covered everything, from when he would officially start to court her to the color of their firstborn child's eyes.

When the Darling family arrived, Fanny immediately was dragged away from her family by her best friend, Lady Penelope de Vere.

They didn't stop until they reached the Queens Walk, where they proceeded more slowly, letting the chaperoning maid catch up.

They had been friends since they first met as little girls during outings in their corner of England, the lovely county of Berkshire. They had been full of mischief, and their adventurous spirits had put them in more problematic situations than anyone ever wanted to remember.

Now they both had turned eighteen and had, hopefully, left all their antics behind, as they had gone with their families to London in pursuit of husbands among the eligible bachelors of the *ton*.

Penelope was the beauty of the two, with blonde hair, blue eyes, and rosy cheeks: the perfect English Rose. Unfortunately, she was the younger sister of the incomparable Charmaine, and therefore her exquisite beauty went unremarked.

However, as Fanny believed, when you got to know Penelope and could see beyond Charmaine, her loveliness inside as well as outside was astounding.

The two girls hooked arms and strolled down the path, enjoying the warmth of the sun. The air was filled with the scent of thousands of wildflowers blooming everywhere in the green grass. Bumblebees buzzed and birds twittered. It was an amazingly beautiful day.

Penelope hugged Fanny's arm. "Oh, this is so exciting," she breathed happily. "Everybody is talking about it, you know, you and your handsome duke."

"Handsome as one of Grand-Papa's Roman statues," Fanny joked, and they laughed, filled with the starry-eyed happiness only young women can feel the day after their first ball.

"It must have been an amazing feeling to meet him again, after all this time. You have talked about him as long as I can remember, and my memory happens to be extremely good." Penelope winked, and Fanny hugged her friend closer as they giggled.

"It was amazing, and at the same time frightening. I knew immediately who he was when I saw him, even though he is now a grown man instead of the boy I remembered."

"Did he recognize you at once, too?"

Fanny rolled her eyes.

"Of course not. He is a man, after all."

"I'm not surrounded by men, as you are, so how men act and how they think are not a part of my knowledge."

Penelope sounded almost as if she were jealous, and Fanny kissed her friend's rosy cheek.

"Just because I have more manly relatives than I can count doesn't mean I know how they think. But I did once overhear a friend of my mother's say men were easy to read, as all they think about is eating, sleeping, and drinking."

"How utterly boring," Penelope said with feigned horror, and they giggled again.

"Enough about me. How was your first ball? I looked for you but couldn't find you."

Penelope lost her smile. She bowed her head and sighed, which clearly told how her evening had been, and Fanny's heart went out to her friend.

Why couldn't those horrible parents of Penelope's see what a treasure they had? Their youngest daughter was a gem among lumps of coal, with her pure heart and a smile that could melt gold.

But all they could see was Charmaine, and as she fulfilled their every dream, they didn't look any farther.

"It wasn't as bad as you think," Penelope said

slowly, knowing all too well what her friend thought. "I still had to wear Charmaine's old dress, and there was no time to alter it, so I had to lift it constantly, as she is quite taller than me. Father danced with my sister but forgot about me, which made me a little upset. However, what hurt most was how my mother noticed his forgetfulness but didn't care. It was more important to her to stand beside Charmaine and be her mother than to drag my father from the gambling tables and force him to dance with me too."

"Oh, Penny!" Fanny stopped and gave her friend a tight hug, silently swearing a holy oath to revenge her friend. Someday she would make sure the other three members of the de Vere family would suffer immensely.

Penelope reached for her handkerchief and used it to dry the tears trickling down her cheeks. "It feels better now that I can share it with you," she sniffed, and they started to walk again toward the end of the walkway. "Everything feels so much better when I am with you."

"Of course it does," Fanny joked. "I am, after all, the most perfect human being to ever set her feet on this earth."

"You are, indeed." Penelope laughed, and with the fragility of the moment over, they continued arm-in-arm in a much better mood, now they had aired the hurtfulness of yesterday's ball.

"What did you think about the Easton Ball besides your family's shortcomings?"

"Oh, it was so grand! It felt like I was in a fairy tale, surrounded by all the elegance of the ballroom and the people in it."

"Wasn't it? I have never seen so many exquisite ladies in my life. And the dresses! I could hardly believe how deep some of the necklines were."

"Did you see the lady in the thin dress that showed her whole body? I overheard Mother tell one of her friends the lady had dampened her chemise to make the outline of her body more visible."

"How outrageous," Fanny breathed, more impressed than shocked.

At the end of the walkway, they turned and started back toward the others. Fanny used the time well, telling Penelope all about what had happened the day before.

Well, not exactly everything.

She didn't tell her friend about the Charmaine part of her evening. And she didn't mention her thoughts about whether Devlin might or might not court her, since she was still a little unsure on that subject.

Besides, Penelope always became upset whenever Fanny said anything bad about her older sister. And suggesting Charmaine was a liar really wasn't a good something.

Instead she dwelled on what Devlin had said and the way he had acted when they danced.

"I felt like I was five years old again," Fanny finished with a dreamy smile. "He made me feel at ease, like I was with one of my relatives, or like now when I'm with you. He is very beautiful, painfully so. It almost hurt my eyes just to look upon him."

Giggling, they hadn't noticed the tall man coming their way until he stopped right in front of them.

They gasped, caught off guard and very nervous about what he might have heard.

He, of course, didn't let them ponder.

"Ladies," he said with a slight bow. "I hope I don't hurt your eyes standing in front of you like this, but I would ask if you could grant me the honor of walking the two of you back toward your families."

He succeeded with something few men had before him—he made them both blush.

Before they knew what to say, he took his place between them, put their hands in the crooks of his arms, and got them walking again. At first they were quiet, too embarrassed to know what to say.

How much had he overheard?

A deepening blush heated Fanny's cheeks, which Devlin of course didn't miss, as she could tell by his soft chuckle.

"Well you really are, you know," she finally managed to say, when she found her voice again, and tried not to look at Penelope's horrified face on the other side of his broad chest.

"I'm what?" he asked. He was clearly enjoying this too much, as he showed no intention of letting them off the hook. The awful man just couldn't resist teasing them a bit more.

"You know," Fanny said, and made a vague gesture with her hand. "Pretty."

That made him stop.

"Now, I will tell the two of you the first rule regarding men." He gave them a hard stare. "You can refer to our looks in many different ways. 'Handsome' is good. 'Good-looking' works well, too. Even 'nice' is a splendid choice. However, never, *ever*, tell a man he is pretty."

Penelope apparently found the subject intriguing,

because she forgot all about her awkwardness and took a step closer.

As the true gentleman he was, he took one step closer to Fanny, who suddenly found herself pressed hard against the side of his body. Her eyes met his for a second, and the smoldering heat that washed over her made her knees go weak.

She didn't care what he said. He was splendidly pretty, and she was almost scared by the power he possessed to affect her by a mere look.

Penelope didn't notice Fanny's obvious discomfort, as she was busy discussing with Devlin about why a man couldn't be called pretty. Penelope by habit was very attentive and didn't miss anything, but this time she did, and Fanny was thankful for it.

She had no secrets from her friend, and usually she told her everything. But this hurricane of strange feelings was new to her, and she had no idea how to describe them.

If she couldn't clarify them even to herself, how would she ever be able to tell Penelope about them?

They started to walk again, slowly strolling under the large trees gracing the walk. The earlier embarrassment was soon forgotten, and the two young women found they had the best source of information about Devlin they possibly could find: the man himself.

"I heard your father died last year, and I'm so sorry for your loss."

"Don't be." He smiled at Fanny. "I'm not."

"Are you not sad about your father's demise, Your Grace?"

Penelope, who hadn't the best connection with her own father, found the subject fascinating.

"No."

Devlin's curt answers weren't as fascinating to hear, though, and Penelope had no choice but to change the subject. Fanny gave her friend a sympathetic smile, as she too had wanted to know more than he was willing to share.

"Have you any other family staying with you in town, Your Grace?"

"I don't have any close relatives, so I am all by myself."

"I'm so sorry," Fanny breathed, horrified over such a predicament as not having any relatives. She would have missed hers immensely if she had not had them.

"Don't be," he repeated softly. "You can't miss what you never had. My mother died when I was a small child, and I have no memories of her. I am an only child, just as my parents each were. I have no aunts, uncles, or cousins, therefore, either."

"Oh," Fanny sighed, devastated over what seemed a fate worse than death, and she saw the other two share an amused look, but she decided wisely enough to let it pass.

Penelope, who didn't want to waste this opportunity to delve deep into the secret world of men, quickly changed the subject. "Is it true there are bets placed in a book in one of the clubs? Bets about silly things like when someone will propose, who will ask who for a dance, and so on?"

Devlin arched an eyebrow, and Penelope looked back with too-innocent eyes, trying to hide her curiosity.

"How is it possible you know about the bets?"

"I have ears." Penelope gave him a fast smile,

encouraging him to tell them more about these all-man secrets. Fanny couldn't help but admire her friend's bluntness; Penelope on a mission was unstoppable.

"Why should I tell you?"

"Why not? There is no harm in telling us. We won't tell anyone else. Right, Penny?" Fanny interceded, and Penelope nodded in agreement, garnering them another amused look.

"What if I don't want to?"

"Oh, come on." Without thinking, Fanny tightened her grip of his arm, and he sent her one of those hot wicked grins, which silently challenged her to do something more than just touch his arm. Blushing, she loosened her grip again, and he made a disappointed face. "Coward," he mouthed.

"Just tell us about the last placed bet you heard about." Penelope flashed him another encouraging smile, and he couldn't stop himself from laughing.

"If I tell you all about the last bet, will you please change the subject, and stop behaving like two annoying flies?"

Both young women nodded solemnly, and he had a sinking feeling they wouldn't let anything go.

"It will be embarrassing for you, though, Pup."

Fanny blushed with pleasure at his use of her childhood nickname and tried to ignore Penelope's knowing smile.

"For me?" she asked surprised. "I am in the book of bets?"

"Yes, you are."

"I wonder about what," she said, and chewed her lower lip, effectively drawing Devlin's eyes to her mouth. The heat of his eyes made her tremble, and his eyes darkened even more when he felt her response to him.

For the first time ever, Fanny wished Penelope would just disappear and take the chaperoning maid with her. She wanted desperately to be alone with her duke, to find out what the burning promise she could see in his eyes was all about.

However, as Penelope wouldn't leave, Fanny took a deep breath to strengthen herself. She had to stop acting like this every time they met. If she continued with this fluttering around him whenever he was near, soon he would think she was in love with him, and nothing could be farther from the truth than her having warm feelings for him.

Nothing.

"Do you want to know?"

"Yes!" Both young women answered in unison.

"Remember, you asked for it."

"Yes! Just tell us!" Penelope was having a hard time staying polite in response to his delaying tactics.

"The last bet I heard about was Lord Danville's. He said I would propose to you, Pup, before the end of this month."

Chapter 8

Fanny didn't know how she managed not to ask "Will you?" but she somehow succeeded, and she was forever thankful for it.

The subject was too embarrassing as it was, and she didn't need to enlarge it into something unbearable.

Meeting Devlin's golden eyes, she saw him silently daring her to ask her question, but she was forever a coward. She didn't have it in her to blurt the question out.

When they reached the picnic area, their acquaintances came to greet them. Devlin nodded gracefully to those he knew, but he did not stop for anyone until he reached the Darling family.

Fanny hid a smile when she saw his surprise that her entire family was there, every single member of the Darlings except her grandparents and her uncle Charles, who almost never left Chester Park. It would take more than her first ball to make those three leave the premises of their country home.

"Why are you so surprised?" Fanny asked, with a tender smile toward her kin, and Devlin looked down at her with his golden eyes. "Don't you remember the tale of the royal family? I know Rake told you."

"The royal family?" Devlin frowned, not remembering this specific tale at all.

"Oh, I love the tale of the royal family." Penelope

breathed dreamily. "It's so romantic, and yet so sad."

"Sad?" Fanny laughed at her friend. "How can you call the lives of my beloved family sad? To me, it is anything but sad. It is all about love."

"I meant the duke's story, of course. Losing a wife so young; it must have been devastating for him. All alone in the world with three small sons. It is a wonder he managed to see it through."

Devlin rolled his eyes over such romantic nonsense, and Fanny had to bite her lower lip, as Penelope looked like she would give anything to be able to kick his shin. Hard.

"Please enlighten me. What is the tale of the royal family? I would venture to say it has nothing to do with King George and relatives?"

"Well…" Fanny beckoned him a little closer as if she was about to spill England's most guarded secrets and not only the history of her family. She had always loved a little drama, and as Devlin gave her an amused grin, she could only guess he did, too. "It was King George who started to call us "the true royal family," and so I have to say he is involved in this, although in the smallest way."

"King George called *you* the royal family?"

"Yes indeed. King George and Grand-Papa went to school together and have been friends ever since. My father, who is the firstborn son of Grand-Papa, is named after King George, who also is his godfather."

She could see he was impressed by her family's close personal connection to the king, but as she had grown up with the knowledge of it, she didn't think so much of it herself. To her, the king was a kind man who every year sent the most wonderful gifts at Christmas.

Or at least he had until his mind started to fail him. Now it had been a couple of years since they last heard from him, and she could only hope he had a good life in spite of his sickness.

"Is your father the reason he called you 'the royal family'?"

"No, the nickname came later, when Grand-Papa continued to sire sons and named them all after kings of England. His first wife, Grand-Mama Georgiana, gave birth to George, Henry, and Charles, and his second wife, Grand-Mama Anna, continued with Edward, William, James, and Richard."

Devlin grinned in acknowledgment.

"I do remember this, now that you mention all the names. Rake did tell me about it. Your poor Grand-Papa, who so desperately wanted a daughter, and all he got was sons."

"And hadn't the fantasy enough to come up with other names than those of earlier kings."

"But didn't any of your grandmothers have any say about what to name the children?"

"Apparently not."

"Hannibal's quite stubborn sometimes, I guess."

Fanny nodded and gave him her cheekiest grin before she put her arm around Penelope's waist to bring her friend into the conversation.

She had to admit she liked the way Devlin made her feel when he watched her so intensely. Having his full attention made it seem as though they were the only two people in Green Park. But Penelope was her friend, and she had started to look a little abandoned.

"Not as stubborn as his granddaughter," Penelope said with a faint smile, which faltered when the golden eyes centered on her.

"It runs in the family." Fanny smiled.

Devlin looked at the large collection of people, all related to her in some way or another, and for one unguarded moment she could sense the envy he felt.

It saddened her that someone could be so lonely. He had no close relatives. How alone he must feel.

She looked at her loved ones and couldn't think how life would be without them. They were such a close family, and they all shared the same homes, a highly unusual arrangement.

Their country home was the ancient castle, Chester Park, where Hannibal ruled the world and where they all stayed, off season. When in London, they all used the townhouse at Berkeley Square, an enormous house that took up almost an entire block.

"Ah, there is my family." Penelope interrupted Fanny's thoughts and gave her friend a warm hug. "I'll have to join them before they get worried. It was very nice to meet you, Your Grace. I do think we will see much more of each other in the future."

As Devlin bowed, Penelope curtsied and, before Fanny could stop her, twirled around and disappeared among the surrounding socialites.

Fanny gave Devlin an awkward smile, not knowing what to say to him now, when it was only the two of them. He was so magnificent, and if she could, she would gladly have stood there for the rest of the day, simply gawking at him.

He was sartorially perfect in every detail, and she guessed not one single strand of his black hair dared to move from its place and disrupt the perfection. His clothes were the height of fashion, and everything sat exactly as it should. If she hadn't known better, she would have guessed they had been sewn upon him.

"You are lucky to have so many people who love you," he said.

"I know. They are a colorful group, but I love them all dearly, without any restrictions whatsoever."

Devlin nodded, sadness spreading over his beautiful face, and she wished she could do something to ease his loneliness.

"It must be so hard for you, since your father passed away."

"We were never close, so there was nothing hard about it at all."

His golden eyes lost their emotion and turned cold and dead, and she cursed silently. She should never have mentioned his father. Of course she knew all about his hateful relationship with his father. Uncle Rake was a perfect source whenever she wanted information about anyone, and especially about Devlin. What had she been thinking?

She tried to backpeddle. "It can be hard, even if you are not close."

He looked down at her, curious about what she meant.

"You lost your father, and even though you were as far away as two people who know each other can be, he still was your father. As I see it, a very big part of your life is now missing."

"I didn't need him when he was alive, and I rejoice now when he is dead. There is nothing more to it."

Yes, there is, she wanted to yell, but she held her tongue. Now wasn't the right moment, and she certainly wasn't the right person. It had to be someone who had known the old duke, someone who knew what Devlin had suffered.

Someone such as her Uncle Rake.

She looked at her uncle as he stood talking to her father and promised herself to talk to him about Devlin. The faint horror in Devlin's voice made her scared for him, and she wanted to make sure he didn't close it all deep inside.

She sighed, and then blushed when he looked down at her with a grin. Of course he had heard the sigh.

"Is there something bothering you, Lady Francesca?"

"Only the same old things, Your Grace."

His grin became more wicked when she followed his teasing lead, and he leaned closer, until she almost could see the stubble on his chin.

"Do tell me, Lady Francesca, what these old things might be?"

She leaned closer to him, until she felt his breath against her face. She saw his eyes change again, becoming warmer until they were burning as liquid gold.

"Many things bother me, Your Grace, but only one thing haunts me day and night."

"Do tell me," he whispered, mesmerizing her with his soft tone. "What can haunt a young lady such as yourself?"

"Pretty men, Your Grace."

He blinked, and blinked again before he threw his head back and roared with laughter.

The chatter around them grew quiet for a moment before the mumble restarted excitedly, and Fanny had no problem guessing the new topic of conversation.

Devlin, too, noticed the sudden interest given to them, and he drew back slightly, keeping some distance between Fanny and himself. He offered her his arm, and she put her hand lightly in the crook of it, enjoying the feeling of the muscles beneath her fingers.

"You are lucky to have such a close, loving family," Devlin said lightly, as if the hot teasing hadn't happened. "I must admit I am most envious."

Fanny couldn't help feeling a little disappointed.

The intense minutes earlier had been so interesting, and she was indeed curious to know what would have happened if the moment hadn't been lost. But she followed his lead again and kept her voice light.

"I think I can remember Uncle Rake telling me that you have an aunt?"

"Yes, well, a cousin once removed, to be precise. Her name is Delia."

"Well, that's nice. You have someone."

"Not as nice as you think. Delia is my mother's cousin, and she lives with her two children in my home in Herefordshire."

Fanny searched her memory. She knew she had heard the name of Devlin's ancestral castle mentioned. What was it? Oh, yes.

"Pendragon is the name of your country home, isn't it?"

"Why, yes."

He didn't have to be so pleased that she knew what his country home was called. But he obviously was.

He gave her a knowing smile, and she couldn't stop her treacherous cheeks from turning red.

"But you have two cousins—second cousins, to be more precise," Fanny realized a little late. "Are they of the same age as you?"

"No, they are younger, more of your age. I hardly know them, as I was already living at Eton when Delia's husband died and they had to move in with us. And as I continued directly from school to the army, I haven't spent much time with them as an adult, either."

"That's so sad." Fanny couldn't stop feeling sorry for the threesome forced to live in a faraway castle when they lost husband and father.

Devlin, who obviously didn't share her feelings, snorted.

"No, it is not sad at all. They have had comfortable lives at Pendragon for almost fifteen years now and should be thankful instead of demanding."

"Demanding?"

"Delia, my selfish little aunt, thinks I should bring them to London now my father is dead and has no more use of them at the castle. She writes to me every day, and sometimes I feel I am drowning in the pile of letters."

"Why not give in to her wish and bring them here? I can understand how your young cousin must be looking forward to having her own debut season."

"Not as long as I'm alive."

Fanny took a step away from him, and looked at him in shock.

"Don't you think you are being selfish? Think of your poor aunt, forced to live all those years in the countryside, longing for the pleasures of London, believing her life would change with your father's death..."

Devlin arched an amused eyebrow at her choice of words, but she didn't let him interrupt her.

"You must bring them here to London, so they too can continue with their lives."

"You think?"

"Yes, Your Grace. So is my wish."

Devlin must have found her words amusing, as he laughed again, another head-turning laugh that made her heart skip a beat.

"Before you decide what you're wishing for, I think you should consider the situation. You see, my aunt is desperate to come to London, but not for her daughter's first season. No, she is afraid I will marry before she has a chance to convince me otherwise."

"You must have misunderstood her. I can't think she wants to convince you not to marry. I think she wants to be a part of your marriage, as the only living relative you have."

Devlin gave her an odd smile. It was filled with warmth and something that strangely enough seemed to be pride.

"You have a kind heart, Lady Francesca."

"Thank you, Your Grace. But I still think you are acting selfishly."

"She is afraid I will find someone to marry before she has a chance to get here and force me into marrying her daughter Amelia."

"Not as long as I'm alive."

Fanny winced as she realized she had snorted the words aloud. Horrified, she closed her eyes and took a deep, shaky breath.

What was wrong with her? Why on earth had she said those mean-hearted words straight out, and why had she said them to him?

She felt embarrassed, so utterly devastated, and

wished she were anywhere but here. She wished she had courage enough to look up at him, to meet his eyes to see what he thought about her outrageous remark.

Why had she said it?

Bloody why?

Chapter 9

Devlin looked down on the top of Fanny's head, which was all she let him see after blurting out her wonderful remark.

Oh, how he adored her.

He wished she would look up at him, but as her whole body screamed how embarrassed she felt, he didn't force it. If he'd had any doubts earlier about her being the right choice as the wife for him, they were all gone now.

He admired her immensely. Her honesty, her rightfulness, and her kind heart were everything he ever could wish in the woman who would raise his children.

He had left Pendragon with anger and refused to read any of the letters his aunt showered him with, all because of a young girl he didn't want.

Then, by some strange twist of fate, he found himself longing for the company of another young girl, and without hesitation he had thrown himself into the society swirl he loathed and even gone to a picnic.

A picnic, for goodness' sake.

And, worst of all, he, who found peace in his solitude, was now surrounded by her family, all fifty, hundred, or thousand of them. They, of course, were all pretending to ignore him, but he could feel their probing eyes whenever he looked another way.

Fanny let go of his arm and, still without meeting

his eyes, mumbled something inaudible before leaving his side for the table where the food was placed.

Caroline Darling, the lovely Marchioness of Newbury, approached him with a sweet smile. She invited him to join their company for luncheon, and he thanked her courteously, grateful for a reason to stay close to Fanny.

But before he had a chance to move toward his desired wife-to-be, he was surrounded by some of the younger Darling men and dragged away to a set of chairs, where he was forced to sit down in a not-too-gentle way.

"Having a nice afternoon?" Sin asked, deceitfully polite.

Before Devlin had a chance to answer, Jamie and Sebastian sat down facing him, giving him their best fake smiles. He glared at them, refusing to back down.

Another man sat down beside him, and by the look of him he also was a Darling family member. The same dark brown hair and light gray eyes as most of his relatives, and just as tall and muscular. As he was about Rake's age, this probably was one of the younger brothers, Edward or William.

He could feel more men silently standing behind him, but he refused to turn around. That might show weakness. It wasn't very hard to understand what it was all about.

They were trying to intimidate him, and he would rather die than let them know they succeeded all too well. Instead, he kept up his assumption of indifference, a skill he'd polished during his time in France, and to his satisfaction, that seemed to make the men rather frustrated. They couldn't know he had learned the hard way to keep his face blank, to not give away any emotions.

They were, in Devlin's mind, too innocent to be aware of all the malice in the world. They had grown up surrounded by an overprotective family, and probably not more than one or two of them had been anywhere outside England.

"So the lost heir has returned to society," Sin said, a little less politely.

Sebastian wasn't as polite. "We all thought you would return to claim your place in society last season, but you were nowhere to be seen. One would think a son would honor his father by at least being present at his deathbed."

Devlin could tell the thought of not standing by one's father's side as life slipped away was something they had a hard time understanding. Their ignorance came from always being loved and cherished, and the unexpected jealousy he felt made him a bit incautious with his reply.

"As he never thought it was important to be a part of my life, I saw no importance in rushing home to be a part of his, especially not to honor him by standing at his side during his last breaths."

That baffled them.

"How can you not honor your father?" Edward-or-William asked, astonished.

"Yes, I was thoroughly enjoying my afternoon," Devlin said to Sin, responding to his first question and ignoring the rest of them.

Rake, who had always had a good feeling for when Devlin needed to be rescued, stepped through the wall of relatives and looked at the group with feigned surprise.

"How come you're gathered here, when our lovely ladies stand over at the sandwich table all by themselves and without protection? Well, except for George and Harry, but they are too old to be able to fight off the persistent suitors."

Sin didn't take his gaze from Devlin's face.

"We are a little busy here. Why don't you go and protect the ladies instead of interrupting this very interesting conversation."

Rake lifted one perfectly arched eyebrow at his nephew but didn't do as he was asked. Instead he turned to Sebastian, and with a wicked smile he continued, "And here I thought you all detested the young Mr. Pembroke because he was a leech and a fortune hunter, but instead you let him walk away with Fanny without even a blink."

This time he got a reaction.

In a second, all five men were up on their feet and on a new mission, to rescue Fanny from the leech. Rake sat down beside Devlin, stretching his long muscular legs in front of him.

They sat quietly for a while as Rake watched his relatives walk all over poor Mr. Pembroke, and Devlin tried to decide how to answer Rake's questions.

He knew there would be questions.

Their friendship was too good for Rake not to ask him about his intentions. But was Devlin ready to admit openly he wanted to court Fanny?

Last night he had decided he would marry her, that she was the perfect bride for him. And, more importantly, she would be a wonderful and loving mother to their children. Her family would never let her down, and she and the children would always be protected and cherished, as they well deserved.

This morning he had been a little unsure whether his feeling from the night before had been nothing more than an extension of the delight of meeting her and her family again.

But all bewilderment had disappeared like butter in sunshine when he met her today.

She was perfect in every way.

As if she could feel him looking at her, Fanny raised her head and met his gaze for the first time since she'd blurted out her wonderful outrageous words. To his pleasure, it seemed her earlier embarrassment was gone, and she gave him a slow, sweet smile that made him ache.

He wanted to kiss those lush lips and make her whimper with the need for him. Something must have shown on his face, because suddenly she blushed and looked away, and all he could think about was kissing the sensitive spot beneath her ear.

"You have to stop looking at her like she is a piece of cake. One could easily make the assumption you have thoughts about her you're not supposed to have toward a young debutante, especially one belonging to your best friend's family."

Devlin groaned silently.

Of course Rake would have seen him drooling all over Fanny. To be honest, he had not been very subtle about it, as even Fanny had noticed, and she was standing several feet away.

He looked at Rake, but the friend still had his eyes locked on the men who now were dragging poor Mr. Pembroke away from the Darling family. Fanny looked a little frustrated, and he guessed she wasn't too pleased with how her family was behaving toward her suitor.

"I would never do anything to endanger our friendship," he pointed out firmly, forcing Rake to look at him.

"No?"

"Of course not. You know me, Rake. I would never do anything to someone who means something to me."

Rake was quiet for a while, pondering what Devlin had said.

"I haven't seen you in more than five years. Why should I believe nothing has changed between us, and believe that you still are the man you were when we last met?"

"Why would I be here if I had anything but honest intentions toward Fanny?"

Rake suddenly sat straight up, staring at Devlin with disbelief. "You want her."

Devlin rolled his eyes. "I thought this whole conversation was about the fact that I want Fanny."

Rake shook his head and stood up, forcing Devlin to look up at him. "No, this conversation was all about you lusting for her, and me letting you know I'm aware of it. But now we are discussing you marrying her—and that, my friend, is a completely different matter."

Devlin could see the thought of courtship and marriage rattled his friend, because Rake couldn't stay still. Instead he paced to and fro in front of the chairs, obviously brooding about what he'd just heard.

As the other Darling men now had Mr. Pembroke chased away far enough, they were heading back toward their original victim, and Devlin knew he hadn't much time before they would be all over him again.

He rose and forced Rake to stop pacing by standing in his way.

"Do you think I have a chance?" he asked in a low, serious voice. Rake looked at Fanny, who now was whispering with her friends again. Now and then they would steal glances toward them, obviously talking about Devlin.

He snorted. "Of course you do, you bloody fool. She is completely awed by you, and would probably throw herself over a puddle of mud just so you wouldn't get your pretty feet dirty." He sighed deeply before he continued, "It's not that I would mind if you became a family member by marriage and not only in spirit. The thing that makes this whole affair feel strange and awkward is who we are talking about: my Fanny."

"So what do you want from me?"

Devlin could see there was something on Rake's mind, but his friend had trouble getting the words out, and before he had a chance to say more, Sin and Sebastian reached them.

Fanny's brothers immediately started to brag about how they had extracted Nicholas Pembroke from Fanny's presence. Jamie, Raleigh, and the two men who were probably Edward and William also joined them, and before he knew how it happened, he too was somehow extracted from the gathering of Darlings and away from Fanny's vicinity.

He looked at Rake, and his friend mouthed "White's," and Devlin nodded. He would have to wait a couple of hours, but then he would meet with Rake in peace and quiet, and they could talk about the situation.

His thoughts were interrupted by Lady Charmaine

de Vere, who all too obviously was trying to charm him into courting her, and he sighed quietly before he put on an interested face.

No one ever won anything by being uncivil.

Chapter 10

"Don't you think they make a striking couple?"

Fanny ripped her eyes from Devlin and Charmaine to glare at Emma Archer, who had joined her where she stood at the food table, pretending to ponder what to eat while watching the too-gorgeous couple.

Of course *she* thought they were a perfect match, as she was one of Charmaine's worshippers. She was supposed to think well of her friend. It wasn't Emma's fault Charmaine was an ogre.

"They are really quite handsome, both of them," Fanny replied diplomatically, trying hard not to reveal how envious she was of her archenemy.

But in vain, as Emma's small knowing smile told without words. Fanny guessed it wasn't too hard to figure out, as she had been staring at them with fire in her eyes for several minutes.

"I wouldn't be surprised if there will be an announcement not too far in the future," Emma said superciliously. "Charmaine is too beautiful to remain unengaged for too long, now that Hereford has finally returned to England."

Fanny faced a temptation to blurt out something stupid, like telling Emma how she'd overheard the conversation in the restroom, or saying that Devlin certainly didn't act like a more-or-less-engaged man when he was with her. Instead, she changed the subject.

97

"So you are Sebastian's guest today? I must admit I found it a bit strange when I heard about you two, as I didn't even think you knew each other."

Emma blushed, not at all happy with Fanny's choice of subject. "When your brother heard I was going to miss today's picnic, he nicely enough asked me to join your family. It was courteous of him, because I like picnics and would have been sad not to attend."

"Oh, really?" Fanny snorted. "And here I thought it was just because Mother felt sympathy for you and forced him to accompany you without regard for his feelings about it."

She regretted her harsh words as soon as they left her lips, but it was too late. Emma turned pale with shock, obviously without a clue that Sebastian had been coerced into inviting her.

Fanny started to apologize, but Emma murmured an almost inaudible, "Please, don't," before she turned abruptly and left.

"Emma?" Fanny groaned with embarrassment, feeling lower than low. It wasn't Emma's fault Charmaine and Devlin could be courting. And it certainly wasn't Emma's fault Fanny felt upset over Devlin gazing a bit too admiringly at Charmaine. She had done nothing but be a true friend. It was Fanny who was behaving like a fool. She surprised herself by her own behavior. She had reacted like a woman madly in love, one who wanted to mark her territory, not the well-behaved debutante of good family she was supposed to be. Was this how you knew you were in love?

"What's the problem, my dear?"

Rake put his arm around her waist as he joined her at the food table, and she welcomed his loving embrace. He kissed the top of her head, and she sighed again, but this time it was a contented sigh. He had always been her favorite uncle and her best friend, ever since she was a little girl.

"I heard Charmaine tell her friends she was being courted by Devlin."

"What?"

It was amazing how much better she felt, just because of Rake's obvious surprise.

"Do you think it could be true?" she asked him and almost held her breath, waiting for his answer.

He didn't answer her at first, his eyes darting from Devlin to Charmaine, as if just looking at them would give him his answer.

"No, I don't think it's true. Or, to put it a little more honestly, I know it isn't."

"How can you be so sure?" she asked, although she knew the only way he could know was if Devlin himself had told him about it.

But Rake was not interested in retelling his conversation with Devlin, as his head was filled with the delicate problem of the incomparable Charmaine.

"What I would like to know is why Charmaine tells such a lie? She can have anyone she wants, so why go for Devlin? And why entrap herself with a snare of lies? It is quite a big thing to tell your friends you are courted by someone, especially as she has no reason at all to believe it will actually happen."

"Doesn't she?" Fanny frowned toward the conversing couple. "I disagree with you there. She has all the reasons in the world, starting with the obvious one. She is the most beautiful young woman of the *ton*. Men with lesser titles than Devlin's have married a pretty face to make the family heirlooms look good when she carries them."

"So young, and yet so full of knowledge of the crudity of the real world." Rake grinned at her. "I just wish you would use this rare wisdom more randomly and not save it only for Charmaine."

Fanny ignored the remark about her random intelligence, as her head was filled with the delicate problem of Charmaine and her maybe-suitor Devlin.

"All those proposals she has received from most of the unmarried men of the *ton* must have gone to her head. Otherwise I can't think of anything to make her so confident about Devlin wanting her."

"He can't have met her much, as he came to London at the end of the last season and didn't attend any of the official social functions," Rake said as he pondered Fanny's words. "And as far as I know, they haven't met during the off season, as Devlin has not been anywhere near London or Berkshire. I guess I have to agree with you. She must be relying on the fact there is no one who can match her beauty. She must think a proposal is only a couple of days away if she plays it right. I mean, just look at them. She's practically showering him with attention, and any other man would have been down on his knees already, begging her for mercy."

"But not Devlin?"

Rake smiled. "No, not Devlin. You see, I know from a really good source that his interest is captured by another woman, one who knocked him off his feet yesterday."

Fanny blushed, feeling very pleased with her uncle's answer. So Devlin had told Rake he was interested in her? How nice.

She looked at the gorgeous couple again, and this time she met Devlin's gaze. He gave her a wink and a smile, and all her doubts disappeared. Rake told the truth, she was certain of it, because Devlin would not be so openly flirtatious with her if he were courting the woman at his arm.

Fanny blushed, and she could tell Devlin found her reaction funny, as she could see his shoulders move as he chuckled.

Charmaine, catching the direction of his glance, apparently didn't like her beau looking at another woman. As she walked farther from Fanny, Devlin, being a gentleman, had no choice but to follow.

However, this time Fanny didn't mind.

She had her answer. Devlin was not courting Charmaine. For the moment, he was all hers, although she was realistic enough to take it for what it was, an attraction. The season had just begun, and there was too much going on during the next three months to guarantee the attraction would last.

But for now, she and Devlin had started something, and she could hardly wait to find out what would become of it.

With a last glance at Charmaine, who hung on Devlin's arm flaunting her most flirtatious smile, Fanny said, "I never thought I would say this, but somehow I feel sorry for her." She frowned. "She is the most beautiful person ever to set foot in an English ballroom, and yet she has to lie about being courted. Penny says Charmaine has had over a hundred eligible bachelors asking for her hand, but she has refused them all, to everyone's surprise. I can't help but agree with you. There is something more to it."

Rake nodded thoughtfully.

"Penny has been wondering why she keeps saying no," Fanny continued. "When Lord Dane asked for her hand, she refused him, too, and Penny got really worried, as she knew he was very special to her sister. She said Charmaine had once admitted she wouldn't mind moving to Yorkshire, where he has his country estate, if he ever would propose. Nevertheless, when he finally did, she told him no."

Rake looked at her with astonishment.

"Really? Lord Dane?"

"Penny said she turned him down in the most brutal way, and it is such a mystery. One day she was madly in love with him and spoke nothing but good about him. But the next day she called him every horrid name she could think of and said she didn't want to hear his name again."

"How strange. I know Lord Dane, and he is a good man, honest and kind. His fortune is quite large, and his family is well connected. He would have been a really good choice for a girl without a dowry to speak of."

They looked at Charmaine where she stood, laughing and flirting with Devlin and her constant ring of other suitors. She was perfect, not a hair out of place. She looked just like the stunning diamond of the first water that she was.

And yet both Rake and Fanny pitied her.

"Well," Rake mused. "Maybe we should talk to Penny and ask her if she knows something more, so we can stop this scandal before it happens. Our friends in the *ton* will destroy her if they ever find out she lied about being courted by Devlin. They like nothing better than to knock a goddess off her pedestal."

Fanny directed their steps to where Penelope stood with Lord and Lady Nester, and one moment later they were chatting amiably.

Penelope's mother was of an agreeable personality but a little naïve and too easily impressed. Penelope loved her dearly, but sometimes she got impatient with her vagueness.

Her father, on the other hand, was the jolly kind, and his loud, booming laughter could always be heard over any crowd's chatter. Fanny didn't know much about him, other than that he wasn't a rich man, and that he was impressed with her family.

He always made a big fuss about her whenever she paid Penelope a visit, sometimes so much it became awkward and embarrassing.

Lord Nester was extremely pleased when they joined his little group, and Fanny thought he would have hugged Rake if his wife weren't at his arm.

"Lord Richard," he beamed. "How nice of you to join us!"

He nodded lightly toward Fanny, not quite so impressed by her, as he had known her since she was a wee little girl.

"It's our pleasure," Rake drawled, and Fanny had to bite her lip to stop the laughter that threatened to burst out over his obvious lie. "Have you been enjoying the picnic, my lady?" he asked Lady Nester.

Before the good lady had a chance to open her mouth, her husband gave his loud, booming laugh.

"Of course we have. It has been a real treat. The

ladies have most certainly outdone themselves this year, turning this boring park into such a wonderland of flowers and colors."

Lady Nester opened her mouth again, but her husband continued to ignore her.

"And the lemonade…" He kissed his fingers and continued in the worst French accent ever heard, "*C'est magnifique*."

"Yes, very good indeed," his wife agreed, bobbing her head, clearly giving up any thought of having an opinion of her own.

"Pity, though, Charmaine isn't here with us. She would have loved your company. But she is so popular, you know, and we can't hold her to us more than a few minutes before someone ushers her away. But for you, Lord Richard, we can call her over."

Lord Nester waved his hand toward his eldest daughter, and Penelope looked nauseous. Her father wasn't the best with etiquette, and Fanny knew Penelope sometimes found him terribly embarrassing.

Rake saved her from having to endure her father's shouts by grabbing hold of Penelope's hand.

"We just want to borrow Penny for a short while, and we will soon be back with her. If it's all right with you, of course?"

Before Lord and Lady Nester could say anything, Rake practically dragged the girls away, heading toward the outskirts of the picnic area, where they could talk more privately without anyone overhearing.

"I'm so sorry," Penelope breathed when they halted. "He is a little too eager sometimes, and tends to forget himself."

"Nothing to speak of." Rake shrugged.

Fanny let go of his arm and went to a stone bench at the side of the walkway, where she sat, gently spreading the skirt of her gown. Penelope joined her, and Rake paced to and fro before them, as he had a habit of doing when he had something on his mind.

He was a delight to look upon, this big, splendid man with dark brown hair and light gray, laughing eyes. After Devlin, he was the most sought-after bachelor in the *ton*. He was not highly titled, as he was a mere seventh son of a duke, and because of this the mamas placed him only second in the most-wanted-for-a-husband list.

Still, no woman had yet made him even consider marriage, and Fanny had a feeling he had no intention of ever getting married. He led a good life as it was, and there was no lack of willing women throwing themselves in his way in their eagerness to put themselves between his sheets.

This was unfortunate for Penelope, since she had been madly in love with him for many years. Rake had never noticed Penelope's admiration. As far as Fanny knew, he had never thought about her other than as his niece's friend.

"Fanny and I feel we have to talk to you about your sister," Rake blurted out, having finally decided how to start this uncomfortable conversation.

"W-what?" Penelope stuttered, caught off guard.

"As you are Fanny's friend, I think there is no other choice for me than to inform you about this first."

He sat down between the two women and grabbed Penelope's hands. If someone else had looked in their direction, they probably would have thought he was going to ask her to marry him, which would have been funny indeed, if it weren't for Penelope looking devastated.

"Oh, my God," she said in a harsh, broken voice. "You're going to marry Charmaine."

Chapter 11

Rake became still.

"No, of course not," Fanny said, rushing in to break the awkward silence. "Rake doesn't even like Charmaine, as you are aware."

Penelope looked from Fanny to Rake, who stared at her with a strange look in his face.

"You're not? You don't?" she asked him with tears in her eyes.

He blinked a couple of times before he let go of her hands and stood up. He opened his mouth, then closed it again as if he didn't know what to say.

Suddenly, without another word, he bowed and left them sitting there by themselves.

"What was this?" Fanny mused, looking at her uncle's disappearing back. Penelope opened her purse and lifted her handkerchief to her teary eyes.

"I'm so sorry, Fanny," she sniffled. "He caught me off guard. It was my worst nightmare coming to life. You know how I suffered last year, when I knew Charmaine was in London where he was too. Everyone always falls in love with her, and I expected him to. But when a full season went by and he hadn't even been courting her, I relaxed, and this really took me by surprise. Oh, God, what will he think of me now?"

Fanny hugged her friend closely, silently cursing Rake for being such a blind fool, and especially for being so stubborn about remaining a bachelor.

This was so typical of the men of her family! None of them could see what was in front of them. They kept their eyes on the horizon, always searching for what they thought they needed, instead of actually enjoying what they had.

"Don't you get upset about this now," she told Penelope. "Rake is one of the most intelligent persons I ever met, and he does wonders with our family fortune, constantly enlarging the already vast funds, according to my father. However, when it comes to feelings, he is beyond naïve."

She gave Penelope her own dry handkerchief, and her friend accepted it with a thankful, if damp, smile.

"What was it you two wanted to talk to me about?" Penelope asked when she had composed herself again. "What about Charmaine?"

"Oh, please don't be angry with me for saying this, but there is no way I can choose not to tell you."

"Fanny, now you worry me. What is it? Please do tell."

Now it was Fanny's turn to stand and walk to and fro before the bench, unconsciously mimicking her uncle. "I think Charmaine has told her friends something I know is untrue, and it is about to backfire on her."

"What?"

"Last night, at the Easton Ball, I went to the restroom to sit down for a while, but I heard Charmaine and her friends coming." Fanny hesitated but decided to tell the truth. "As I didn't want to spend time with her, I hid on the balcony while they were refreshing themselves."

Penelope frowned. "Fanny, you shouldn't go out on the balcony all alone. Someone might see you and get the wrong impression. Think of your reputation, your future. Think about your family."

"I know. You don't have to tell me. It was a stupid move, but I *cannot* stand your sister."

Penelope sighed. She knew this was the truth, so she forced herself not to jump to her sister's defense. Instead she encouraged Fanny to continue.

"They were talking about a lot of things, and one thing was how Charmaine secretly is being courted by Devlin Ross."

"What?" Now Penelope stood, too, her confusion obvious. "I can't believe it. I mean, she's hardly met the man. She once told me he didn't even look at her with the admiration she was used to, and it vexed her a bit. She is a bit spoiled, you know."

"A bit?"

Penelope glared at Fanny, who let the subject drop and continued on with her confession instead.

"As I happen to know Devlin has no intentions toward Charmaine, her lie will soon be revealed. It will be devastating for her if her friends choose to make it public."

Penelope paled as she realized the truth of what Fanny said. She grabbed Fanny's hand and stopped her from pacing.

"Are you sure?"

"Have I ever lied to you?"

When Penelope shook her head, Fanny couldn't stop herself, and she hugged her friend close.

"It's not too late, as the truth is not out there yet. We still have time to stop it. You have to talk to

Charmaine."

"No."

"You have to."

"Please don't force me to tell Charmaine."

"You have to, or else I will. You know as well as I do that she won't believe a word of what I tell her. But she believes everything you say. So, yes, you have to. She's *your* bloody sister."

They stared at each other for a while, both trying to subdue the other with bare willpower. But, as always, it ended with the two of them giggling.

"Oh, Fanny, you're such a treat." Penelope sighed. "Okay, I'll talk to her, but I won't look forward to it. You said he has no intentions of courting her. I have to know—are you certain?"

Fanny's face warmed, and she knew she didn't have to tell her friend anything. The beet-red color would say it all.

Penelope cried out with delight. "Oh, Fanny, really?"

"I don't know what it will lead to, but there is a mutual attraction, and Devlin has acknowledged it to Rake. I don't think he would do such a thing if he were already engaged, or on the verge of proposing."

A shrill whistle sliced through the air, catching their attention. The picnic was over, and Lord Newbury wanted his daughter to join them for the journey home.

Together, Penelope and Fanny walked back through the fields of flowers, thinking about all that had happened in the few short hours of the picnic.

Penelope hugged Fanny again before she left her and joined her sister and parents in their carriage. The lawn was almost empty by now, and Fanny looked through the few people remaining, but Devlin was nowhere to be seen. She couldn't help but feel a little prick of disappointment.

She had secretly yearned to meet him again, if only to say goodbye. If she didn't see him now, there was no way to tell when the next time would be. The invitations she had received so far had been from relatives and friends, nothing to which a bachelor who wasn't an immediate relative would be invited.

The next grand ball was two weeks away, and suddenly fourteen days seemed like an eternity.

Her father was in an expansive mood and enjoyed ordering his brothers about, collecting chairs and tables. At the same time, he succeeded with annoying his poor servants, who couldn't do their jobs with their masters constantly in their way.

Fanny joined her mother, who stood silently in the now empty field, ignoring her husband. Caroline was a radiant beauty, with mahogany-colored hair and shiny green eyes. Fanny had many times wished she had inherited her mother's striking colors, instead of her father's brown hair and gray eyes.

Sin also had their father's coloring, but where the men looked strict and handsome with that, she as a woman looked merely mousy. Sebastian stood out in any family gathering, the only child who had their mother's coloring.

"Have you been enjoying yourself?" Caroline asked her daughter as they strolled toward their carriage.

"I have. It has been most entertaining. So far, I am really enjoying my first season. Everyone is dashing and fashionable, and the clothes are amazing. I can't believe how some of the women put on so much jewelry at this early time of the day. I could hardly make out if they were dressed at all!"

Caroline laughed at her enthusiasm. "Yes, the women of the *ton* do know how to look their best. But I think you and Penelope won the fight, looking so pretty together. Just like a bouquet of flowers. And I wasn't the only one admiring you. I noticed a certain duke who couldn't tear his eyes from you."

Fanny cursed silently over her inability to stay serene, as she could feel her cheeks get warm and red again. There was no way her mother would let it pass without getting an explanation out of her.

"According to Rake," Fanny admitted quietly, "he has acknowledged his intentions of courting me."

Caroline could easily see how much her daughter cared for the man, or rather her own image of him, even though she pretended to be unaffected.

"And how do you feel about it?"

"I must confess I am very much attracted to him, as everything about him is highly appealing to me. And I do want him to court me, because I want to get to know him. I want to see if I'm just as attracted to his personality as I am to his appearance. I was fanatic about him when I was younger, and I seem to fall too easily into the same state of mind as I did then. But I do now understand how falling in love is more complicated than one would think. A person you once knew could today be someone else. A shiny exterior can hide a rotten inside." She winked to her mother. "Just take Charmaine as an example."

Caroline laughed. "I have always felt sorry for the poor girl, as she has not had an easy time with you hovering around, hostile and unfriendly."

"Mother! You are supposed to be on my side, not the fishy ogre's."

Caroline didn't answer the childish remark. Instead she simply looked at her daughter until Fanny made an embarrassed grimace.

"I know. You don't have to say it," she finally admitted. "I have not been very accommodating toward Charmaine. She was such an awful child when we were younger I got kind of used to disliking her. Penelope always tells me there is more to Charmaine than meets the eye, and that I am just being childish. But nobody thinks about how she acts toward me. She is not very nice when she addresses me, either, and so I don't think our poor relationship is only my fault."

"If you are nicer, maybe she will be, too," Caroline urged. "You don't know until you've tried, my dear."

"I suppose you are right, although I think it's a little late for me and Charmaine to be friends. Especially now."

"Oh?"

"Promise you won't tell Papa about it!" When Caroline looked at her with suspicion, Fanny stopped and put her hands on her hips. "Promise!"

"All right, I won't tell your father, as long as it isn't something dangerous to you or anyone else in our family."

Fanny rolled her eyes, but she knew she couldn't ask more of her mother, since she was too caring for her own good. She told her mother what she had learnt about Charmaine's lie, and what Rake had said about the consequences.

Caroline nodded. "You did the right thing, my

dear. Telling Charmaine now makes it possible for her to repair her story with her friends and, by doing so, prevent a terrible scandal before it is too late. For any other young woman, it wouldn't be such a big thing, but Charmaine is, after all, the most sought-after debutante, and thereby an easy target for every envious other woman out there who would love to put an end to her reign."

"Thank you, Mama."

With a gentle smile Caroline climbed into the carriage, now full of Darling men arguing over the best way to stack chairs, and put an end to the conversation.

Chapter 12

"Is this seat taken?"

Devlin looked up from his newspaper and gave Rake a welcoming smile. "I'm sorry you had to wait," Rake continued, as he sat. "Dinner turned into a rather heated occasion. My brothers and nephews couldn't stop arguing about some bloody chairs, and the subject prolonged the whole meal."

It sounded strange to Devlin's ears, having one's meal disturbed and prolonged because of chairs. He had eaten his dinner alone. Bear, who usually joined him when he was at home, had been out on one of his unmentionable escapades.

"Quite a crowd here today," Devlin said, tilting his head toward the other men in the room.

"It's always like this when the Season starts. Every last gentleman in the *ton* comes here to meet old acquaintances and exchange news and gossip."

As a servant passed their table, Devlin ordered two glasses of wine, while Rake lit a cigar and leaned farther back in the comfortable armchair. Neither of them spoke until after the servant had returned with their wine and then left them again in their dark corner.

"I think Penelope is in love with me," Rake said in a voice whose uncharacteristic squeaks and trembles made it clear he hadn't gotten over the shock yet.

"Is it a problem?" Devlin asked. "I thought the girl

was like family to you already."

Rake sat up. "That's just it. She's been around my legs for eighteen years, and not once have I thought of her as anything more than Fanny's friend, or an annoying little sister. But these last months…"

He leaned back again and puffed on his cigar, obviously more upset about the whole thing than he should have been, if he truly thought of Penelope as merely a little sister.

Devlin hid a smile. Rake was already caught in Penelope's sweet web and had not a clue about it. He sent a thought of sympathy to the poor girl, who had an impossible mission ahead of her. It wouldn't be easy to make Rake give up his bachelor ways and instead settle for being a husband and a father.

The thought of becoming a husband brought him back to his own situation.

"Your family left the picnic before I had a chance to say goodbye."

Rake snorted. "As we were among the last ones leaving, I don't think your missed chance to drool all over Fanny was because of us. I would rather say it was because you didn't come forward, although she stood there moping over not seeing you anywhere."

Devlin lit up. "Did she mope?"

Rake rolled his eyes. "Oh, come on, please save me from this. Don't make me talk about things only women find a pleasure in discussing."

Devlin didn't like the reprimand and would have asked more but saw it would be to no use. Rake had no intention of saying more about what his niece did or did not say or do.

"It was that awful Lord Nester who more or less

pushed me inside their carriage when he learnt I had arrived in a paid hack," Devlin admitted with a shudder. "I had to sit beside Charmaine, who 'happened' to bump into me at least twenty times during the short ride. There are few bends on the way from Green Park to Grosvenor Square, and yet the poor girl was thrown around the carriage. Your Penelope—"

"She is not *my* Penelope!"

Devlin looked patronizingly at him, and this time it was Rake's turn to fume.

"Anyway, Penelope tried to converse with me about the weather and other neutral topics, but her old man kept probing about my fortune. He wanted to know how vast it was, and enlightened me on how good it was for me to have so much money as a safety. He even mentioned how he wished his daughters would marry someone with a large fortune, and pointed out that I wasn't married."

Rake laughed, as he had no problem imagining Lord Nester ranting on about money and marriage.

"The man is infamous for all his creditors. Of course he wouldn't mind marrying off his daughters for money."

"Poor Penelope. It must be horrible for a nice girl like her to have such an awful family. I must say this makes me feel much better for not having someone to call family. I am sure as hell not counting Delia as my closest kin."

"I wouldn't either." Rake grinned wickedly. "Not after she tried to climb into your bed. I can't believe she had the nerve, being your mother's cousin and all."

Devlin twirled the red liquor in the crystal glass and shook his head with a chuckle. "You should have

117

seen her face when I told her to take her old wrinkled body and get out of there."

"I can imagine." Rake laughed. "Too vividly."

"I wish she would simply disappear, and take those horrid children with her. Better to have no family at all than have to share the same roof with those three."

"It's hard for me to think of a life without a caring family. I can't imagine life without mine. They might be a little too much sometimes, but they still mean everything to me."

Devlin felt a small prick of envy.

Rake's parents were the safe haven of his life, and Chester Park the one place in his life where Rake knew he would always be welcome. There he could be himself without any strings. For Devlin, it seemed like something out of a fairytale, too good to be true. But for Rake, it was reality.

"I can't imagine being so close to anyone," Devlin said, half aloud, and Rake gave him a sharp look.

"Can't you? I thought you and I had a close friendship."

Devlin emptied his glass and made a gesture to the servant that he wanted another.

"Of course we are. Or at least were."

"Were?" Rake echoed, as if he didn't believe his ears.

"Oh, come on," Devlin drawled. "You have to admit we aren't as close now as we were when we attended school together."

"I don't know whether to laugh or cry over such a ridiculous admission." Rake shook his head, and Devlin frowned at him.

"It's not ridiculous. We haven't seen each other at

all over the last couple of years, and consistency is what keeps a good friendship going. Not absence."

It wasn't hard to see how pathetic Rake found his admission, but Devlin didn't care. "We have both been through things in our lives that have molded us into what we are today," he continued, as Rake stayed silent, brooding. "And since our roads have been very different, I would say you and I are different men now than we were five years ago."

"Maybe," Rake replied, but Devlin could tell he didn't agree at all with his harsh words. No surprise there. Rake had always been the softer of the two.

"You must recognize the truth in my words, don't you?"

"Maybe," Rake repeated, still not admitting to anything. "Yesterday I told some of my relatives how I trusted you around Fanny, but now I think I can't. Or can I?"

"You know you can."

"Can I? You've just spent the last couple of minutes trying to convince me you are not the man I once knew. So how can you at the same time expect me to trust you around my beloved niece?"

Devlin leaned forward and looked deep into Rake's gray eyes in an effort to show him what was inside his heart.

"War changes a man, and I am not the same man I was five years ago. However, some things never change, and you know how highly I honor and respect you, as I always have."

"Five years ago, I would have thrown myself down from the Tower if you asked me to, as I knew you wouldn't ask if you didn't have a really good reason.

Until today I thought I still would have. But now suddenly I feel differently. I'm not really sure of who you are anymore. As you put it, war changes a man, and both Jamie and my cousin Lee are living examples of how war can cripple a man, mentally or physically."

The mention of Rake's relatives who had joined the Napoleonic wars cut through Devlin's erratic thoughts. His heart filled with compassion over the poor men who too had seen the horrors of war and survived.

"Now there's the Devlin I know and trust," Rake said, and Devlin frowned at him.

"Excuse me?"

"And maybe that's what's bothering me."

Devlin had a hard time following Rake's thoughts.

"Now what?"

"Hmm," Rake said, frowning, not answering Devlin. "You haven't changed. Not really. You still are the same person, maybe, only older and more levelheaded. With Jamie and Lee fresh in mind, you seem quite undisturbed for a man who has seen the ghastliness of war."

"How are they?" Devlin questioned softly, ignoring Rake's ranting for the time being.

"Not so good. Neither had any bodily harm, which is a relief. But our beloved Lee, the happy and somewhat naïve young man, has turned into a quiet, brooding fellow. He doesn't talk about what he has seen or gone through, and it puts us all in an impossible position. We all want to help, but no one is able to because we don't know what the problem is. He doesn't even talk to Jamie, who went with him and therefore is well aware of all the horrors our soldiers fighting

Napoleon Bonaparte had to live through."

"Please tell them both they can talk to me anytime they want to," Devlin begged. "I have been to the continent and have seen many things, too. I might be able to understand in a way no one of you, their family, can."

"So how was the continent for you?" Rake resumed his earlier probing, and Devlin couldn't stop a grin. Rake would have made an excellent spy. "It can't have been easier for you than for my brother and cousin."

"It wasn't so bad."

"Wasn't it?" Rake was aghast over Devlin's unusual indifference. "Every other man I have spoken with, including Jamie, has admitted the same thing—it was hell on earth."

Devlin shrugged. "The food was good."

"You must be kidding me!"

Devlin put his wine glass down and gave Rake a hard stare. "If you don't believe my answers, why do you insist on asking me about it?"

Rake was silent for a moment, his eyes never leaving Devlin's face. "I want to get to know you again. As you so nicely put it, you were my friend before you left, and now it feels like I don't know who you are anymore."

"I am the same man."

"You can't be, not after enduring something as awful as war."

Devlin nodded. "One would think so."

"So why aren't you?"

"I haven't been with the army during my time in France, but I have been working for the government."

Rake leaned back, his eyes suddenly filled with understanding.

"Were you one of Basil's Boys?" he asked, surprising Devlin with his insight.

"You know about Lord Saxton?"

"Of course I do. My cousin Drake, Lee's younger brother, is working for him in spite of his youth."

This surprised Devlin. It wasn't common for anyone to know when a family member worked secretly for the ministry.

"You know about Drake?"

Rake laughed. "Of course I do. So does Fanny."

This news upset Devlin. "Bloody hell! You have told Fanny? What if someone grabs her for information, just because she's Drake's cousin?"

Now it was Rake's turn to shrug indifferently.

"Drake needed someone more than me who could excuse him at home. Fanny was the excellent choice. They have always been such good friends, being almost of an age, you know."

"I don't like it," Devlin muttered sourly.

"Well, it's out of your hands," Rake said with great satisfaction.

Devlin frowned at his friend but held his tongue. This was not the place to discuss his, or Drake's, secret work with the ministry.

Rake grinned back, all his earlier resistance dissipated. "This is excellent news, indeed. As I am aware of how Lord Saxton chooses his spies, I also know there is nothing wrong with you. If there had been anything out of the ordinary with you and your life, Basil would never have invited you to join his Boys."

"I still don't like you two telling Fanny, though. Even if it's not in my hands," Devlin muttered as the servant came and fetched their empty glasses. He served them two large brandies instead.

Rake, who would have preferred to talk about Devlin and his escapades in the line of duty, gave in and held back his questions for another time.

"Are you going to make sure it *is* in your hands?"

"I don't know," Devlin admitted honestly. "I only met Fanny last night, and even though the attraction is outstanding I won't ask her to marry me before I spend some time with her and come to know her a little better."

"It sounds like a good plan."

"So can I?"

"Can you what?"

"Court her?"

Rake laughed. "Of course you can. It's not my decision to make, after all."

"But your opinion matters to me," Devlin said. "And if you are against it, I will back down."

Rake smiled, satisfied with Devlin's show of respect.

"You go ahead. I would be honored to call you family."

The special moment was interrupted when Jamie and Sin joined them at their table and started to chat about the horse race they'd attended a few days before. They kept bantering in a friendly manner about which horse was the better one, and soon more of their friends came over to talk, and the evening got better and better.

Devlin looked at Rake, who was telling some outrageous story about a one-armed whore, drawing hoots of laughter from the crowd. Lord, it felt good being back, especially as he had no obligation to his father anymore.

Now he could just concentrate on his own happiness, and he would begin tomorrow by paying Fanny a visit, and maybe catch a kiss or two.

Chapter 13

Of course they waited for her.

Fanny had stayed in her room until she almost missed breakfast, silently wishing for her family to be long gone before she went down to the family breakfast room.

But no.

As if they knew her scheme, they were all there, eating and chatting about nothing and everything. She gave a resigned sigh and sat down in the empty chair between Uncle Harry and her cousin Drake.

A footman brought her a large cup of tea, and she put her hands around the hot cup, enjoying the warmth that spread from her hands to the rest of her body.

Her parents sat side by side at one end of the table, reading together in the social section of the day's newspaper. Her Aunt Diana sat beside them, arguing with her eldest son, Lee, while her husband read the political part of the newspaper and now and then read something aloud to anyone who happened to listen.

Drake was dressed in apple-green clothing—the essence of fashion, as he was telling Uncle Ward on the other side of the table, completely ignoring his unwilling listener's disinterest in the subject. Uncle Liam was in a heated discussion with his brothers Rake and Jamie over how one got rid of leeches, much to Fanny's chagrin.

Her brothers were still arguing over the best way to stack chairs, which didn't surprise her in the least, knowing how stubborn they both were. She made a little wager with herself that they would continue at least until next Saturday, seven days away, before they found something else to dissect.

She loved all twelve of these people so much, even her petty-minded Aunt Diana, and she knew they all adored her right back. She was surrounded with love, and yet somehow she suddenly felt as if there was a small piece missing. Like there was one more chair needing to be occupied for her to be complete.

The thought disturbed her a little, because she could easily guess from whence it originated.

It amazed her how important Devlin had become to her in the last two days. Now all she wanted was to get to know him, the real him. What were his dreams, his plans for life? Where had he been, and how had it made him into the unbelievably charismatic person he was today? And, more importantly, what were his thoughts about stacking chairs...

"Fanny dear, did you see all the beautiful flowers that were delivered to you?" Aunt Diana asked, interrupting her thoughts.

"N-no," she stuttered. She had been daydreaming about Devlin as she passed the foyer and hadn't noticed anything out of the ordinary.

"How could you miss them? They were all over the hallway—I hardly found my way here!"

"Oh, come on, Sebastian, they were not everywhere," Sin mocked, and gave Fanny a what-an-ass look, which only garnered him a bread roll in the head, thrown by his devoted brother.

"They were too," Sebastian growled, while his brother rubbed the side of his head. "I felt like an adventurer exploring an unknown jungle when I came down for breakfast. You, sister dear, must have crushed a lot of hearts yesterday when you kept ignoring all your beaus for your one and only."

"I did not," Fanny gasped.

"Did too."

"Did not!"

"Children, children," Caroline called out with despair. "Please behave. We are trying to enjoy our breakfast."

Sebastian gave Fanny a superior grin, and she almost growled at him for being such a tease. This was the bad side of having siblings who were close to you: they knew exactly what buttons to push.

Caroline seemed to feel she had to excuse her youngest son, and she turned to her daughter with a shining smile. "There isn't a jungle, Fanny, but it's quite a lot of flowers. There were also a stack of calling cards left for us, including some invitations to some especially pleasant assemblies, suitable for a young lady. Tonight we are going to dine with my parents, as you well know, but tomorrow we are invited to a small party where there will be mostly other debutantes and their families, which is an agreeable way to meet new friends."

"Or a subtle way to be able to view your competition," Sebastian inserted, bringing him a harsh glare from his loving mother.

"Oh, come on, Mother," he admonished with a laugh. "You should be the first to admit how the social season is nothing more than a matrimonial market."

"I do not admit to such a thing." Caroline sniffed. "And you shouldn't be so rude. There is more to the Season than matrimony."

"There is?" Sebastian said, with his green eyes wide. His mother, not so loving this time, mimicked his earlier move and threw a bread roll at him. His quick hand caught it in the air, and he bit off a large chunk with his strong white teeth.

"Pig," Caroline hissed.

"Oh, don't I know it," he answered with his mouth full.

His mother gave up the argument with a deep sigh. Fanny bit back a smile, as she knew all too well there was no way their mother ever would win a verbal duel with her sons, especially the younger one. He never seemed to take anything anyone said seriously.

Butler came in through the door and, in a voice as solemn and formal as his person, announced: "His Grace, the Duke of Hereford."

They all went quiet for a second, and then the racket continued. Fanny's heart skipped a beat, and the only thing she could think was how poorly she was dressed. What on earth had possessed her to come downstairs dressed in one of her oldest morning gowns? This was not how she had planned to look the next time she and Devlin met. She had meant to dazzle him with her finest dress, but instead…

George stood to greet their guest, who came through the door looking overwhelmed by the crowded room and the loud chattering.

Devlin bowed his head to his host and the ladies before seating himself in the chair Butler conjured from nowhere and placed at George's right. He looked around the table with a strange expression on his beautiful face until his gaze briefly stopped as it met Fanny's.

She could feel her cheeks turn hot, and he gave her an amused smile. He seemed to enjoy her transparency, but it made him too aware of every emotion she felt.

"You're up and about early," George uttered, as his wife poured their guest some tea. "Is this something you learnt on the continent, perhaps? Lord knows it isn't common here among your peers."

"This is an awful hour to be up and about." Drake let out with a big yawn. "I still can't understand why I couldn't stay in the sack for a few hours more. At least until it's time for the fashionable hour. It would do wonders for my complexion, you know."

"If you would get any prettier, none of us would be able to eat anything. Instead we would just sit here, admiring your perfection."

Drake looked at Sebastian with a little too much eagerness. "You think?"

George ignored the young ones and offered Devlin some ham sandwiches.

"You know," he said as he set the tray down again, "your mother was one of the most beautiful women I ever met, and had she not been already betrothed to your father I think I would have courted her."

Devlin looked surprised; this was news to him. As if George understood how little Conan had told the boy about the mother he didn't remember, he continued with dreamy eyes.

"As you know, she was born in the small village of Compton, not far from Chester Park, and she was the loveliest person, both outside and inside. My best friend in those days, Freddie Aldworth, and I were both seriously in love with her. Our hearts were crushed when we were told she had been engaged to your father since before she was born. However, the information didn't stop us, of course. My father was very upset with me at the time, because we learnt Emily's favorite flower was a pink rose, and as there were loads of pink roses in the garden of Chester Park we picked a few and gave them to her."

Uncle Harry suddenly laughed out loud.

"A few, you say?" He guffawed. "More likely thousands. You and your fellow spent a whole night covering the front of her house with all the flowers. We all were made aware of that as soon as her father came with three wagons and returned them at our front door the next morning. He was spitting mad at you and Freddie, and threatened to stuff them down your throats if you did something like it again."

"Oh, Papa, how romantic of you," Fanny said dreamily. "I do hope Grand-Papa didn't get too upset with you."

"He did get upset, but not because we gave them to Emily. No, he got upset because he was all caught up about Anna at the time. She had told him the day before how she loved pink roses, and so he had invited her to come and look at the ones at Chester Park. What upset him was that he now would have to tell her there was no point in her coming, as there were no pink roses left."

"But what did Emily say?" Fanny asked, not noticing how Devlin too stared at George, waiting breathlessly for the answer.

"Emily, as the wonderful person she was, saved

one pink rose, which she dried and put in her jewelry case, where she kept all her things of great value. As I said, she had such a good heart. When I heard she had passed away only a few years later, the world became a bit dimmer."

George sat quiet for a moment, obviously pondering the past, before he continued. "But it was a true treat for me when you came to Chester Park with Rake, Devlin. You look so much like your mother, you know. You have the same dark hair, golden eyes, and bright smile. It was like getting a small piece of her back. It was quite saddening you only came that one summer. We would have loved to have you there every year. Why didn't you return? I hope we didn't offend you in any way?"

Fanny froze. This was a question she too had wondered. She had been terribly upset all those years ago when her hero—and future husband—didn't return to her.

"My father never cared whether I came home during the holidays, until he heard I'd spent a summer with your family. I don't know why it bothered him, but I had no choice but to obey him, as he was my legal guardian and I had no say at all."

Rake, who had been listening, now asked quietly, "Why didn't you tell me? I thought it was something I did wrong, because all you told me was that you didn't want to come with me again."

"I told you I *couldn't* come home with you again," Devlin said. "But you never asked me why."

Rake nodded thoughtfully, and Fanny leaned back in her chair. Was this why? All those tears she'd spent when he didn't come back, and now she was told it

Jennifer Wenn

hadn't been his own choice.

Maybe her mother was right, years ago, when she told Fanny she should stop wearing her heart on her sleeve. Everything that happened wasn't because of her.

As breakfast came to its end, the Darlings one after another left the family breakfast room. Slowly it grew quieter, until only Fanny and her parents remained with Devlin. They were well aware of why he was there without anyone saying it.

"Do you want to tell us what gives us the honor of welcoming you to our humble home today, Hereford?" George pretended innocence but with a wicked smile. "Or shall I just tell Fanny to go and get dressed and tell her maid to get ready for a walk in the sun?"

"Papa!" Fanny protested, embarrassed over her father's forwardness, but Devlin only laughed.

"I would really enjoy your daughter's company for a ride in the new phaeton I just bought, if it would be all right with you, sir? Unfortunately, there won't be any room for her maid."

"It would be just fine—or, what do you say, my dear?" he asked Caroline, who nodded with tears in her eyes.

"Fanny, dear, why don't you go upstairs and get yourself ready? We will await you in my office."

Fanny nodded to her father. She had to restrain herself from running until she was out of sight. Then she took the stairs two steps at a time, and in a second she was in her bedroom shouting orders to her maid Nell, who just smiled and shook her head at her young mistress' obvious hurry.

Fanny rummaged through the dresses in her large wardrobe. What should she wear?

132

She wanted to make a really good impression. She wanted to show him she wasn't just a debutante or the little girl from his past but a grown-up woman who would make an excellent duchess.

In the end, she picked one of the new mousseline gowns she and her mother had ordered from the seamstress when they arrived in London. It was a lovely pink color that she knew fit her complexion and didn't render her pale and colorless.

Nell helped her with her matching bonnet and coat, and Fanny rushed down the stairs again, heading for her father's office, only to be stopped by her mother in the hallway.

"You do look beautiful," her mother said, obviously pleased with her daughter's appearance.

"Thank you, Mother," Fanny breathed, and kissed Caroline's cheek before she continued down the corridor. Giddy, almost too excited, she couldn't stop smiling.

It was unbelievable she had met him only two days earlier, because now he was all she could think of. She was so caught up in her thoughts she bumped into the men who stood in the hallway waiting for her. All her four younger uncles, her two cousins, and her two brothers stood there with determination written across their handsome faces.

She caught herself before she rolled her eyes. She guessed she had no other choice but to listen to whatever they wanted to say, and she had a pretty good idea what was on their minds.

"Yes?" she asked, trying hard not to show her impatience.

Sin was pushed forward by the others, obviously

being the one chosen to deliver the message they thought she needed to hear. He opened his mouth to speak but closed it again. A minute or two passed with him standing there squirming and not speaking one syllable.

Now and then one of the others would poke Sin in the back, and he would turn around and glare.

"Oh, come on! Devlin is waiting for me, you know," Fanny said, when she had reached the absolute end of her patience.

"You can't let him fondle you," Sin finally blurted out.

Fanny was mortified.

"I can't believe you just said that!" she cried out.

"Oh, for heaven's sake!" Rake gave in. "What your daft brother is trying to tell you is that you must be aware Devlin is a libertine, and as such he might make some sort of pass at you. If he does, you must be quite clear that you won't have anything to do with it, and you must demand that he return you here at once."

Fanny didn't know what to say. She knew they only talked about this because they cared for her, but this was a bit too much.

"A man can get carried away when he is attracted to a woman. A man as experienced with women as Devlin is will be too much for an innocent like you, and you won't stand a chance," Edward clarified from somewhere behind Sin. "Before you know it, you will be on your back with your skirts over...*ouf!*"

"Too much information," said his twin, William, after he'd punched him in the stomach. Drake came forward and took her hand, and his long slender fingers held hers in a surprisingly strong grip.

"We know what someone as experienced as Devlin can do to someone who is as innocent as you, and to not be able to be there to prevent it from happening scares the hell out of us. Your mother forbade us to go with you, follow you, or send someone else to be closer to you than a mile, so we are fumbling in the dark here."

Fanny closed her eyes and counted to ten before she glared at her relatives. They shrank back, all eight of them, and she walked by them with her head held high.

When she had passed them, she turned around and put her hands on her hips, giving each one of them a hard stare.

"Never talk to me about this again."

When Sebastian opened his mouth, she threw out a wagging finger and said with the angriest voice they'd ever heard from her, "Never, ever, ever!"

She turned and left them standing there in the hallway and didn't halt until she stood in front of the office door. With a deep breath to calm her nerves, she knocked and entered the room.

Her father gave her a welcoming smile she almost missed because of the magnificent man who rose and bowed his head politely toward her.

George put a loving arm around her slender waist, bringing her close to give her a small peck on her head. "Off you go, and have a nice time."

Fanny smiled shakily toward her father, unable to find her voice, as excited as she was.

Devlin offered her his arm, and she put her hand lightly on it, feeling the hard muscles shift under her fingertips. He led her outside to a shiny new phaeton behind the loveliest pair of white horses she had ever seen.

"It's beautiful," she breathed. "I love its elegant simplicity, so perfect for a duke!"

Devlin smiled at her exhilaration and followed her as she fluttered around the carriage, stroking the smooth surface, before she went to the horses and petted them. One buffed his muzzle against her head, almost pushing her bonnet off, but she only laughed.

When she looked back at Devlin, he was again staring at her with that strange combination of pride, admiration, and contentment. He held out a hand toward her, and she grabbed it with a sweet smile.

His thumb caressed her fingertips as they rested in the palm of his hand, and she blushed even more. Looking deep into his smoldering eyes, she knew she would have kissed him if they hadn't been standing in public outside her home. A glance at the front of the house informed her that almost every window was occupied by a family member looking down at them, and she let out a little frustrated sigh.

As she climbed up and sat down in the carriage, she waved her hand toward her onlookers and had the satisfaction of knowing she'd surprised most of them, as they took an automatic step back before they came forward again to wave hesitantly back.

"Bloody family of mine," she muttered to herself, and Devlin, who had just settled beside her, looked at her curiously. She gave him an apologetic smile.

"My family can be a little too much sometimes. I know it's because they care about me, but being the only young female, surrounded by all these men who want to protect me against everything, can get rather annoying."

"They do it because they love you."

"I know, and I am most thankful for the love they bestow on me. But sometimes I can't help but wish they would give me some freedom. Some things you need to find out by yourself."

"Learn by living?"

She laughed, pleasantly surprised. "Why, yes. 'Learn by living.' Oh, I have to remember this saying, so I can tell it to them the next time they are going to give me some unwanted advice."

Devlin laughed. "You must promise me you won't tell your brothers, or the rest of your obnoxious relatives, that it was I who gave you the idea."

As the carriage started to move, they shared a smile. Somehow it suddenly became them against the world, and both felt excitement over what was going to happen next. Their future was an unwritten page, and it was now up to them to fill it.

Chapter 14

They drove silently down Mount Street and turned right on Park Lane, where they continued until they reached the Grosvenor Gate to Hyde Park. Once inside the large park, they turned left, and Devlin let the horse walk slowly down The Ring, heading for Rotten Row.

It was still too early for the fashionable hour, so they were practically alone, overseen only by a few nannies exercising the children in their care. Fanny smiled and waved to the children, who waved back with the enthusiasm only children show.

The morning was so beautiful. The sky was all blue, and the sun spread its golden light, making everything seem more colorful.

Or maybe it was the company.

Devlin was, if possible, even more devastatingly handsome than he'd been the day before. He was perfect all over, from his modern windswept hair—his valet had probably spent an hour creating that perfection earlier this morning—down to the shiny Hessians embracing his muscular calves.

"Do you always have such loud breakfasts at your home?" Devlin asked.

"Oh, it wasn't loud. They were very quiet today, all because of you."

This caught Devlin's attention. "Because of me?"

"Why, yes, they were trying very hard not to talk

too loudly, so they wouldn't miss what you and Father were discussing."

Fanny almost smiled as she saw his amazement. She guessed it was also not easy for someone who was used to being alone to understand how, in a household where thirteen persons lived, one had a hard time to find some solitude. You weren't even safe in your own room, as they all were too used to being able to walk through any door without thinking twice.

If you wanted solitude, you had to lock your bedroom door or hide in the attic.

"Don't you ever get bored with each other?" Devlin asked, obviously fascinated with the subject.

Fanny shook her head. "No, not bored, exactly. Of course, we sometimes can get a little tired of each other, but I imagine living all alone has its ups and downs, too. We would all rather live together, and sometimes get frustrated over not being able to have some peace and quiet, than live alone and wish there was someone else there."

"What if you marry someone who has no relatives of his own? Won't you feel somewhat lonely?"

She looked at him from the side, but his eyes were glued to the road as if her answer wasn't the least bit important to him, which only made her think maybe it was.

She chewed on her answer for a bit, as she felt the importance of it. If she said she wouldn't mind the solitude she would tell a lie, but telling him she would hate the solitude would be untrue, too.

If their relationship developed into something more constant, she guessed this would become an issue for her, so she decided not to make her answer too deep, but not completely untrue, either.

"My first wish would be for him to move into our home too. But as most men have their own houses, I guess I would have to start my own large family, so there wouldn't be just the two of us. I mean, when one has ten children one can't possibly feel lonely, can one?"

"My God, ten children?" Devlin chuckled. "I can't help but feel a bit sorry for this future husband of yours, though I suppose he'd be quite happy with the making of all the offspring."

He looked at her, and her insides turned warm and breathless from the heat of his golden eyes.

It was such a two-sided feeling.

One part of her wanted to throw herself at him and kiss him wherever she could reach. But another part of her didn't like how easily she reacted to him, as if she had no self-control at all.

As if he could read her mind, he looked at the road again and continued lightly, "Anyhow, he must have a large income, or else he won't be able to keep you and the children in food and clothes. Seeing how gluttonous you all were at breakfast made me realize how being a part of your family could impoverish even a good-sized fortune."

Fanny pretended to be upset. "Oh, you awful man! How can you say such a thing about my lovely family."

This brought her a glance with a raised eyebrow. "Oh, really?"

She made a face toward him. "Yes, really. But my future husband won't have to fret about money, as I'm told that I am the wealthiest heiress this side of the turn of the century."

"You're an heiress?"

Fanny looked at him with surprise, as his astonishment was real. He obviously had no knowledge of her large dowry. It made her feel good—too good, almost. It was nice to be wanted for her own person, not for all the money that came with her.

She'd had quite a number of suitors over the last few years, ever since she started to join her relatives in different assemblies at home in Berkshire, and not one of them had been interested in anything more than her money.

But Devlin was.

"My family has made sure I will be bringing quite a nest egg into my future marriage."

"You mean your father has seen to it."

"No, my family."

He looked at her, not really believing her.

"Ordinarily it's the father who provides his daughter with a dowry."

"But my family is not an ordinary family." She smiled at him.

He laughed and nodded, obviously agreeing with her just to vex her, but she was too happy with their bantering to be annoyed with him.

They met another carriage, and Devlin nodded politely as they passed. The ladies in the other carriage were staring with their mouths wide open and forgot all about being polite back.

"Oh, no." Fanny sighed. "Of course we had to meet Lady Easton and her friends. Now everyone will know we went for a ride today, thanks to that obnoxious woman."

"And this is a bad thing?"

This time she took a good look at him. He didn't look at all like the cold libertine duke whom everyone talked about. When she thought about it, he hadn't been acting at all like one with her since they met at the Easton Ball. Instead, he had been open, friendly, and had made sure she was aware of how interested he was in her. He even embraced her family, even though some of them treated him like a pariah.

No, she didn't have any problem with others in the *ton* knowing he courted her. She wanted to spend time with him, to get to know him better. If she continued to feel as wonderful with him as she did now, she would eagerly accept his proposal, if it came. Good Lord, she would probably not hesitate to ask him to marry her—as she had thirteen years before—if she was sure he was the one.

"No, Your Grace, I don't feel it's a bad thing."

Again their eyes locked, and this time he was the one who apparently had to rip himself out of a daze. After a deep breath, he cursed softly.

"If only there were somewhere we wouldn't be seen by others," he mumbled, and she felt like she would burn up with the need to feel his arms around her and his lips against hers.

Devlin's thoughts weren't as innocent. He was already picturing her naked, moaning for him to come inside her, uniting their bodies. His eyes went down to her chest, admiring the heaving of her full breasts, and his hands ached with the need to slip inside the bodice and fondle their softness.

Unfortunately, it was just at this moment another carriage came up beside them, and a cold voice interrupted their passionate thoughts.

"For your information, this is a public park."

Devlin became rigid, and he turned slowly.

There, in an elegant phaeton, with his wife beside him, sat Devlin's boss at the war ministry, Basil Sinclair, the Earl of Saxton. He could feel Fanny leaning forward, and to spare her the embarrassment he pushed her back with one hand, so the elderly couple wouldn't see who his companion was.

"Lord Saxton," he said, startled over Basil's disapproving posture.

So he had been ogling Fanny a bit too hotly, but he hadn't touched her, had not even been too close to her. There hadn't been anything scandalous about his behavior. He was a highly titled English nobleman, and as such he was supposed to court young ladies. Hell, he was even allowed to court married ladies.

"How nice to meet you, my lord. I haven't seen you for quite a while now."

He gave Lady Saxton a genuine smile she didn't notice. She was too busy, almost snapping her neck in her attempt to see who was with him. He had always thought of Lady Saxton as one of the friendliest and most likable ladies of his acquaintance, and her evident curiosity now took him by surprise. He felt Fanny move behind him, and again he held out his hand, forcing her to stay hidden.

"We have been out of town for a couple of days, attending the funeral of a very good friend, and just came back yesterday evening."

"Please accept my condolences," Devlin sympathized.

"Thank you," Basil said solemnly.

"Who died?" Fanny asked.

Devlin closed his eyes, resigned.

Of course she couldn't stay quiet. Here he was trying to save her from the embarrassment of meeting the eyes of a couple who had seen them drooling all over each other—and he had almost succeeded—when she opened her lush little mouth. However, to his surprise, Lord Saxton did answer her question nicely enough, and Devlin opened his eyes again.

"Lord Plumber."

"Oh, poor Lady Plumber! She must be terribly upset."

"She is," Lady Saxton interjected. "We didn't want to tell you about it before the Easton Ball, but now it won't matter. That is why we haven't visited you and your family during your first week here in London, but we couldn't leave her all alone."

"I understand." Fanny smiled, and both Lord and Lady Saxton smiled back to her, a loving smile one only bestowed on someone close. Like a relative.

"Do you know each other?" Devlin asked suspiciously, and Lord Saxton glanced at him with a mixture of condescension and humor. Was the man laughing silently at him?

Fanny wasn't as subtle; his dear little dove laughed and whacked him on his shoulder.

"Of course we know each other, silly. These two lovely people are my maternal grandmother and grandfather."

Oh, my God.

Devlin didn't know what to say.

This was his commander, for goodness' sake. The only man alive who knew everything about him.

Every dirty little detail.

There was no way Lord Saxton would let Devlin marry his granddaughter, with that knowledge. Especially considering how easy it was to see by just looking at Lord Saxton how the man adored Fanny. He wouldn't sit back silently and not interfere.

The ladies were chatting about the funeral, and Devlin could feel Lord Saxton measuring him.

"Your Grace," Lady Saxton said. "I would be forever in your debt if we could swap carriages for a little while, as I haven't seen my dear Fanny for some time, and I would love to catch up with her for just a few minutes, if I may?"

Devlin nodded, and soon Fanny sat in her grandmother's phaeton, hugging her closely, and Devlin had Lord Saxton beside him.

"Why don't we roll a bit," Lord Saxton said, and Devlin did as he was asked, filled with dread.

They drove silently down Rotten Row. The commander wasn't known for backing down on an unpleasant situation, but Devlin had to wait until they had turned around at Kensington Gardens before Basil ended the uncomfortable silence.

"We love all our grandchildren, but Fanny is special, and because of this, I must ask you what your intentions are."

"Marriage."

"You hardly know her. How can you be so sure?"

"I don't know for sure, but I thought I would find out while courting her. If she still seems perfect, I will ask her to marry me."

"What if she declines?"

"Then I guess I will have to go on with my life without her."

Lord Saxton looked at him sharply. "You don't seem to care about her answer."

"What do you want me to say?" Devlin asked angrily. "Do you want me to declare how much I love her, and how I will never harm her in any way? I can't tell you this, because I don't love her. Not now, but I might later, when I know her better. Bloody hell, I just met her!"

He took some deep breaths to calm down, before he continued. "It feels very strange telling you this, as you are her grandfather, but I have never lied to you before, and I am not about to start now. There is something about her that attracts me immensely. When I'm with her, everything is right, and I am content and at peace. She makes me feel whole, as if I've found the one missing piece in my life, the one I've always been looking for. I don't know if this will fade as time goes by, or if by some wonderful luck I happened to meet the one person in the world who is my perfect match."

"All right," Lord Saxton said with an indifferent shrug, and Devlin halted the horses and turned to look at his commander in surprise.

"All right?" he asked hoarsely. "Is this all you have to say to me?"

"What more do you want me to say?" Lord Saxton questioned with an unreadable smile.

Devlin threw out his hands in frustration.

"Something."

"Like?"

"Now you're toying with me," Devlin growled.

Lord Saxton nodded his head to a passing acquaintance, ignoring Devlin's obvious puzzlement. Instead he swept his hand toward the horses.

"You are aware we aren't moving, I hope? Otherwise, I might have some objections regarding your sanity."

As the carriage slowly moved forward again, Devlin realized he'd never felt so unsure of himself. He had always trusted his own judgment, a necessity when one grew up with an abusive father and no one to lean on. This uncertain mood of the last couple of days was wearing him down.

His work as a spy had utilized and enhanced his ability to rely on himself and trust his own decisions, something he had not found overly easy at the beginning of his secretive career despite his background. But Lord Saxton's patience and gentle guidance had helped build his confidence, and for this Devlin was eternally grateful.

Lord Saxton's integrity, devotion, and sharp intelligence were something Devlin admired deeply, and though he might have hesitated to admit it, he looked upon the older man as a father figure. The commander had one rule for all his spies—total honesty. At the start, they all had to sit down with Lord Saxton and tell him everything about themselves, so he had a chance of guessing what path they would go if he lost contact with them or needed to rescue them.

Devlin had a hard time opening up, but in the end, he surrendered himself to Lord Saxton's capable hands, and in some strange way it was a relief for someone finally to be privy to the long-held secrets. Someone cared about knowing his thoughts, actions, and most intimate details, and it had given him a feeling of immortality. His life wouldn't be forgotten if he wasn't there to live it.

But what was good in war wasn't as good elsewhere. As Fanny's grandfather, Lord Saxton might have a hard time filtering all he knew about his granddaughter's suitor. It wasn't hard to see how much he loved Fanny, and his immediate acceptance of the courtship alarmed Devlin. No one who knew every bad thing about him would let his beloved little girl closer to Devlin than a mile.

"How can you accept me?" he finally asked, terrified for the answer.

"How can I not? You are a good and honest man, and I know you would never do anything deliberate to hurt Fanny. I know what you have done during the war, but that was war. In England, among the *ton*, you are a different man, and this is a different situation. Other things matter here, and when you, the number one eligible bachelor, court my granddaughter, how can I object? But none of this affects my opinion of you as a suitor for Fanny's hand. Not at all."

This surprised Devlin. "How can it not matter? All my beliefs, everything I've done, makes me into this person I am, and nothing can change it. I wouldn't think of it as lightly as you seem to do, if this was about my granddaughter."

Another small smile passed Lord Saxton's face. "But you keep forgetting something, Devlin. Something more important than anything you have said or done."

"For heaven's sake, what?"

"Fanny."

Devlin fell back in the seat, dumbfounded. "Fanny?"

"You keep forgetting about her, don't you?"

"I don't understand."

Lord Saxton fixed Devlin with a hard stare. "Fanny is my granddaughter and I love her dearly, but more importantly, I trust her with my whole heart. She has a head of her own and will never accept your proposal if she is not sure you are the one she wants to spend the rest of her life with. Besides, she is part of a very large and overly protective family, who won't let her marry anybody without letting her fight for it. And I tell you, Fanny only fights for the things she really believes in, and you are obviously one."

That explained it, Devlin thought, a bit shaken. He had not once thought about her part. He had been too occupied with his own. Fanny was too levelheaded to fall for flattery and pretty words, and she was too well protected to be allowed near anyone who could be a threat.

"It will be good for you, you know," Lord Saxton continued, "to belong to someone and to start something new. Your children will never have to suffer what you did because of your father, and I know you will appreciate your family more than most other men do, because of him."

"You are right about this," Devlin agreed. "My father's malevolence will not have any influence on my future children. I will make sure of that."

Something in Devlin's words struck Lord Saxton as off-key. "How will you make sure of this?" he asked carefully.

"By not being there to pass on Conan's malice further."

This caught Basil off guard. "Whatever do you mean, 'by not being there'?"

"Just what I said. I will make sure nothing I have

learnt when I was a child will be passed on to my children, and I will do this by not being a part of their upbringing. I will leave them in the hands of my wife, capable hands, hopefully, and by staying away, I will not affect them in any way."

Lord Saxton was speechless. How could Devlin think he could stay out of his own children's lives? "So you're going to hide your wife and children in some vast country estate, or what?"

Devlin chuckled, apparently amused. "Of course not. Can you imagine me trying to hide Fanny somewhere? Besides, you or the rest of her family would never let that happen."

Lord Saxton almost laughed straight out but managed to hide his mirth from the younger man. The moron actually thought he could leave his wife with her family, and, by doing this, he would be making sure of his children would be raised in a loving and caring environment.

As if Fanny ever would let it happen. Poor Devlin, he didn't stand a chance. She would never let him miss his own happiness.

Chapter 15

"So, tell me everything about you and your splendid man," Frances Locksley Sinclair, Lady Saxton, urged her granddaughter as they watched the carriage with the men slowly drive away.

"There is not much to tell." Fanny laughed. "We met at the Easton Ball, and he has since made it clear he wants to court me."

With a loving smile, Lady Saxton looked at the granddaughter who was named after her. The young woman was already spellbound by her suitor, and it was not difficult to see that he was just as mesmerized by her.

Her husband was very fond of Devlin Ross, and Lady Saxton didn't need any other evidence to know this was a good man. She had complete faith in her husband's discernment. She knew he would never trust someone as much as he did the young duke if he had any doubts about him.

"I do confess," Fanny continued with a dreamy look in her gray eyes, "I find him most attractive. As you can see, he is after all a magnificent man. But more importantly, I find I like his wit and his intelligence. When I talk to him, I feel as though there is nothing I can't tell him. He has a tendency to sarcastic or ironic comments, but as you are aware, I'm quite used to those."

"I have to agree with you, my dear. He is a most handsome man, and I could sit here and admire him the whole day. But what's more important is that you connect with him on another level than mere appearance."

"Oh, we do connect, Grand-Mama. I think the reason is all because of his friendship with Rake. Devlin lets me in and opens up to me in a way I don't think he has ever done to any other female. You know, I never thought my libertine relatives would be a good thing when it came to me meeting a possible future husband."

They giggled as if they were two young girls, not one young woman with her grandmother. But that was the way it always had been.

Lady Saxton possessed a young mind, and with all her experience, she was the perfect friend for a young woman on the verge of adulthood.

She was a very attentive grandmother, and sometimes she showered her three little nuggets, as she called Sin, Sebastian, and Fanny, with a little too much love. But as they adored her right back, no one ever complained.

She was a good listener and never told a secret. Therefore she was probably the only one who always got the whole truth from her grandchildren.

"Do you think he is the one?" Lady Saxton asked, with a curious gleam in her beautiful green eyes. "Or might you finally give up and accept Mr. Pembroke's hand in marriage?"

"There is one thing you can be sure of," Fanny said with a dejected sigh. "I will never marry Nicholas Pembroke. Don't misunderstand me. I do like him. He is a nice man, and he has a good heart. If I hadn't met Hereford, I might at least have considered him as a future husband."

"Your heart is too soft, my dearest girl." Lady Saxton hugged her granddaughter close. "I don't know where it comes from."

They sat silent for a while, still with their arms around each other. It was not good etiquette, this closeness they shared, but somehow they had never found themselves bothered enough to care about what everyone else thought.

"I do look forward to tonight's dinner." Fanny smiled. "Is there anyone else besides our family joining us?"

Lady Saxton looked at her with a knowing smile.

"No, I haven't asked your beau there, as I thought we should keep it in the family. It will only be your parents and brothers, a nice small family gathering."

Fanny nodded, secretly relieved. She needed time to think about the whole Devlin situation. The Easton Ball two days earlier had been her first social event in London, and since then Devlin seemed have been everywhere, and she needed time to think. She needed time to find out how she felt.

She was desperate for solitude, because when he was nearby all she could think of was him, and her heart beat faster than normal. He made her dizzy and stupid, she thought, with a wry smile.

Some friends of Lady Saxton's halted by their side, and Fanny let go of her thoughts of Devlin. He would be back in a moment, and she needed to think about something else for a change.

As her grandmother was a popular woman, they

soon were surrounded, and time passed too quickly. Soon the men had returned, and Lord Saxton helped Fanny into Devlin's carriage again.

She was aware the crowd took in every small detail concerning herself and Hereford, what they said and what they did. It wouldn't take long for everyone in the *ton* to be informed.

Even Charmaine wouldn't have a chance to miss it, and Fanny found that thought comforting, in a kind of malicious way.

When the carriage started to move again, she asked Devlin kindly to take her home. He looked at her with a mix of astonishment and suspicion, but she was too tired to care right now.

She needed her solitude.

She needed time to think.

In silence they headed back to Berkeley Square and the beautiful townhouse which belonged to the Darling family. Devlin plucked insecurely with the reins, as if he had something to say but didn't know how to say it.

Fanny put her hand on his to get his attention, and he immediately became as still as a statue.

"Please do forgive me," she begged him with a sweet smile. "I feel I'm quite weary. I'm not used to this overbooked schedule my family keeps while here in London, and I do need my rest now so I will be able to manage at tonight's dinner."

"Where are you going tonight?" he asked tightly.

"To a family dinner at my grandparents' house. It will be only my closest kin."

"Oh."

She had no idea a simple "oh" could sound so abandoned, and she almost invited him right then and there but stopped herself at the last minute. They both needed this time apart. It wasn't forever, as they would probably meet again tomorrow.

"I will attend the Crofts' dinner party tomorrow."

He looked up into her eyes, and she thought she would drown in their golden warmth.

"I don't think I've received an invitation," he said with a smooth voice that was like music to her ears. He leaned a little closer to her, and his lips were slightly parted. She could feel his warm breath stroking her face, and she closed her eyes as she lifted her face to his.

A loud shout woke them, and Devlin barely missed driving straight into a salesman's carriage. He begged the angry man for forgiveness before they continued down Curzon Street. The near accident loosened up the tension between them a bit, and they laughed, relieved nothing had happened.

"What are you doing tomorrow morning?" he asked when they calmed down.

"Mother is terrified over the possibility I might have too small a wardrobe, and has insisted we will spend the day over at Bond Street. We must do anything to avoid the worst scenario possible—that I would have to wear the same evening dress twice. However, Monday is free, as far as I know."

"Unfortunately I have some business to attend to during the first part of the week, and I won't be back in London until Wednesday."

Now it was Fanny's turn to say an abandoned "oh."

"I guess we'll meet at Almack's, then," she said ruefully.

"Oh, God, no," Devlin moaned.

"What is it with men and Almack's?" Fanny cried. "All my male relatives look like I'm talking about purgatory and not an assembly where one meets acquaintances to dance and have fun."

"Fun?" Devlin asked with a ridiculous expression on his face.

Fanny rolled her eyes.

"Fun?" Devlin repeated, clearly not understanding the best thing about Almack's.

As he halted in front of her home, she turned and glared at him.

"Yes, fun. You will come to Almack's Wednesday evening, and you will do it in good time, before eleven, and I might save a dance for you."

He gave her a slow, earthshaking smile.

"What if I want more than one dance?"

"You d-do?" she stuttered.

"I do."

"You do…"

"Um-hm."

"That's nice."

"Sure is."

The heat in his golden eyes made her feel warm all over, and, mesmerized, she leaned closer to him. Just as she felt his warm breath against her face, a well-known voice cut through the intensity of the moment.

"Oh, for heaven's sake."

They broke apart to gaze down at Rake, who stood on the sidewalk looking disgusted. Devlin couldn't stop a smile, and his friend shook his head.

"It's unbelievable. You must be completely head over heels for the little one. You wouldn't actually try to kiss her outside our house if you weren't."

He held out his hand, and Fanny grabbed it as she stepped down from the carriage. Her uncle gave her a peck on the nose, before he with one step elegantly climbed up and sat down beside Devlin.

"Take me away, Devlin. Let me save you from destroying this grand-looking vehicle with drool."

Fanny winked at Devlin before she ran lightly up the steps to the front door.

"Ladies don't run, they walk, Fanny. Walk," Rake shouted instructively to her disappearing back as the carriage rolled away.

The last thing Devlin heard before she closed the front door behind her was her laughter, which nestled around his heart like a warm blanket. He was so filled with his own brewing happiness he didn't notice his friend's foul mood.

Chapter 16

Fanny closed the door behind her and gave Butler her bonnet and coat. He graciously accepted them and pointed toward the parlor.

This was obviously not the time to run up to her room and throw herself on her bed to daydream about Devlin the rest of the day, she thought, as she went to see who her visitor was.

Penelope was waiting for her in the salon, looking alarmingly pale and worried. Fanny immediately sat down beside her and took her wringing hands in hers.

"Penny, what is it? What's wrong?"

The compassion in Fanny's voice broke the last of her friend's strength, and Penelope started to sob. Deep, heartbreaking sobs. Her body shook with each breath.

Butler came in with a tea tray and set it down on the table in front of the sofa before he just as quietly left the room again, closing the door softly behind him.

Fanny caressed her friend's back until she calmed. Then she poured her a soothing cup of tea spiked with a hint of her father's best brandy.

Penelope grimaced as she tasted it, but she sipped at it anyway, as if she needed the fake strength the alcohol could give her. She looked a wreck: her hair was a mess, and her dress looked as though she had slept in it. Something had happened, and she was going to talk about it even if Fanny had to force it out of her.

Penelope had always been the strong-willed and courageous one of them and Fanny the merry and ingenious one. This breakdown was as far from the normal Penelope as could be. Her family had never cared about her, so she had been used to taking care of herself since her earliest childhood and was not afraid of challenges.

But this Penelope was completely defeated.

"Dearest, dearest Penny, what is it?"

No answer, just a sob or two.

"Please tell me what it is. Has something happened to your parents?"

Penelope shook her head, still not looking up.

"Charmaine?"

Penny nodded, and Fanny paled. Oh, Lord, she had forgotten all about yesterday's conversation about Charmaine and the big lie of being engaged to Devlin. Fanny took hold of Penelope's chin and forced her to meet her eyes.

"Penny, did you talk to Charmaine?"

Another nod and a sob.

"What did she say?"

"Sh-he got u-hupset…"

Not so hard to figure out. Fanny repeated, "What did she say?"

"She lied, Fanny. To-hoo me."

Merciful heavens!

"She has never lied to me before. Never."

Penelope stood up to pace to and fro in front of Fanny. "This time she lied straight into my face and denied everything. She said you were the liar, but I know her. I could tell by looking at her she made it all up."

"I'm sorry, Penny."

"Oh, no, love, don't be sorry. It's not your fault. In a weird, unhappy way, I'm glad you told me. Something is terribly wrong with my sister, and now I'm at least aware of it."

"Did she tell you the truth at all?"

Penelope sat again, with a thump. "No. She just stood there in front of me, looking all angelic and indignant whilst accusing me of being the worst sister ever. Then she floated away into her room, and I didn't see her until this morning, when she ignored me as much as she could. It was one of the worst breakfasts ever. My parents never talk to me, but Charmaine usually says a word or two. This time it was as if I weren't even there. Invisible to my own family."

Fanny sat back, confused. So Penelope got upset over her sister and her family ignoring her, but it was obvious she hadn't gotten upset enough to turn into this sobbing creature now before her. There had to be something more to it, something more than a fight with her selfish sister.

Suddenly a thought popped into her head.

Rake.

He had left the house as she came home, and so he must have met Penelope. When she thought about it, he had seemed a little distraught. He had let her off the hook very easily for almost kissing Devlin, especially since he normally was very restrictive about her.

"You met Rake."

It was a statement, not a question, and Penelope nodded hesitantly.

"What did he say?"

"He kissed me."

"What?" Fanny said not believing her ears. "But this is good news, isn't it?"

She got no answer.

"You have been in love with Rake as long as I can remember, so why is it a bad thing he kissed you?"

"It's bad because he doesn't want a wife."

Fanny snorted. "It's just his stupid stubbornness. He will come around before you know it."

"No, he won't."

"Of course he will. He likes you. He always has. We just have to push him a bit so he realizes it faster, as the men in my family can be frustratingly slow in mind sometimes."

"He told me he wanted me."

Fanny shrieked with excitement, and Penelope clamped her hand over her friend's mouth to keep her quiet.

"But it's good news," Fanny said when she was allowed to speak. "It really is! Rake would never say something so emotional if he didn't mean it. Oh, Penny, can you believe you will now become my real sister? Or aunt. Or whatever… We will be family!"

Fanny let out a loud happy sigh.

"He told me he would buy me a nice little house in a good neighborhood, and he promised he would make sure I never lacked anything."

"What?"

"He asked me to become his mistress. His kept lady."

Penelope started to sob again, and this time it was Fanny's turn to walk to and fro in front of the sofa.

"The bastard. The sick, awful, horrible moron."

Penelope smiled through her tears. She couldn't

help herself, as Fanny sounded ready to kill as she swore between her teeth.

"I know."

"That evil, selfish…man!"

"I do so agree with you." Penelope sniffed.

Fanny sat down again, this time looking very determined. "He can't do this. Not to me, and definitely not to you. You are my friend, and this is the worst insult he ever could give either of us."

Penelope nodded solemnly. She agreed wholeheartedly with her friend. This time Rake had gone too far, and it felt good for Fanny to take her side.

"Please, Fanny, don't do anything stupid. I know how you sometimes throw yourself into situations too quickly. This time it's your Uncle Rake, your all-time favorite, and you don't want to lose him just because you overreacted to something stupid he said."

"Of course not," Fanny reassured her. "I know too well a direct attack won't help when it comes to my family members. You have take the sneaky way, and snare them slowly until they are caught and can't come loose. But there is one thing I want to know before I do anything."

"What?"

"Do you still want him? As a husband, I mean?"

"I don't know, Fanny, truly I don't. If you had asked me an hour ago, I would have told you a loud yes, but now I hesitate. He hurt me. He insulted me in the worst way a man can, by removing all my dignity and my honor. In a few words, he belittled me into nothing."

Fanny put an arm around her friend.

"I know, dearest. I know. However, promise me, if

you change your mind, do tell me, and I will make sure I won't rest until he understands how stupid he is."

They laughed—a forced laughter, but at least they were trying.

Fanny gave Penelope her handkerchief and watched her friend as she dried her tears. What on earth had been on Rake's mind? Humiliating her best friend, a girl he had known for his whole life? What was the matter with her uncle? She knew he wouldn't have acted like this if he had been his normal self. He was, as his nickname said, a rake at heart, a libertine and a drifter, but still…

He always behaved with the best of manners and had, out of respect for his family, never had a mistress of their acquaintance. Asking a family friend to become his mistress was an outrageous act, and it didn't make sense for Rake to have done so.

She knew he had mistresses, and she even knew the name of his current one, too, though she would never tell Rake.

He would die of mortification.

She didn't know how Penelope managed to live with the knowledge of Rake with another woman, as she never would be able to live with a man who had another on the side.

She froze as the thought of Devlin in the arms of a mistress came to her mind. Why hadn't this bothered her before? Maybe because she hadn't thought about it. The subject had never come up.

Did Devlin have a mistress?

Her heart screamed "no," but her head said "probably." He was a man, and she knew all men had either wives or mistresses. Sin had once told her about men who had both, and she had promised herself never to marry such a man.

How little she knew about the man she thought she would like to marry.

Now she knew she had to talk to Rake.

First she would ask if Devlin had a mistress, and then she would demand that he answer any question she had about her beau. She knew she could ask Devlin her questions, but she always seemed to forget everything whenever he was near. All she could think about was kissing him.

No, it was Rake she needed to talk with, and she would make sure she got the whole truth out of him. He had never been able to deny her anything, and she would make certain he didn't start now.

Penelope deserved the truth, and so did she.

Chapter 17

Devlin walked through the entrance door to Almack's just as the doorman was about to close it at eleven o'clock.

The patronesses, who had been about to leave their spot at the door where they stood to greet the arriving guests, flirted wildly with him, and he managed to withhold a dejected sigh. Since his return to London only a couple of hours earlier, he had been surrounded by ladies of all ages and social standing, and all of them wanted a piece of him.

He was tired.

The last three days had been hard. He and Drake had gone to Bath, searching for a man someone had named as a suspected French spy, a man who had been surprisingly hard to find. When they finally located him, he wasn't connected to France at all, and they had obviously been misled.

So they had rushed back to London and to Lord Saxton's office, only to be met with the news of a break-in. The thief had got his hands on some top-secret papers.

Lord Saxton had been furious and had asked Drake and Devlin to search through the whole building for any clues as to who the thief was and how he had been able to penetrate their most highly protected office. They hadn't found anything, and Devlin had almost given up joining Fanny at Almack's when Lord Saxton suddenly remembered they hadn't slept for three days and sent them home.

Devlin had rushed as fast as he could home to wash and change clothes before throwing himself into the carriage waiting outside. He'd barely made it in time.

He managed to get rid of the patronesses without being too rude and started to hunt down Fanny. The ballroom at Almack's was filled with London's finest, and it wasn't easy separating one white-clad debutante from another. Slowly he walked through the crowd, nodding to the faces he recognized and stopping only when he had no other choice.

The dance floor was filled with couples. He had walked almost to the other side of the large room when he finally spotted the lovely young lady he had been seeking.

Fanny was dancing with Nicholas Pembroke, gracefully moving with the music. She wore a beautiful white gown laced with knitted flowers. Pearls graced her neck, her ears, and her hair. She laughed at something her dancing partner said, and Devlin caught himself smiling in response.

She sparkled; there was no other way to describe her.

He had thought about her a lot, as there was not much else to do when one was riding all the way to Bath and back. But even though she was fantastic in his dreams, she was even better in real life. It was hard to understand why she was called homely. To him, she was anything but that.

The dance ended, and Nicholas Pembroke, as the obedient beau in desperate need of being accepted into the family, walked Fanny back to her parents where they stood in the midst of all the Darling relatives. Devlin almost smiled when he saw the Darling men throw themselves around the poor Mr. Pembroke, like wolves over their prey.

Fanny was immediately cornered by a bunch of suitors who almost tripped over each other in their rush to reach the fair maiden who just happened to be a very wealthy heiress.

George, looking quite disgruntled, was held back by his wife as Fanny again was dragged away to the dance floor, this time by the notorious womanizer Lord Burnsville. Devlin growled to himself, watching how the man kept looking too often and long at the gentle curve of her breasts. Some people might think Burnsville quite handsome, with his strawberry-blonde hair and square shoulders, and Devlin had known a certain amount of liking for the chap, as he was a jolly good fellow.

But that all ended the second Burnsville put a lingering peck on Fanny's fingers, and she blushed.

Devlin didn't like it at all.

She wasn't supposed to be blushing when other men gave her a peck on her hand, as it was just common flirting. But she was, and he couldn't help but frown at her.

Unfortunately, she was too caught up in what Burnsville was whispering in her ear even to realize Devlin had arrived. So maybe he was a wee bit late, but at least he was there. At Almack's, for goodness' sake. If this didn't tell her of his devotion for her, nothing could.

He again made his way through the crowd, until he

reached the small doorway leading to the ladies' restroom and, further in, the patronesses' meeting room. Sooner or later she would head for the restroom, and he would be ready.

Luck was on his side, as he had to wait for only two more dances, and two more suitors, before Fanny excused herself and headed his way. He hid in the meeting room until she came out from the restroom into the empty hallway. Then he pounced. Before she knew what was happening, he grabbed her arm and dragged her into the meeting room, where he closed and locked the door.

She had no time to react. As soon as the door was locked, he dragged her into his arms and did what he had been yearning for since he first met her in the darkness of the Easton balcony.

He kissed her.

His right hand pressed the small of her back gently, forcing her body to yield to his. His left hand found its way into the curls of her hair, holding her head. His lips slanted across hers, forcing them to open so he could ravish her mouth with his tongue.

Fanny's hands were on his shoulders, her nails digging into the cloth of his eveningwear, leaving marks that would last for days. As he deepened the kiss, she moaned. Unwittingly she pressed her body and lips even closer to his. His hand found its way to the modest neckline of her debutante dress and, with a contented sigh, he did just what he had dreamt about earlier.

He let his hand dive in and gently caress the softness of her full breasts. She became rigid for a second, as the sensation hit her, before she staggered against him, her legs not managing to hold her upright.

Without letting his lips leave hers or his hand leave her breasts, he nudged her to the couch, where they sat—or rather fell—down, and he placed himself on top of her, forcing her legs apart with one of his knees.

She kissed him back with so much enthusiasm it almost did him in. But somewhere in the back of his head he knew a roll on a sofa wasn't the way he wanted to take her virginity. He would never forgive himself. He wanted her first time to be in his bed, with his ring on her finger, and so he drew back just a little, to gain some space between them.

Her disappointed moan almost made him change his mind, but he hardened himself and sat up, leaving her lying on the sofa in a lovely, breathless mess.

"What was this all about?" was all she managed to ask as she sat up.

"This was for forgetting me."

She looked up from straightening her bodice, and he almost kissed her again as he looked at her blushing face with its swollen lips made for kisses.

"Forgetting you? Whatever do you mean?"

"You were dancing with every eligible bachelor, and a couple of those not so eligible, and not once did your eyes search the crowd in hope of finding me there."

"You can't be serious." Fanny laughed. "How should I ever be able to search the crowd while dancing? I would knock down most of the other ladies, while turning in the dance, if I looked for you instead of concentrating."

Devlin drew his fingers carelessly through his hair, completely destroying the windswept coiffure his valet had fought to attain. Turning to Fanny, he watched her try to straighten her own hair. She sent him a shivering smile while putting every curl back in its place.

He gave her a lust-filled grin, and she turned fiery red and wet her lips with her tongue. He moaned, and before he could stop himself, he leaned forward and captured her lush lips with his, kissing her thoroughly without touching the rest of her body.

When he finally let her go, she looked at him in a dreamy daze. He took her chin in his hand, and forced her to look deep into his eyes.

"You have to marry me now, you know," he said seriously.

She nodded, tears filling her eyes. He knew it was crazy, as they had only known each other for a few days, but it felt so right.

She was the right woman for him, so why wait? Why continue with courting her, while watching others do the same, when he could have her neatly engaged to him and thus safely his? He stroked her tears away with his thumbs, and she put her hands around his, savoring his touch against her cheeks. It was amazing how such a simple gesture could mean so much to him.

"I'll try to make you happy," she whispered softly with a tender smile, and he had to kiss her again for being the wonderful person she was.

"Happiness is my job," he finally managed to say, as he looked down into her gray eyes. "Yours is to be crazy in love with me, for the rest of your life."

She blushed even deeper, and he put a last kiss on the bridge of her nose before, with a sad sigh, he removed his hands from her and helped her straighten her appearance.

When they had destroyed the last evidence of their

hot embrace, he slipped out through the door, and Fanny followed his lead a couple of minutes later.

****

As Fanny entered the ballroom, she found Devlin in the midst of a heated discussion with her uncles and brothers. She sighed and joined her parents, who were listening to the younger men with indulgent smiles.

"Can you believe they are arguing about the best way to get rid of him, with him right there, overhearing every word?" George chuckled, and Caroline just shook her head.

"Men," she sighed. "They are impossible beings, and especially the Darling men. I don't understand why they must always argue about everything."

"Because it's fun," George drawled, and his wife looked at him as though he were ridiculous.

"Fun?" she repeated. "You think they are having fun?"

George shrugged. "I don't think they are having fun. I know they are. It's just a heated discussion, nothing more. It's all about being the one who says the final word."

Caroline snorted.

"I believe you, because you Darlings never know when to quit."

"And this is why we Darling men are the best, because we always continue until we have finished our personal crusades," George replied, and gave his wife a wolfish grin that made her blush prettily.

Before Devlin's kiss, Fanny wouldn't have thought more about it. But with that hotly burning sensation still in mind, she understood what her father was telling her mother between the lines, and she too blushed.

Fortunately, her father was too busy making love to her mother with his eyes to notice his daughter's telling blush.

Fanny's heart swelled with love as she watched her beautiful parents, so apparently in love with each other after all these years. And they were not at all bothered about the unfashionable way they showed it to everyone.

This was what she had always wanted for herself, especially as she had seen her friends' parents behave in a more we-are-married-now-and-I-have-to-cope-with-it way.

She sneaked a peek at her secret fiancé-to-be. Devlin was looking at Sin with an amused grin, as her brother was trying to convince Uncle Jamie how kidnapping and hiding a man somewhere in the dungeons at Chester Park indeed was the best way to get rid of an unwanted suitor. Jamie was more for selling him as a slave, to be shipped off to the West Indies.

He fit in, she realized, as if there had always been a spot there among her relatives, just waiting for him to fill it. Even the Darling men had noticed. Otherwise they wouldn't have been arguing so openly in front of him.

When they were really against someone, they just whisked him away, not looking back. But with Devlin it was different, as they were dragging him into the discussion, forcing him to argue for himself.

Fanny felt tears fill her eyes again, and she sighed at her own silliness. Devlin wouldn't have a hard job getting her crazy in love with him, as she was a goner already. It was amazing to think she'd met him only a week ago, but so much had happened so fast, and she was caught: forever and ever his.

Just then Devlin happened to look at her, seeing her teary-eyed happiness, and he gave her a genuinely happy smile that went straight to her heart and made it skip a beat.

Lord, he was such a beautiful man. There was not a man in this ballroom who looked half as splendid as he did. Not even her own relatives, whom she always had thought were the handsomest of men. He was the essence of elegance, in his black tailor-made evening wear, and she noticed she wasn't the only female who ogled him. Most of the women around him couldn't help but cast a glance in his direction. As he stood there, a little wicked smile playing on his full lips, he looked like an ancient Roman statue, too beautiful to be true.

The music stopped playing, and the dancers moved away from the dance floor to make room for new couples, and she saw Devlin catch her father with a question in his golden eyes, and George nodded.

Without a word, Devlin held out his hand to her with a secretive wink, and blushingly she gave him hers. He led her out onto the dance floor, joining the other dancers in the beautiful country dance.

Fanny usually loved to dance, despite the need to concentrate on the steps, but dancing with Devlin was pure heaven. Every time their hands met, electricity flowed through her body, and she tingled all over.

Devlin obviously felt the same, because he couldn't take his eyes off her, instead drenching her in their honey-colored heat. He brushed his arm against her chest as he passed her in the dance movement, and she couldn't stop shivering with delight. Her whole body yearned for his hands and that wonderful sensation they had given her earlier, in the meeting room.

When the dance ended, he had to give her up to the beau who had written his name on her dance card earlier, but as soon as the card had an empty spot he danced with her again.

Everyone in the ballroom noticed what was taking place. The handsome and powerful Duke of Hereford was courting the rich and well-connected heiress Lady Francesca Darling, apparently with her parents' approval.

"I guess I'll be having a visitor soon." George whispered to Caroline, who looked as dazed as her daughter did as she watched the couple twirl by.

"Do tell me, brother dear, what will your answer to the man be?" Rake asked, having overheard George's comment.

"When it comes to Fanny, I'll guess she will shoot me in the foot if I say anything other than yes. She is spellbound by him. I mean, look at her—she is so happy, one would think she will never be able to stop smiling again. I will of course ask her of her opinion before I give him any answer, but I think we all know what the answer will be."

Rake nodded slowly.

"But what do *you* think of Devlin?"

George frowned.

"It's complicated. He is her perfect social match, as she is the granddaughter of a duke and daughter of a marquess. Honestly, I would have a really hard time giving her away to a man of lower standing, such as

Mr. Pembroke, if he had been her choice. Personally, I like Devlin. Or at least I think I do. I keep thinking of him the way he was during the summer he spent at Chester Park, and I'm afraid I will miss any flaws in his character just because it was a long time ago. People do change, you know."

"He hasn't changed so much," Rake mused, "Not really."

"No?"

"In my opinion, I would say he's better now, as he has done his wild days. Now he is ready to settle down. And one thing is for sure. He will never do anything to make Fanny or any future children unhappy, as he had the worst childhood imaginable."

"I wouldn't say that," a familiar voice interrupted. Lord Saxton appeared from nowhere, suddenly standing between them, watching the couple who had eyes only for each other.

"Whatever do you mean, sir?" George frowned.

"Conan succeeded so thoroughly with his patronizing of his son that Devlin has got a rather stupid idea of how his own presence would affect the one he loves, in a bad way."

George and Rake stared at him, not really understanding what Lord Saxton was trying to say.

"Devlin thinks Fanny and eventual future children would be much happier without him, so he will make sure they will be influenced by her loving family instead of by him."

"What?" Rake said hoarsely.

"I know." Lord Saxton shook his head. "It's so stupid."

"Goodness me." George could hardly believe his

ears. "How can he ever think she will be happier without him by her side? And his children happier without him? They need a husband and a father, not someone who comes to wish them happy birthday once a year!"

Rake shook his head. "It is the dumbest idea I ever heard of, but somehow I'm not so surprised. I know all about how awful Conan was toward Devlin. All the small, petty things that small boy had to endure under his father's roof."

Lord Saxton nodded in agreement.

"He needs love, something he has lived his whole life without. But in his urgent need to make everything right, he is going to make himself even more miserable, and probably Fanny too."

Rake lifted his head and looked at his niece, who was just giving her courting beau another dazzling look that made Devlin's eyes darken into darkest brown, and then he smiled.

"Don't worry. It will never happen," he said slowly.

"No, it won't," Lord Saxton agreed, all too aware of what Rake meant, as he himself had come to the same conclusion the day before.

"She'll never let him."

"No, she won't."

George looked from one to another and threw out his hands in despair.

"What?"

Lord Saxton whacked him in the back, making his son-in-law stumble by the force of it.

"You know your daughter. Fanny will never let him slip away to some faraway corner to lick his wounds while telling himself he's doing something for the greater good. Your daughter is a resourceful young woman and will probably drag him home again with a good grip of his ear."

"Ah," George breathed, enlightened. "No, she will never let him have his way. She is too used to being surrounded by everyone to let him play the sad knight in shining armor."

"Do you think we should tell her?" Rake asked Lord Saxton.

"No, don't spring it on her now. It's not something that affects their relationship nor their perfect match. Personally, I think this is the only bad thing about him, and you should let her try to handle it herself, if it ever will come to it. And then, and only then, should we tell her, just so she knows it's not about her."

George looked hard at his father-in-law. "How do you know him so well?"

"He's one of my boys."

This caught George by surprise. "He is?"

"And clearly one of the best. He has done more for his country than anyone ever will know."

"Does Fanny know?"

Lord Saxton shrugged. "I don't know, and I'm not going to ask her. I think it's up to him to tell her, if she doesn't already know about it. It's all about trust, you know."

"You are a good man, sir," George told the only man alive who had the ability to make him feel like an awkward little boy.

"I know," Lord Saxton said as he left them, heading for his wife and daughter.

Chapter 18

Fanny lighted the candle beside her bed and closed her eyes with a happy sigh. It had been such a wonderful night, filled with romance and laughter.

And two wonderful and surprisingly hot kisses.

She sighed happily again.

Those kisses had moved her world. Nothing would ever be the same again. Now she could hardly wait for the next secret meeting, and the next hot kiss.

She had been a bit upset with him for scaring her when he dragged her into the meeting room, but all anger had vanished when his lips claimed hers. Nothing in her most vivid fantasies had been even close to how wonderful it had been to be in his arms.

She couldn't help wondering if this was how everyone felt when they kissed someone, but something made her think it wasn't.

She was in love with Devlin, and it must make some difference, she thought. For example, when her uncles kissed their mistresses, she was sure it wasn't the same. Those women were only there to fulfill the men's needs, not to enlighten their lives.

Sin had, without going into too much detail, explained to her the difference between a wife and a mistress. He'd said that most married gentlemen had other women on the side, because men's needs were much stronger than a gently bred lady could fulfill. It hadn't sounded like something bad, even though she had promised herself never to marry a man with a mistress.

But the thought of Devlin kissing another woman was like a fist in her gut, and the hatred that filled her heart against this other woman, whoever she might be, scared her.

What if Devlin would refuse to get rid of his possible mistress? Would she be able to live with it? She guessed it was something she would have to endure as his wife, as anyone's wife, but she didn't like the thought at all. She knew she wanted Devlin as husband, to share the rest of her life with him. So maybe she would be able to endure another woman, as long as she had Devlin in her life.

She frowned in the darkness, not as happy anymore.

A sound disturbed her thoughts. Was it a tap on her window? She lay quiet, perfectly still, listening for it to repeat, but could hear only the pouring rain outside.

Just as she came to the relieved conclusion it had been merely her imagination, another tap was heard, and this time there was no mistake about it. Fanny sat up, her heart beating faster than a galloping horse's hoofs, and tried to see the window through the thick curtains that surrounded her bed.

Her fear of darkness immediately made her think of monsters, and for a second she considered putting a pillow over her head, but the thought of someone entering her room when she couldn't hear or see made her cast the idea away.

The next tap was harder, as if someone was

desperately trying to get her attention. With shaky breaths she got out of bed, slowly heading toward the window.

As she passed the fireplace, she grabbed the poker and, with it in her hand, felt more secure.

The next tap wasn't just one tap but more like thunder. She guessed there was no danger lurking, as it was so noisy her brother Sebastian, who had the bedroom next to hers, probably would have heard it if he were home.

Without losing her grip on the poker, she pulled the curtain aside as fast as she could, to surprise the intruder, and then she screamed.

Outside her window, on the thin windowsill, sat Penelope, drenched by the rain. Fanny tried to open the window, but to her despair it was caught, and she had to pry it open with the poker. With a terrible crash it flew open, and Fanny tumbled backwards as Penelope fell into the room.

Before either of them could speak, Fanny's father came storming into the room, closely followed by most of her other relatives. They stopped short as they spotted the soaked Penelope on the floor beneath the open window.

"What on earth are you doing here?" George bawled. "Are you out of your bloody mind? This is the third floor you've entered. The *third* floor! What of all stupid things in the world could make you do such a bloody idiotic thing?"

Caroline put her hand soothingly on her husband's arm. "How are you, sweetie?" she asked with a voice full of motherly care, and Penelope sobbed in response.

Caroline kneeled in front of Penelope and opened

her arms, and the weeping young woman threw herself into them. Over Penelope's shaking shoulder, Caroline gave the men a look that clearly told them to get the hell out of there, and after muttered comments they left with little protest. Tears were best left to a woman to handle.

Rake stayed on, though, ignoring his sister-in-law's forceful stares, and helped Fanny up from the floor.

"Is Lord Newbury angry with me?" Penelope sobbed, and Caroline shook her head.

"No, sweetie. He was just upset because he got a little scared. First, all the noise from Fanny's bedroom was frightening, and finding you had climbed to the third floor... You could have fallen and been killed!"

"What were you doing out there?" Fanny asked, and Penelope looked up at her friend with tear-filled eyes. When she spotted Rake still in the room, she started to tremble, and this time Caroline obviously didn't want to let her disobedient brother-in-law have his way.

"Get out. Now!" was all she said, but Rake didn't obey. Instead, he took a step closer to her, letting go of Fanny.

"No."

Penelope started to sob again, and Fanny rushed to her friend to comfort her. When Penelope fell into her friend's waiting arms, Caroline relinquished her and rose slowly to confront Rake. He glared back, his face hard and obstinate.

"Now," Caroline said.

This time he didn't answer at all, and his gaze never left Penelope.

"I said now!" she snarled between closed teeth.

And with more force than anyone could have imagined in her small body, she shoved Rake hard on the chest, so hard he lost balance and tumbled backwards through the doorway. Before he could recover from his astonishment, Caroline closed the door in his face, and locked it.

Mother and daughter helped Penelope out of her soaked clothes and into one of Fanny's thicker nightgowns, and made her sit down in the armchair next to the fire. As Fanny put more wood into the fire, Caroline rang for Nell, who immediately was sent for a tray of tea and something to eat.

Caroline placed herself in the armchair facing the young woman she had known for so many years and whom she loved dearly, almost as much as her own daughter.

Penelope was a mess. Her wet hair was tousled all around her white face, where a large bruise covered her left eye and cheek. She sat with her legs under her, looking more like a small girl than a full-grown woman.

"First I want to tell you how climbing up to Fanny's bedroom was incredibly stupid and dangerous," Caroline admonished. "And I want you to promise me that you will never do something like it again."

Penelope nodded forlornly, as she too was well aware of how her actions were beyond rational comprehension.

"That said," Caroline continued, "I urge you to tell us what you have been through. You have a bruise on the side of your face that clearly has the shape of a large hand."

"Please," Penelope cried. "Don't make me tell you.

I don't want to go through it again. Please let me just forget all about it."

"Penelope de Vere, there is no way I will let this be. I love you dearly, as you have always been like a sister to Fanny, closer than a friend. I will not let you leave this house until I know what happened to you. I will give you the choice of telling me alone, if that would make it easier than having to tell me and Fanny. But I tell you this, my girl—if you don't tell me now, you will have to answer to me *and* my husband tomorrow."

"Mother!" Fanny's exclamation held shock at her mother's coldness.

"Fanny, your friend has been beaten, and I can't and won't take it lightly. I'm not acting this way because I want to hurt Penelope. I do it because I care about her."

"It's okay," Penelope whispered to Fanny before looking up into Caroline's distressed eyes. "Not now, please. I haven't got any strength left. I'll speak to you in private tomorrow, if you don't mind."

Caroline went to her, gave her a warm hug, and kissed her white, cold cheek before opening the door for Nell and the tray of tea. When the maid had gone, Caroline followed her and closed the door softly behind her.

Fanny poured a cup of tea and gave it to Penelope, who accepted it with a weak smile. They sat silent, enjoying the tea and the fire while thousands of thoughts rushed through their heads.

"I'm so sorry, Fanny," Penelope said, finally breaking the silence. "I had nowhere else to go."

Fanny gave her a reassuring smile.

"You know you are always welcome at our home, and I am most grateful you came here in your hour of need, but we do prefer you use the front door."

Penelope giggled, not being able to withstand Fanny's friendly banter. "I'm sorry I wasn't able to attend the Almack's assembly this evening. We had another invitation, which my father insisted we should accept, and nothing I said could make him change his mind."

"I missed you dearly." Fanny smiled. "Something wonderful happened, and you weren't there to share it."

This caught Penelope's attention.

"Oh, dear, what happened?"

"Devlin kissed me."

"What!" Penelope squealed, forgetting all about her own situation, as was Fanny's intention. "How was it?"

"It was wonderful." Fanny sighed. "I can hardly explain how wonderful it was."

Penelope frowned, thinking. "But where did he kiss you? There is no privacy at Almack's."

"In the patronesses' meeting room. He surprised me when I had been to the restroom, and he dragged me into their meeting room, and he kissed me."

Fanny sighed again, dreamy-eyed, and something envious flared over Penelope's face before it vanished again.

"Did he just kiss you?" Penelope asked curiously, as she had never been in this kind of situation herself. Fanny blushed, and Penelope had her answer.

"Did he…" Her voice trailed off, as she knew not how to continue.

"Oh, Lord, no!" Fanny laughed, embarrassed. "But

by his choice, not mine. Penelope, it was amazing. I've never felt anything like it. He overwhelmed me completely, and if he hadn't been such a gentleman, I think we would have had to be married anyway, but a little sooner than we expected."

"Marry?" Penelope said, shocked.

Fanny nodded.

"Oh, Fanny," Penelope breathed happily, and gave her friend a tight hug. "This is indeed the most wonderful news!"

Fanny beamed, too happy to know how to respond. Her happiness was obvious, and at first Penelope beamed with her, until apparently something ugly grew in her mind, forcing her to remember what had happened to her and pushing all the happiness away. Fanny immediately noticed her friend's distress and got down on her knees in front of Penelope, taking her small cold hands into her own.

"Please, Penelope, tell me."

Penelope leaned back, resting her head against the back of the armchair. She closed her eyes tightly, and Fanny watched sadness and pain cross her face. She was silent for such a long time that Fanny jumped when she finally said something.

"My father has this friend he has known since he was a young man. They have never been close friends, to my father's despair, as the other man, Lord Bolton, is very rich and well connected in Essex, where he resides. This noble gentleman has been married three times, and all three times his wives have died suddenly after a few years of marriage, and without giving him any children. Now he is searching for wife number four, and of course he remembered my father has two daughters, one of whom is claimed to be the most beautiful woman ever. So he invited us to his townhouse for dinner. Father would never say no to Lord Bolton, so yesterday we joined him for dinner. Fanny, he was such a repulsive man! He is just as old as father but looks more like he is old enough to be my grandfather, or even my great-grandfather. Father smirked and smirked, but Lord Bolton hardly looked at him. Our host was too busy drooling all over Charmaine. She was admirably nice to him and didn't even mind as he tried to look down her bodice."

She sat quiet for a while, and Fanny knew she must be bracing herself for the next part of her story, the one where it all happened.

"If you don't want to tell me more now, we can continue tomorrow." Fanny said softly, not wanting to put her friend through too much anguish.

Penelope's smile was full of love. "It is okay, my dear. I'd rather say it now and have it done. I don't think I can sleep without getting some of it off my chest."

"Whatever you wish is my command," Fanny said reassuringly, and Penelope hugged her warmly and thanked her for being such a good friend. Again she sat back, and this time she stared into the fire unseeingly.

"After dinner, Mother, Charmaine, and I were ushered into the salon, as the men were staying behind for their usual port. We didn't have to wait a long time, though, before father came and told us we were leaving. As we got up to go to the front door, he stopped me and told me he wanted to talk to me in private, and we were left alone by the others."

Penelope's voice became hoarse with emotion, and

she drank some of the now-cold tea before she took a deep breath and continued despite a cracked voice.

"He told me I was to stay, as he and Lord Bolton had an agreement. Lord Bolton wanted Charmaine for his next wife, but my father had surprisingly told him no, as Charmaine was meant for another man. As I understood by my father's explanation, Lord Bolton got very angry and threatened to lock me and my parents in and have his way with Charmaine anyway, and thus force a marriage. My father..."

Penelope took a deep shaky breath.

"My father," she continued, with an impressive show of strength, "made a bargain in order to keep Charmaine and her virginity intact, and Lord Bolton reluctantly agreed to it, still upset but at least still my father's friend. Father told me I was to stay behind while my family went home. I was told to do anything the man wanted me to do, and when he was done with me I was to send my father a message, so he could have a servant fetch me and drive me to a small estate in Wales, where I could stay for the rest of my life."

Fanny didn't know what to say. What Penelope told was incomprehensible. It was too much for a mere eighteen-year-old overprotected girl to take in. She put her head on Penelope's shoulder, closing her eyes as tears of compassion fell on her friend's nightgown.

"I cried and begged, but nothing I said seemed to affect my father. He turned his back to me and told me this was the least I could do to keep my sister chaste. When I tried to grab him, to force him to stay and listen to me, or preferably take me with him, he shoved me so hard I fell backwards and hit my head on something. I must have fainted, because when I woke up again I found myself lying on a bed in an unknown bedroom."

She started to cry, and Fanny could only hold her friend, to help her through her pain.

"I was so scared, Fanny! I didn't know what to do, and then Lord Bolton came by with his snickering footman and told me to stay put, as he had other appointments planned. You should have seen his evil face when he told me what he would do with me when he came back—it was terrifying. And they left me there alone, waiting for a fate worse than death."

"Oh Penny," Fanny moaned, filled with dread for what her friend gone through.

"I was desperate to get away from there," Penelope continued bravely. "When I found an unlocked window in an adjoining bedroom, I could hardly believe my luck. I climbed out through it and made it down to the street, where I ran as fast as I could until I reached my father's house here at Berkeley Square.

"But, as I grabbed the knob of the front door, I realized I couldn't go home. My father had given me away to Lord Bolton. I know what a stubborn man my father is, always bound by the honor of his word, and I knew he would send me back. So I came here, but when I was about to knock on your door, I saw a ladder someone nicely enough had forgotten, so I moved it to where your room is, and the rest you know."

"Oh, Penelope," Fanny cried, devastated for her friend's sake.

"I have nowhere to go. I can't go home again, for I am not wanted there. I have no other relatives I can live with. I might be able to work as a governess, but who would hire me? If this comes out, I will be destroyed in the eyes of society."

"Oh, come on," Fanny said angrily. "Now you are just being stupid. You can stay here, and so you shall. I don't care what anyone says about you, or if your reputation is damaged forever. You are my friend, and you will always be."

Penelope gave her a small smile, and although Fanny could see she didn't believe her, she decided not to continue to argue the point. Penelope was clearly fatigued and on the verge of falling asleep, so Fanny kept quiet, and a few minutes later Penelope was sound asleep in the comfortable armchair.

Fanny grabbed a thick blanket and tucked Penelope in neatly before she climbed into bed, thinking about what Penelope had told her. She could hardly believe something like this could happen in these modern times. It was unbearable.

She sighed deeply, feeling drowsy, and then she too fell asleep.

Chapter 19

Lord and Lady Newbury sat silently in the marchioness's salon, staring at their daughter with disbelief written on their proud faces.

Fanny, who had been just as shocked when she heard Penelope's story the night before, stayed quiet following her recital of the details she'd learned. Her parents obviously needed a chance to digest the whole ugly truth.

Earlier, when she awoke from a night filled with nightmares, Penelope had still been sleeping soundly, and Fanny had dressed herself quickly before sneaking out from her bedroom without disturbing her exhausted friend. To spare Penelope the pain of telling her horrible story again, she had sent a maid to collect her parents, so that she instead could tell them.

Her parents never said a word. They didn't interrupt her once, which told her more than anything how much it affected them. Finally George woke from his numbed state and took his wife's cold hand. "I'll kill him."

Caroline shook her head. "No, you won't. He is not worth it."

"No, he isn't, but Penny is."

"Please, Papa," Fanny begged, as she leaned forward and put a hand on his knee. "Don't do anything stupid. This is so hard for Penny, and she would never be able to live with it if more evil came out of it."

George looked at his only daughter. "What if it had been you in such a situation?" He shuddered, then nodded.

"I'm going to talk to her," Caroline said as she arose and headed toward the door. "Don't do anything without telling me, and don't tell anyone else. Especially not Rake."

George turned toward his daughter with a frown. "Why not Rake?"

"Oh, come on, Papa," Fanny said, not believing her ears. "You know why."

"No, I don't," George answered, bewildered.

Fanny didn't answer, though. She was trying to sort out this horrible situation of Penelope's in her head.

"I can't believe it happened," she whispered hoarsely. "He's her bloody father! He should love and protect her, not sell her."

George went to Fanny and hugged her closely for a long time, the father needing to reassure his daughter that his love for her was true and the daughter needing to feel fatherly love truly did exist.

Butler came in, his grave face more serious than ever.

"Lady Nester, for Lady Newbury."

George froze. His gray eyes darkened with a seething anger he could hardly control, and Fanny shook her head at him.

"No, you won't," she soothed him quietly, before she told Butler to send the woman in.

George released her and strode to the fireplace. He grabbed the mantel with as much strength as he could muster, until his hands turned white from the effort.

To Fanny it looked as though he was trying to keep from hurling himself upon the woman who walked through the door.

Lady Nester stopped short as she saw who was waiting for her. "I came for Lady Newbury," she shrilled with a slightly hysterical voice.

"My mother is occupied, for the moment. Maybe I can help you?" Fanny asked politely, not sure how otherwise to approach the older woman.

Lady Nester looked ready to faint. She was obviously looking for her daughter and didn't know how to ask them for her without letting them know she was missing.

Fanny took pity on her. She knew this woman had not been a part of Penelope's nightmare last night, as it had all been Lord Nester's doing, and she must be devastated by now. The poor woman probably had not a clue of the arrangement he had made and why her youngest daughter hadn't gone home with them.

If Lord Nester could behave so outrageously toward his daughter, one could only assume he behaved in the same selfish and unethical way to his wife.

"My mother is upstairs with Penny, trying to sort things out."

Lady Nester paled as relief washed over her tired face. For a short moment her angst was visible, before she turned stark white and fainted dead away.

George rushed forward and, in the last possible second, caught her head before it hit the floor. He lifted her up with a grunt and carried her to the sofa.

Fanny turned to Butler and told him to get smelling salts, and then she gazed down at their guest.

"Poor woman," she said, filled with compassion.

Her father snorted in a most patronizing way. She ignored that completely. He, like all her occasionally tedious male relatives, could sometimes behave in the most childish way. Her mother had more than once sighed over their lack of dignity when they snorted and rolled their eyes too much in public.

Lady Nester, who slowly regained consciousness, was soon sitting up, fanning herself with a silken handkerchief. She looked flustered and uncomfortable, understandable since her family had just had an enormous crisis.

"Is there anything I can do for you?" Fanny asked, carefully choosing her words.

Lady Nester glanced quickly at her before she shook her head.

"Do you want me to get Penny for you?" Fanny asked, trying to get the silent woman to speak, a seemingly impossible mission.

"N-no," Lady Nester stuttered, startled, surprising both Fanny and George. "Please don't fetch her. I just needed to know where she was, and if she was all right. I was so afraid…"

They waited for her to continue, but instead she started to gather her things, seeming in a sudden frenzy to leave.

"Are you sure you don't want to see Penelope? She had quite an awful night yesterday and may really need her mother."

The sorrow in Lady Nester's eyes was unbearable as she shook her head, unable to speak. Her distress was obvious, and Fanny didn't argue with her. Instead she picked up the gloves and the reticule Lady Nester had dropped when she fainted and was rewarded with a wobbly, thankful smile.

Not until the lady was about to leave the room did she ask her, "Would it be acceptable for Penny to stay with me for a while? I am finding it so reassuring to have her around during my first season, to share this with her. I would be forever thankful."

Lady Nester stopped in the doorway and looked back over her shoulder at Fanny, who stood there, young and pretty, her back straight, ready to fight for the friend she loved so dearly.

"Maybe it even could be possible, to avoid complications, for Penny to stay with me for the rest of the Season? Perhaps the rest of this year, so I won't feel lonely?"

Lady de Vere nodded, her gratitude visible. "She may stay as long as she wants. I'll let it be known among our acquaintance." With one last half-smile, she disappeared through the door.

George looked surprised.

The woman had managed to astonish him, and Fanny was thankful he had kept quiet during the short visit. His rudeness would have ruined the meeting. Now, when the visit was done, she was glad he had decided to stay put, as she knew he had needed to hear this.

They sat down and talked quietly about the visit until Caroline rejoined them. When they told her about it, she was just as relieved as they had been, and so was Penelope when she was told. She did cry a bit for her mother and sister. She would miss them.

Penelope was given the bedroom next to Fanny's, even though they always had shared a room during earlier overnight stays. But this time was different, and

Fanny guessed her friend needed solitude more than she needed her. But it almost broke her heart when she heard Penelope turn the key in the lock until it couldn't turn anymore.

She walked into her own bedroom, now cleaned by the servants and showing no evidence of the night's events. At the window, she looked down at the ladder still standing against the front of the house. She shivered at the thought of how the distressed Penelope had climbed it in pouring rain with her heart shattered into thousands of pieces.

Fanny leaned her forehead against the glass of the window, finding its coldness soothing for her pounding head.

What would Devlin think about this?

Would he be just as outraged as she was, or would he think of it as nothing, because a father's right was unbreakable? She realized again how she knew next to nothing about him. Nothing that mattered.

The things she did know about him were tidbits told to her by others. Devlin was exasperatingly secretive about his private thoughts, and he had up until now told her only his most shallow ones.

She was going to marry him, and yet she knew so little about him. What if he turned out to be another Lord Nester? She, as his wife, would have no say whatsoever. It didn't matter how much her family loved her. They too wouldn't be able to do anything about her situation.

The husband had all the power, and the wife none.

She closed her eyes, telling herself she was stupid. He wasn't like Lord Nester. Deep inside her heart she knew it, but what had happened to Penelope had brought doubt to her mind, and she couldn't shrug it off. She hadn't it in her to go back to the innocent girl she had been at Almack's last night.

When the distant sound of the doorbell was heard in the background, she knew it was Devlin on his way to her father. Her beau was there to ask her father for her hand in marriage, and she knew her father would agree without hesitation, as he thought Devlin was the man she wanted for husband.

But was he?

Could she trust her life and the lives of her unborn children to a man who might or might not turn into a beast as time went by?

When Nell came to get her, she still had no answers to the questions that roamed in her head. She couldn't stop wishing she could send her maid downstairs again, to tell Devlin she wasn't feeling well and ask him to come back some other day. But sending him away was no option, especially as she had already agreed yesterday to marry him.

When she entered the library where Devlin and her father were waiting for her, she felt her treacherous heart skip a beat when she saw him. He was standing in front of her, tall and magnificent, his golden eyes showering her with his warmth.

She gave him a wobbly smile and could have cried over the frown that slowly took away the lighthearted happiness he had shown when she walked through the door. George grabbed Fanny's hand and, with his other hand, took hold of her chin, gently forcing her to look into his eyes.

"Hereford has asked me for your hand in marriage, and I told him you have my blessing, as long as you are willingly giving him your acceptance."

Her father was offering her an easy way out, and she felt tears running down her cheeks. Silently, he wiped them away before he kissed her gently on the forehead and left them alone in the library.

She could feel Devlin watching her, trying to discern what was wrong. When they parted last night, she had been exhilarated and had almost jumped up and down with excitement. But today she was standing in front of him no more than an empty shell of a human being.

"Your father gave us his blessing, and now it's up to you, if you will have me?" Devlin broke the awkward silence.

She closed her eyes and took a deep breath before she turned and looked at him. For the first time, she really looked at him, not falling into her normal spellbound stare at the wonder of him.

He was a tall man, muscular and fit. His hair was dark brown, almost black, and his eyes golden. His skin was smooth and unblemished, his nose straight and aristocratic, his lips firm and yet unbelievably soft.

She knew he was a graceful man who moved easily anywhere, and his hands were large and strong but yet tender. If she closed her eyes, she could still feel them caressing her breasts and gently stroking her neck.

"Do you?" he asked again, not managing to wait for her answer.

"I don't know," she whispered, before she started to cry. She sat down on the sofa, and hid her face in her hands. "I'm so sorry."

She heard him move and felt the sofa shift as he sat beside her. He grabbed her hands and forced them gently away from her face before he bent and kissed her softly on her cheeks, wiping the tears away with his mouth.

The tenderness he showed her made her cry even harder, and in one swift movement he lifted her up and placed her on his lap. He put his hand on her head, and forced her gently to rest her cheek against his heart. Silently he waited for her to finish crying, while he hugged her closely.

When the last tear had dried, she took a deep shaky breath and managed to give him another wobbly smile. He smiled tenderly back, stroking a loose strand of hair away from her face.

"You know, even with your eyes puffy from all the crying, and your nose as red as ripe strawberries, you still are the most beautiful woman I have ever seen."

His loving words went straight into her heart, and she felt a few of her worries easing away.

He placed a soft kiss on the tip of her red nose, and when she didn't object, he put another on her cheek. She gave him a small teary-eyed smile, and was rewarded with a soft kiss on the other cheek.

She leaned closer to him, and slowly and as lightly as he possibly could he placed a chaste kiss on her soft lips. She looked into his golden eyes, enjoying the warmth they showered upon her, and before she could stop herself, she kissed him, deeply.

Her tongue thrust into his mouth, ravishing it, and his moan made her feel dizzy with the need of becoming one with him.

When he moved his arms to pull her closer, she grabbed them and forced them back toward the back of the sofa. She turned around in his lap, and straddled him, not once stopping the sultry kiss.

Not until he was panting with the need of her did she lift her head. She looked down at him, and all the marvelous feelings that made her feel hotter than fire must have shown in her face, or her eyes, because his eyes turned darker, mimicking the fire inside of her.

"I'm burning," he whispered hoarsely, as his hands hardened their grip of her arms.

"Really?" She gave a little smile, hoping it looked just as sultry as she felt, and his breathing became deeper and shakier.

"You are so beautiful," he breathed again, looking at her with awe, and she knew she was silly for being so pleased with his exclamation, but she was.

Extremely so.

She wet her lips with her tongue, and the moan escaping him told her how much he liked her innocent action.

"Not as beautiful as you," she whispered, as she leaned closer to him again and kissed him.

His response was immediate and honest, as he growled with pleasure over her brazen behavior. The kiss lasted for the longest time, and when they finally broke apart, she could hardly breathe. Strands of her hair had escaped her coiffure, and she tossed her head to clear them from her face.

"God," he groaned, as the movement made her shift in his lap. "You have to sit still, or I won't be able to hold back anymore."

She looked inquisitively at him, with her head to one side, and he groaned again.

"If you don't stop looking at me like that, I can't be held responsible for my actions."

"You can't?"

This was becoming more than interesting, she thought. He almost growled at her as his eyes fell to her heaving breasts. She had not a clue what was about to happen, but she realized she didn't care.

She trusted him.

A stone fell from her heart, as the truth settled in her mind and eased her worries.

She *did* trust him. Completely.

So what if she didn't know so much about him? She had the rest of her life to spend learning all she could. All she needed right now was him.

"I keep forgetting you are a virgin," he grunted, as his hands moved from her arms toward her breasts. "You sit here in my lap looking at me like a trained seductress, with your swollen lips parted and inviting and your gray eyes black and passionate."

"Oh."

She gave him a surprised face, as this was news to her, and he grinned and gave her a fake suspicious look in return. "Because you are, right? A virgin?"

She laughed over his joke, and threw her arms around his head in a joyous hug. She felt his face against her breasts and tried to lean back, feeling a little embarrassed over her wanton behavior.

"Ah, my little minx," he smiled wickedly, showing her without words how much he enjoyed her wanton behavior, and all her discomfort disappeared. This time she didn't stop him when he let his hands slowly lift her skirt, caressing her knees and her thighs until he found his hot goal. Instead she kept her head back and closed her eyes as she let him have his way with her.

Without thinking about what he was doing, he

pushed her down on her back, got rid of all the fabrics between them, and pressed his manhood against the junction of her legs, feeling the soft tissue stretching to make room for him. Her sudden cry made him stop, and he closed his eyes, begging for patience and restraint.

"I'm sorry," he whispered to her, as he made the final thrust through her maidenly barrier.

He caught her shout in his mouth, kissing her until he could feel her responding to him again. When she was moaning with passion instead of crying out with pain, he started to move with his hips again, and was rewarded with a gasp of pleasure from her.

Faster and faster he thrust, until he could feel her tremble beneath him. With a growl, he made one last powerful move that sent him all the way to the stars and back.

When they both could breathe normally again, he sat up, not wanting to crush her with the weight of his body. When he saw the blood between her thighs, he winced.

"I'm so sorry," he said again. "I didn't mean to hurt you."

She gave him a slow smile, filled with contentment and shook her head slowly as she sat up. As he got dressed he glanced at her, not knowing really how to behave.

Her forlorn behavior when she'd arrived in the library earlier had spooked him. It had made him feel strangely unsure of her. Her passion had caught him off guard, and although he had already promised himself not to touch her before their wedding night, he hadn't been able to withhold his passion.

"Well," he said slowly. "Now I guess you won't

have a choice but to marry me, and preferably as soon as possible."

She turned around, now fully dressed, and looked at him seriously. "I will marry you, because I think I can love you with all of my heart when I get to know you better, but at the same time it scares me. I can't help wondering if I ever will…"

Devlin froze as her voice trailed off.

"Don't you think you can love me?" he asked hoarsely, not really wanting her to answer his question, as he was too afraid of the answer.

She rolled her eyes at him in a very Darling way, and he relaxed. "No, stupid, I am more than halfway in love with you already—and stop the smirking. What scares me is the feeling of not knowing you."

He couldn't stop a relieved laugh. "My dearest Fanny, you must be joking. Of course you know me."

"No, I don't. Not what you truly think about anything, not your feelings about a variety of subjects."

He could see this was extremely important to her, so he sat down and put his feet on the table in front of the sofa.

"All right," he drawled arrogantly. "Question me."

She couldn't stop herself from giggling as she settled again on the sofa at the other side of the table, facing him. She chewed on her lower lip, and to his surprise he felt himself hardening again.

"Stop it," he whispered.

"Stop what?"

"The chewing."

She looked at him blankly.

"It's rather enticing, and if you don't want to have me all over you again, you need to stop."

This time she understood what he meant, and she blushed prettily. "I wouldn't mind," she finally admitted shyly, and before he could stop himself he jumped over the table.

He ripped her clothes, aching with the need to penetrate her, and sighed loudly with contentment as he slid into her. She was still wet, and he soon had her losing control and screaming his name into his mouth.

This time they were too loud, and they barely had time to straighten their appearances before George and Caroline came through the door to find out what Fanny's answer had been. Her shy, happy smile told them everything, and they hugged her closely.

Caroline immediately started to talk about the wedding, wanting Devlin to say what his preferences were, and she exclaimed at her luck when he told her she could do whatever she wanted, as he trusted her judgment.

Caroline slapped her husband's arm when he mumbled, "Are you really sure you do?" to Devlin before she bustled out, hunting for paper to do lists about everything, including a list of her lists.

George pounded Devlin on the back and invited him to White's for a drink, and Devlin couldn't say anything but yes, as he was practically dragged away by his future father-in-law.

Fanny just smiled and shook her head, a bit relieved to have her solitude, because she needed time to think. The passion she had felt in Devlin's arms was starting to fade, but this time she didn't let herself fall back into her earlier misery.

Devlin had said he would tell her everything she wanted to know, and she believed him.

Being her mother's daughter, she rushed to her room and started to write down a list of all the questions she wanted to ask him.

She wasn't going to forget anything.

Chapter 20

The following months were the happiest in Devlin's life. Every day turned out to be more precious than the day before, and it all was because of the wonderful minx to whom he was betrothed.

Even Fanny's colorful family was happy for her, although her brothers and uncles were patronizing whenever they had a chance. His patience seemed to be endless, though, because he only smiled at them, not once showing how irritating they were to him.

It wasn't the constant bantering that disturbed him, because he knew exactly how to close his ears to their nagging voices. No, it was the way in which they effectively made sure he and Fanny had no time alone that he found most disturbing.

Even Fanny had agreed with him, as he sighed over the obnoxious crowd that followed them during an innocent stroll down Rotten Row. Sometimes her family was a little too much.

The passion of the proposal day still haunted him, both day and night. A couple of times he had even dreamt about her—so vividly he had stained his linens. She was such an odd mixture of innocence and sultriness, and he sometimes thought she must have a secret twin sister.

They spent most of the days together under the surveillance of one or more of her relatives. She held on to his promise of honesty with an admirable stubbornness, and asked him every question she could think of, and he answered her truthfully, as promised.

He told her about his job for Lord Saxton, with his commander's blessing. It had caused him more than a few bad moments, though, as he had to convince her it wasn't a good idea at all for her to start working for the war ministry too.

The mere thought of her in danger made him nauseous, and he even thought about quitting completely himself, so she wouldn't do anything stupid, like trying to save him if she thought he was in danger.

In the *ton*, the engagement between the Duke of Hereford and Lady Francesca Darling was a sensation without end. Wherever they went, they found themselves the object of gossip.

Fanny shrugged everyone's excitement away, only intriguing Devlin further. Her indifference toward the pettiness of other people was something fresh for him, and her honesty was like balm on his scarred heart.

As the Season passed and May turned into June and then July, it was soon only a couple of days until the wedding, and they travelled to Chester Park. To have the ceremony performed at the family's country estate had been Fanny's only demand. Her Grand-Papa Hannibal would prefer not to make the trip into London, she had declared. He never liked to leave the castle's grounds.

It had been harder than ever to find solitude together with Fanny at the castle. Hannibal Darling, the Duke of Berkeley, was even more patronizing than all his offspring together. His cold eyes, under those bushy eyebrows, didn't miss a thing, and every attempt Devlin made to spend some time with his fiancée alone was met with failure.

Not until the last day before the wedding did an opportunity present itself. Hannibal had invited all the servants and everyone living on the vast lands surrounding the castle to a wedding party. The evening was calm and amazingly warm, and the dark blue sky was full of twinkling stars.

In the barn, close to the stables, long tables had been set and decorated with loads of flowers. Such enormous quantities of food had been placed on the tables it would have taken at least three times as many people to eat it all.

Children were laughing and running everywhere, and the adults grew louder and laughed more easily the more ale they drank.

The Darling family sat in the midst of the tables, interacting with the servants as if all were equals and not masters and employees.

As the evening grew darker the dance started, and the bride and groom were ushered up onto the dance floor for the fastest country dance ever played. One after another, more couples joined, until the floor was filled with a twirling mass of happy, laughing people.

When Devlin realized they all were too busy having fun to waste time watching the soon-to-be-married couple, he grabbed Fanny's hand, giving her a wicked grin. She blushed, but he need not have worried whether she was willing to go with him, as she practically dragged him outside, where they disappeared into the darkness outside the barn, away from searching eyes.

Silently they ran together over the dewy lawn until

they came to the small gazebo hidden among large magnolia bushes.

Fanny giggled as she climbed the two steps. His hands were already on her clothes, undressing her. Hot with passion, he turned her to face him, and she threw her arms around his neck, pressing him closer to her as her lips found his.

Waves of passion hit him, and he moaned and gave up undressing her. Instead he lifted her, pressed her against the wall, and in one swift motion thrust inside her. He felt her bite into his shoulder, and he knew she was trying to keep quiet as passion overtook her body and mind. But when the ecstasy reached its climax, she couldn't stop herself, and her scream mixed with the groan that left his own lips.

They fell to the floor together, panting, their hearts racing, too content to care about the cold, hard wood beneath them, where they lay still until their breathing became even, and they could move again.

Devlin lifted his hand and felt a strand of Fanny's hair, enjoying its velvety softness. In the moonlight filtering into the gazebo he watched her as she lay with closed eyes, and he savored every second of their solitude in this special moment.

As he had many times before, he sent a thank you from his heart to whoever had put Fanny in his way. She was such a lovely young woman, and he adored how she continued to surprise him every day.

And he adored how she truly enjoyed making love, not only for the passion but for the closeness it gave them, the intimacy they shared. He could hardly wait for the rest of their life together, where moments like this would be his as often as he liked.

As if she had the same thought, Fanny sighed happily, and Devlin couldn't help but chuckle.

"You look like a cat that just ate a mouse," he said with a laugh.

"I feel so good right now, I can't help it."

"My pleasure, I assure you. Whenever you need me, I'll be at your service."

"Well, how nice of you." She winked. "And as I intend to need you for the rest of my life, you had better go and get some rest, because starting tomorrow you are all mine."

Something warm filled his chest as he looked at the young woman beside him. He felt an overwhelming urge to hold on to her and never let her out of his sight.

It was amazing how she completed him. She was the last missing piece in the puzzle of his life. He could hardly believe she had been at his side for only a couple of months. He seemed to have known her forever.

He enjoyed her company much more than he had ever thought possible, considering she was a woman. Deep inside, he sent out a heartfelt wish for it to take some time for her to get pregnant.

He really didn't want to live without her. Somewhere during the last months he had fallen in love with her, something he had thought impossible earlier this year. She had knocked him off his feet, and now he was standing here eagerly waiting to fulfill her every whim.

"Starting tomorrow, my dear, it's only you and me," he murmured, and kissed the faint freckles on her nose. And he just had to kiss the freckles on her cheeks, too. When he tried to kiss her mouth, she laughed and pushed him away. He let out a disappointed growl, making her laugh even more.

"No, no, my dearest almost-husband, don't you start kissing me again. I'm still unwed, and as such I must live by my parents' rules. And the most important rule right now is to not stay out of their sight too long!"

He gave her a wicked grin, and tried to reach her again, but she slipped away with light laughter. Before he had a chance to react, she was on her feet, straightening her clothes.

"And by the way," she continued, while stroking away the wrinkles in her skirt with her hands, "it won't be just you and me in the nearest future. Don't you remember? I told you about my family's yearly get-together, which we have in the beginning of August."

He must have looked just as bewildered as he felt, because his lovely bride-to-be frowned at him.

"What?" He smiled.

"You forgot!" she cried out as the truth hit her. "How could you forget about something as important as this?"

His smile vanished as he stood to face her. "I have had many things on my mind lately, as you are well aware."

"One would think that courting me would mean you remember what I tell you, especially about important things such as family gatherings we are to attend."

"You are important to me, not your family!"

"My family is important to me, and if I am important to you, they should be too."

He looked at her teary-eyed face, not really understanding what her problem was. So what if they missed the family gathering? They had it every year.

They could attend the next year, or even wait for the year after that.

She was almost a married woman, and as such she should know her husband was now her family, not the heap of relatives she had grown up with. He shook his head at her silliness. She obviously didn't like his indifferent attitude, and turned her back to him.

Without a word, he left her standing alone in the gazebo, not once considering a continuation of the discussion.

He needed a drink. No, better make it two.

Lord, he longed for tomorrow, when the ceremony was through and they could be on their way to Pendragon. If luck was on his side, they could leave before high tea and reach as far as Swindon before they needed to stop for the night.

He'd had enough of her family over the last couple of months. Solitude, with time to think things through, had become a necessity. His life had reached a crossing, and he nourished a desperate need to figure out which way to go.

Tomorrow he would have a new responsibility in his life, a wife, and he wanted—no, he needed—time to come up with a plan as to how to handle her with the care and respect she deserved.

When he entered the hallway, he called out orders to the sour-faced butler Ivanoff, who stood at the bottom of the stair, before continuing to his room.

He smiled toward Bear as he closed the door behind him. His aristocratic valet arched an elegant eyebrow at his friend's obvious happiness.

"You look content," he grinned, as Devlin seated himself on the bed, facing him.

"I know I do, and amazingly enough I really am content. For the first time in my life, I know what I want and need in my life, and it's Fanny. She is such a wonderful person, and I can't keep myself from smiling when I think about her. She is a handful; I won't lie about it, but at the same time, she is not too hard to handle. However, more importantly, I have no doubts about her turning into a perfect duchess, with a little loving molding."

"Mold her into perfect?" Bear chuckled. "And here I thought she already was perfect."

Devlin looked at his friend sideways, a bit unsure with him for the first time during their friendship.

What did Bear mean? Did he have a crush on Fanny too, or was he only trying to tease? It was hard to say.

To save himself from illogical tantrums, Devlin decided to ignore the other man's remark. Instead he leaned back and closed his eyes, continuing with their conversation as if he'd never had doubts.

"I want a wife who will be feared, loved, and respected, and who would never be close to doing anything that could be called a scandal."

"Then I guess you have found your perfect duchess, as Lady Francesca is born into respect, and she would never do anything wrongful against you, or your marriage."

Devlin smiled without opening his eyes. "When I think about our immediate future at Pendragon, a wave of contentment washes through my body. Fanny and I didn't have much time before the announcement of our engagement. Since it became official, we have been guarded closely by her family, and the only thing I can think about now is to have her to myself. I'm so bloody relieved we're leaving for Pendragon tomorrow that I don't even feel at all bothered about her wanting to stay on for a while. As my wife she will respect my wish."

Devlin could feel uneasiness oozing from Bear, and he tried not to be affected by his friend's feelings. Tomorrow he would have the right to do whatever he wanted with Fanny, and if his wish was for them to leave, she had nothing to say about it, thank God.

How amazing it would be to have someone to come home to after a long day managing the large machine that a holding like Pendragon was. She would always be there, just for him, eagerly awaiting his arrival.

"You do realize she has a will just as strong as yours, and she won't back down if she thinks you are wrong?"

"Nothing to get excited over." Devlin snorted. "I am, after all, the man in this marriage, and it's my right to have it my way. She will have to bend."

"Oh, indeed?"

Devlin opened his eyes and gave Bear a hard look that his friend just shrugged off before, without another word, he stood and left the room.

Devlin muttered with indignation as he undressed without the assistance of his pretend-valet and, naked as the day he was born, lay down on the satin sheets. He could hear the music playing in the barn as he closed his eyes.

Bear's anxiety had affected him more than he liked. What if his friend was right? What if life with Fanny as he pictured it wouldn't be just that—as he pictured it?

He sighed deeply and shoved his newly found doubts aside. It didn't matter what Bear said. He was going to marry her anyway. And maybe life wouldn't be as pleasant at first, but he wouldn't fret about it.

He was a patient man. Sooner or later he would have his way.

Chapter 21

Fanny sat at her dresser, looking at her image in the small mirror. She looked disheveled, with her hair all mussed and the dress slightly torn and dirty. She looked a mess—and it was kind of a relief, as she felt like a mess.

What had happened down in the gazebo? It had been as if she had tried to talk to a wall.

A brick wall.

A very inconsiderate brick wall, with no respect for her feelings or for the traditions of her family. How could he forget about the upcoming family gathering? They had it every year, and she had told him about it twice.

Twice, for goodness' sake!

She grabbed her hairbrush and started to work through the tangled knots in her hair with swift, almost brutal movements, so that her scalp ached satisfyingly.

A part of her wondered why she was surprised. They had been talking constantly for months, and not once had he interrupted all her questions with one about her. He hadn't even asked her why she had been so upset the night of his proposal. He still didn't know about Penelope and how her friend's situation had affected her, and she had a sinking feeling he wasn't interested in knowing, either.

All in all, she had started to doubt if they were such

a perfect match, despite what everyone kept telling them. How could they be, if he wasn't interested in her? A part of her wanted to cancel the wedding, but the other part wanted to know if such doubts were reason enough.

She looked at the wardrobe where her bridal gown hung for display. It was such a beautiful gown, with layers upon layers of heavy ivory silk. The seamstress had outdone herself this time and created a gown worthy of a princess.

Or a duchess.

She sighed, a deep pitiful sigh, before she quickly changed into her nightgown, threw a shawl around her shoulders, and sneaked out into the corridor. She knocked softly at Penelope's bedroom door before opening it to slink in and over to her friend's bed.

Penelope stirred sleepily as Fanny slipped down under the quilt.

"Is everything okay?" she yawned.

"I have doubts about marrying Devlin, and I need you to tell me I'm stupid."

Penelope moved slightly to offer her friend a little more space. "You are stupid."

"How can you call me stupid, when you haven't even been told why I am upset yet?"

"Easy. You are my friend, and I want to humor you the night before your wedding."

"As my friend you are not supposed to humor me. You are supposed to tell me the truth, and nothing but the truth. And you are not supposed to call me stupid."

Penelope moved to a more comfortable position, as if she could sense this was going to take some time. "So, what happened?"

"He's not interested in me!"

Penelope gave Fanny a look that clearly told exactly how ridiculous she found the comment. "You can't be serious."

"I am." Fanny said, a bit hurt over how lightly her friend seemed to take this. "He doesn't listen to a word I say, which is quite upsetting since I have been talking constantly for months."

"I have to agree with the truth of your words, as your voice has been a constant companion since he proposed to you," Penelope mused, and hid her face under her arm, as she was attacked with a pillow.

"Today we were talking about the wedding, and he told me how much he looked forward to spending time with me alone, when the whole wedding thing finally was over. When I reminded him gently about the family party we always have at Chester Park every August, and told him how we are to stay here for another week, he was genuinely surprised and quite aghast about it."

"Well." Penelope pondered. "I too would have been a little vexed about having to stay put for another week, when all I wanted to do was to take my new bride home."

"But he has no right to be vexed," Fanny cried out, startling her friend.

"For goodness' sake, Fanny." Penelope rolled her eyes. "He wants to be with you! Why are you so upset? If someone I loved made a little fuss about not being able to have me all to himself, I would thank my lucky stars for finding this man, not be upset about it."

Fanny glared at her friend. "I. Do. Not. Love. Him."

Penelope rolled her eyes again, not answering such

an obvious lie.

"I don't!"

"Yes, you do, and stop denying it."

"I don't."

"Well, if you don't, why are you so upset about him not listening to you?"

"Because I thought he respected me."

Ah.

"Fanny, dearest," Penelope said with her softest tone, silently wishing her friend would come to her senses again. "Being upset about finding out you won't be able to have your new bride all to yourself is not in any way disrespectful. You know this is the truth, if you only let go of this childish tantrum of yours."

"I've already told him about the festivities twice during the last week, so I still do think I can have as many tantrums as I like over the fact he apparently didn't hear a word I have said."

"I have to admit, that is a bit disrespectful."

"Thank you."

Silence ruled in the bedroom for a while. The dying fire in the old fireplace cast a soft yellow light over the ceiling above the large bed, and the shadows seemed to be dancing to the faint music still drifting from the barn.

"I don't know what to do," Fanny said quietly, in a hoarse, tearful voice. Penelope rolled over and hugged her tightly.

"Do you love him?"

Fanny nodded. This was not the time nor the place for pretending not to.

"Then marry him. If you don't, you will regret it for the rest of your life. He is a good man, and he cares very much for you. And you know you will never find anyone better or more suitable."

"Well…" Fanny laughed drowsily. "I can always marry Mr. Pembroke."

Laughter filled the room, effectively wiping all sadness away, and when Caroline peeked in an hour later, they were both sound asleep.

She stood by the bed for a little while, watching the sleeping beauties. Her only daughter mumbled something in her sleep, just as she had done since she was a little girl, and tears over times now gone forever filled the loving mother's eyes.

Never again would she be able to stand at her daughter's bed watching her sleep. Fanny would now be sleeping in her new home with her husband.

If she only could turn time back and relive these past wonderful eighteen years again, she would do it in an instant. She was happy for her daughter's marriage, and she would celebrate tomorrow, but this was her night of mourning.

She bent down and kissed her daughter's cheek, her nose on the soft flesh smelling the faint scent that was Fanny's.

The daughter was still too young to understand how much her life would change now, but the mother knew and could only hope she would have as little friction as possible during her installment as the new duchess. With tears running down her cheeks, she quietly left the room.

Chapter 22

Francesca Darling Ross, the Duchess of Hereford, was so angry with her new husband she couldn't even look upon him.

Silently she stared out through the window of the carriage, watching the countryside slowly pass by. She was worn into pieces from keeping herself behaving like a lady instead of the furious woman who raged within.

He had tried to talk to her at first, awkward attempts to reach through her anger, with reasonable arguments about why he had decided they would leave as soon as the wedding ceremony was over.

But when she didn't react to his words, he gave up and stayed just as quiet as she was.

One would think four days of silence would decrease her anger, but instead it had grown, and now as they drove up the road leading to his ancestral home she was practically seething. She had done everything she could think of to make him as angry as she was. She had even locked him out from the rooms he had rented for them at different inns throughout their journey.

But he had not said a word about it.

The first night he had knocked for a few minutes, begging her to let him in. But when she refused to reply or open the door, he left. She had spent the rest of the night wondering where he had gone and imagining him sharing a bed with some barmaid.

The following nights he had left her alone.

Absurdly enough, his meekness had made her even angrier. If he cared as much about her as he said he did, she thought he could at least try a little harder.

Not just give in and ignore her.

On the day of their wedding, her new husband had practically dragged her into the carriage before any of her relatives had a chance to object. As their carriage got underway with impressive speed, her family had been left outside the church openmouthed with shock.

She hadn't even had a chance to say goodbye to her parents. Tears filled her eyes and she wiped them away harshly.

****

Devlin saw her movement, and felt as if his heart were being slowly crushed.

He had been so sure leaving without too many emotional farewells would be the best thing for her, as she never had been without her family before. But now, as he saw her pain, she made him feel like the worst human being ever to set foot on the face of the earth.

He was an awful, selfish ogre who not once had thought about her or her feelings. He was too used to living by his own head, not answering to anybody, and he guessed he had a lot to learn when it came to being a husband and belonging to somebody.

The wedding had been beautiful, and his chest hurt with pride in this wonderful young woman who was his bride. He adored her so much he almost cried when the archbishop pronounced them husband and wife.

Her equal happiness had been obvious, as she

jumped with joy, and he had thought himself the luckiest man alive—only to destroy everything with one bad decision.

He looked out through the window as Pendragon came in sight. The ancient castle stood on the top of a gigantic rock at a point where the River Wye did a large turn, not far from Symonds Yat, with an extensive view for miles in every direction. It was a large castle, though not as enormous as Chester Park. Still, it was large enough for one to be able to get lost among the winding corridors and small stairs.

His father had never liked the ancestral home with its towers and pinnacles, and had preferred the shallow home in London. Maybe this was why Devlin always had thought of Pendragon as his safe haven.

As the carriage stopped in front of the castle, he could see all his servants and his aunt and cousins standing at the front stairs, waiting for their new mistress.

He closed his eyes with distress.

He had yearned for the day when he would arrive home with Fanny, in a haze of newlywed bliss. Instead he would have to drag his hate-filled new wife through the crowd. It would probably be a spectacle to delight Delia and her children. His happiness had never been in their prayers.

He took a deep breath to brace himself as a footman opened the door. Immediately everyone's gaze was glued to the opening. He climbed out and waved to the cheering servants, before he turned and met Fanny's gray eyes for the first time in days.

There was no hatred, as he had thought, only grief and disappointment. He held out his hand to her, and when she snorted, disgusted with him, he whispered, "Please."

Something unreadable flickered across her face, and she sat still as a statue for a minute, her eyes not once leaving his.

Without a word, she put her hand in his and climbed out of the carriage. She gave the servants a shaky smile, and they cheered again for their master and their new mistress. Without letting go of her hand, he led her up the stairs, introducing her to the housekeeper Mrs. Blair, the cook Mrs. Stone, and the butler Jarvis.

Fanny smiled shyly to everyone and stayed close to Devlin, giving the servants the unintended impression that she found strength and security with her new husband, and so also starting the rumor that this young bride was indeed in love with her husband.

Devlin stopped in front of Delia, Simon, and Amelia, who effectively blocked the front door. The two ladies curtsied elegantly, and Simon bowed deeply, a worthless show of respect, as they had never shown him any before.

Fanny bowed her head slightly, aware of her own standing in the eyes of these relatives of Devlin's. He had never said it, but she had read between the lines when he spoke of his childhood, and she understood how these three had joined against him and made much of his early life miserable.

Even though she was angry with him, she would never give them anything to hold against him. As quickly as he could, Devlin whisked her away before they had a chance to talk to her, and she forgot them immediately as she entered the foyer.

It was the size of a ballroom and breathtakingly beautiful. A perfect circle, with a stair that curved its way upwards to more than five floors. At the roof hung the largest chandelier Fanny had ever seen, spreading its soft light.

Three doors, four if you counted the front door, led to primary points of the compass, with the front door at the south. The floor was of white marble, partly covered by thick carpets, and Fanny forgot all about her anger for a second as she gasped with delight.

"Oh, Devlin, it's so beautiful!"

The housekeeper, Mrs. Blair, beamed with delight over her mistress's obvious admiration, and Devlin had to turn slightly to hide his grin over his wife's easy conquest.

"There is not one house in all England who can boast of having anything equal to this room," Mrs. Blair confided to her new mistress. "And you should know, Your Grace, there is rumors going 'round how this, the oldest part of the castle, actually is the true Camelot."

"Really?" Fanny breathed, genuinely impressed.

"This very room we are standing in is said to have been the large hall of the old castle, and it is said the round table was placed in the middle."

"Oh!"

Both stared at the round stone that marked the middle of the floor, awe in their eyes, and Devlin had to cough, this time to hide his laughter. There was of course no truth in the tale at all, but Mrs. Blair loved to dazzle guests and visitors with it. He could find no harm in it, so he had let her be.

The housekeeper was a warm and caring person with a heart large as London, and she had been there his whole life. Delia and her children didn't get along with Mrs. Blair at all, as the housekeeper loathed his aunt, and if this wasn't a sign of a good head, then he didn't know what was.

"You know," Mrs. Blair told her newest audience. "There is a cave, not so far from here, called King Arthur's Cave. It is said to have been a sanctuary to our former monarch in times of desperate need."

"If you'd like, we could go for a ride and search for the cave," Devlin told Fanny, and she threw herself in his arms, hugging him tightly.

"Yes, thank you," she cried out happily, and he closed his eyes, enjoying the feel of her curvaceous body against his. But Fanny couldn't stand still and soon released herself from his arms and almost danced around the room with excitement.

"You know," she confided to Mrs. Blair, "King Arthur is one of my favorite historical persons, and it's amazing he actually has been here in my new home."

"My, my Devlin," a sarcastic voice accosted from behind. "I would never have thought you would end up marrying a dimwit."

Devlin turned to stare angrily at his aunt. She stood, flanked by her children, just inside the front door. Delia had a way with words, and he had a sinking feeling she would do anything she could to make Fanny feel small and inferior.

She walked slowly and gracefully across the floor until she stood face to face with the young duchess, who now had everything Delia ever had wanted. Hate and envy filled the older woman's eyes, and she gave Fanny a falsely sweet smile.

Devlin sent Fanny an apologetic shrug, trying

without words to tell her how sorry he was over his aunt's behavior. How would Fanny ever be able to handle this woman? He knew Delia, and she was trying very hard to intimidate Fanny. By the look of it, she was succeeding. Fanny was too kind and good-hearted—and too young and inexperienced—to know how to handle a slight such as Delia's.

"Delia..." he began but was rudely interrupted by his aunt, who seemed unable to stop herself now as she had the full attention of her prey.

"Are you a dimwit, child?"

"N-no," Fanny stuttered, taken back by the older woman's profound contempt, and Devlin wanted to throttle his aunt for behaving so patronizingly toward his young wife.

"Your Grace," Mrs. Blair interceded gently before he had a chance to react, effectively breaking the tension between the young duchess and the aunt. Delia sent her a hateful look, but the housekeeper pretended not to notice. "You must be tired. Let me show you to your bedroom, where you can rest for a while. Dinner will be served in an hour, and you will want to use the time well, since you have been travelling for so long."

Fanny nodded gratefully and followed the housekeeper without another word.

Devlin watched her leave, not turning to face his aunt until Fanny was out of sight. He knew he had to confront Delia sooner or later, and it was better to have it over and done.

Fanny would never be happy here as long as his aunt lived under the same roof. That left only one possible choice: his relatives had to go. He could tell from Delia's frantic look that she too knew this.

This was the final battle, which could only have one winner, and he could tell she thought she had every available trump card. She would fight like a cat to be able to stay here and act as his hostess.

"Never again look upon my wife in such a discourteous manner," he snapped, his eyes cold and filled with disdain. Delia flinched, but held her back straight, as if strengthened by her children, who hid behind her.

"I didn't know it was discourteous to show one's true feelings," she sneered.

"Fanny is innocent in this. If you have a problem with my marriage, you can direct your concerns toward me."

"*If* I have a problem? Of course I have a problem with you marrying someone else, when you have practically promised to marry your cousin."

"I have never promised you or Amelia anything."

Amelia stepped forward and grabbed her mother's hand, pulling it back in an obvious attempt to hold her back.

"Dearest cousin," she said in her smooth, ingratiating voice as she moved gracefully to her mother's side. "Please, is there really any reason to use such harsh words? You should be more polite toward my mother, who has nursed you and loved you since you were just five years of age. After everything she has done, you should be grateful, not hateful."

Amelia offered him her sweetest smile, and it was as though he stared a viper in the eye. When he was younger he had thought Amelia as sweet and innocent as she looked. But through the years he had learnt her true nature. His aunt was an angel in comparison to her

227

daughter.

Ignoring the little chit, he locked eyes with Delia. "You have until luncheon tomorrow to remove yourself, your children, and your personal things from my premises. If you still remain here, I will tell my servants they are free to force you off the Pendragon holdings."

Delia gasped with horror. "You can't mean this! Where will I go? I have no money, no connections…"

"It's not a concern of mine," Devlin spat. "You have spent over twenty years under this roof as a leech, grabbing everything you can and never returning anything. I don't owe you a thing."

Delia looked ready for a nervous breakdown, and her hands clutched his jacket in one last desperate try to win him over and force him into taking his words back. "You disgrace your mother's memory," she raged. "I'm the only living relative you have. How can you even think to send me to a life of misery?"

"Your son inherited money from your late husband. Why don't you use that instead of living large on mine?" Devlin replied, fully aware of how Simon long ago had gambled every penny away. He knew his relatives were poorer than church mice, but he didn't care.

Delia sobbed, defeated. She had lost the war before it began. If she had put her own pride aside and shown the young duchess some warmth, this wouldn't have happened. But apparently she had assumed he'd married her only because he had to, without caring for his wife.

She let go of his jacket and fell to the floor, unable to stand on her two legs. Simon and Amelia rushed to help their mother, who obviously was in deep distress.

Devlin turned to leave, but his conscience knocked on his shoulder, begging him to make a clean cut. With a sigh he turned again toward the threesome on the floor.

"I have a small house in London where you can stay until either you remarry or one of your children marries into a new home. My wife is a woman with a large heart, and for her sake will I grant you a thousand pounds per year to use as you feel necessary. My carriage will drive you to the nearest inn, from whence you can take the coach to the city. My obligations to you end there, and you will never contact me or any of my family again."

And with this he left them staring at his retiring back, one with teary-eyed gratitude, one with hatred, and one with greed.

Devlin didn't look back once.

Chapter 23

Fanny gave the kind housekeeper one last grateful smile before the door closed and she finally was alone in the spacious bedroom that according to Mrs. Blair was the duchess's private boudoir. She blushed as she saw the large bed centered on one of the shorter walls, facing an enormous fireplace where an armchair was conveniently placed. A small desk stood between two of the large windows, ready to be used for writing letters to her family.

One door led to her private wardrobe, where Nell, her maid, would later put all her clothes, and another door led into the duke's bedroom, where Devlin resided.

Slowly, hesitantly, she walked to Devlin's door and put her hand on the handle. It wasn't locked, and it opened soundlessly. She peeked into the dark, manly room dominated by another large bed.

Bear was emptying a trunk and didn't notice her, so she closed the door again, not sure how she felt. She should be really angry with her husband, but somehow this wonderful home and the respectful greeting by the servants soothed her.

Now she couldn't help but look forward to exploring the grounds of her new home with him.

She went to one of the large windows and looked out over the beautiful Hereford countryside. It looked just as golden in the sunset as Devlin's eyes.

A knock on the door interrupted her thoughts, and when she turned she saw Mrs. Blair had arrived, carrying a large tray.

"His Grace thought you might be tired, so he told me to bring you something to nibble upon."

"Oh, Mrs. Blair, how nice of you." Fanny smiled, relieved that she didn't need to face Devlin's awful relatives again.

"Don't thank me," Mrs. Blair said as she walked toward the door. "Thank your husband. Now eat, and I will have a bath prepared for you." She glanced over the room with a hard eye, bobbed a curtsy, and left.

By the time Fanny finished her meal, a large tub had been placed in front of the fireplace and the servants who brought it had bowed and left her alone.

She squealed with delight at the steaming hot water and wasted no time in tearing off her dirty clothes. Then, with a loud sigh of contentment, she stepped into the tub and eased down into the water. For a few moments of pure relaxation she let the warmth soothe away the tensions of travel before she grabbed the soap left on a chair nearby and covered herself with bubbles from head to toe.

****

Devlin closed his bedroom door and sank back against it with a deep sigh of relief. It felt so good to finally stand up to his horrible aunt and send her on her way.

He knew he had been much more generous with her than she deserved, but it felt better for him this way, knowing they wouldn't be homeless and without funds. Or at least they would have funds until Simon had gambled all the money away, but they would still have a roof over their heads.

He sent Bear away, not in the mood for dissecting everything that had happened so far, and was just about to change clothes when he heard the soft splashing from the other bedroom. Images of what was going on beyond the closed door flared before his eyes, and suddenly he wasn't so tired anymore.

He stepped to the door and opened it soundlessly.

In front of the fireplace, his wife sat in a large wooden tub. Her eyes were closed and her head rested against the brim of the tub. She was the image of beauty, reminding him of a painting of a Roman goddess he had seen when visiting friends in Italy.

Before he could change his mind, he silently undressed and crossed to the tub, looking down at his wife, aware of the possibility that she still was too angry to want him there. But his body yearned for her, and his heart and soul needed her, and he would take a chance.

Water poured over the floor when Devlin settled down into the tub that was barely large enough for the two of them. Fanny opened her eyes in shock as she sat up, almost knocking her head against his chin, wiping at her eyes furiously to glare at him from the opposite side of the tub.

"Hello, love." Devlin grinned.

"Wh-what…"

He gave her a sympathetic smile. "Yes, my love?"

"What do you think you're doing?"

"Oh, just taking a much-needed bath."

"Not in here you aren't!"

"Why not?"

"Why not? Because it's my room and my tub and my water and..." She crossed her arms over her chest and sank down into the water, staring angrily at him, looking just like a small pouting child, and he grinned back.

He could feel the side of her thigh against his foot, and he moved his toes slightly, arching an eyebrow at her as she gasped. She wasn't as insensitive toward him as she liked him to think, and the thought echoed through his body and made him hard.

He put his arms around her waist and dragged her up onto his knees, one leg on each side of his hips so that his member immediately found its special sanctuary, and he groaned as he thrust deep inside of her.

Fanny grabbed his shoulders and bent her head backwards as he drew back and pushed in again. Twisting her hair between his fingers, he brought her mouth down to his and kissed her with every ounce of the heat built up in his body, his loins, his heart. Her kiss replied in kind, and he squeezed her buttocks with his other hand. As he lifted her up and down, passion tore through their bodies until it became unbearable and he filled her pulsating body.

Fanny almost fainted, and she sank down on top of him, savoring the wonderful contentment that spread throughout her body and weighted all her limbs. He kissed her on the nose, and all she had power to do was to give him a faint smile back.

"Thank you," he whispered into her hair.

"Mmm-hmm," she mumbled back, too lazy even to speak.

"I can't imagine how it would be making love to

you in a bed, when it's so good in a bathtub."

She lifted her head and looked at him blankly. He almost stopped breathing. What if she turned on him now? What if she suddenly remembered her anger at him and forced him away?

He didn't know how to live without her anymore. She somehow had become like air to him, an absolute necessity for life.

She looked at her bed and back to him, and a small hope started to burn in his heart. A smile grew on her face, and she leaned closer to him, her lips so close to his he would only have to pucker to kiss her.

"Why don't we try it?"

He caught his breath. Was she implying what he thought she was implying?

She grabbed her towel, and before he could stop her she was out of the tub. She moved closer to the fire, closing her eyes with delight as the heat slowly dried her body.

When Devlin had climbed out from the tub, she went without hesitation to the bed and sat on the edge, holding out her towel. He rushed to her side to grab the towel and in a second was dry and in bed beside her, kissing and fondling her.

****

When Mrs. Blair and a couple of maids later came to get the tub and its water, they found the duke and his duchess sound asleep.

In silence the maids carried away the water in buckets and mopped up the wetness on the floor before a couple of footmen came in for the tub itself.

Just as silently, they all left the room, leaving only Mrs. Blair.

The housekeeper looked at her master and mistress one last time, enjoying the protective way the duke held his young wife even in his sleep, before she too left the room.

Chapter 24

When Fanny woke the next morning, she was alone in her large bed. She closed her eyes again and couldn't hold back a grateful sigh.

She wasn't ready to face Devlin after last night's passion. She needed time to think it over herself before she could confront him with it.

She was still upset with him for selfishly dragging her away from her family, but she wasn't as furious as she had been the day before. Maybe it was this magnificent new home of hers, or the wonderful staff she met yesterday.

Or maybe it was simply the incredible lovemaking they had shared at the end of such an emotional couple of days.

She didn't know, and right now she didn't care.

What she wanted to do was explore her new home. What she had seen of Pendragon when they arrived had made her think of fairytales, and she wanted to see if it looked the same in sunlight.

She tugged the cord for her maid, and twenty minutes later Fanny was tripping lightly into the breakfast room, the way shown by a kind and smiling servant, only to find it deserted. She had been sure she would find her new husband here, but Devlin was nowhere to be seen.

She lingered at the breakfast table for a long time,

reading the paper and looking out the window at the panoramic view it offered, but still no Devlin in sight.

When the servants had cleared the table, she strolled out into the circular foyer and was immediately ushered by a footman into an elegant room nearby. She was told it was called The Duchess's Parlor—therefore, hers from this moment onwards.

She stood inside the closed door and took in the lovely room decorated in soft pink and cream nuances, and like every other room she had seen so far in the castle it was utterly feminine and harmonic.

She sat down at her lovely desk, which faced the window and gave her a fantastic view of the landscape surrounding the castle. She opened the drawers and found pens and ink, as well as papers, neatly stacked.

She cast a longing eye at the door again, as if she could magically force Devlin to open it, but as it continued to stay closed, she started to write letters to her close ones instead. She didn't have much to tell them yet, but she knew her family, and if she didn't send them a note letting them know she was still alive and not thrown into a dungeon, they would come here to save her from whatever harm they could imagine.

A visit from her brothers and uncles now, as she was starting a new life with Devlin, was a wonderful thought but not very practical, as they would interfere with everything and keep her busy nonstop.

She spent the morning in her new chamber, writing letters until her fingers ached. When Mrs. Blair brought her a tray with tea and thin cucumber sandwiches, she was more than grateful for the intrusion and persuaded the housekeeper to sit and take a cup with her.

"I was starting to feel a little abandoned," she

confided to Mrs. Blair. "My husband has been nowhere in sight all day, and I'm used to being surrounded by my quite large family."

With a tender smile, the housekeeper patted Fanny's hand. "You just arrived here last night, Your Grace. In time you will find your place, and everything will seem much easier for you."

"You think so?" Fanny must have looked as forlorn as she felt, for she received another motherly pat on her hand.

"Of course you will."

Fanny sighed deeply and took another sip from her cup. "I must confess I do miss the presence of my husband. I haven't seen him at all today, as he had already disappeared when I woke up this morning."

"His Grace usually spends his days with his supervisor, Mr. Brown. Whenever His Grace has been away, they tend to lock themselves inside the office and go through all the ledgers thoroughly. Sometimes we don't see the two of them for days."

"Oh."

Mrs. Blair chuckled over her mistress' obvious disappointment. "Now, now, dear child. Don't you fret over this now. His Grace will soon be finished with the past happenings of Pendragon, and he will be all yours for the evenings."

"I guess I'll just have to find myself something to do during the days."

"Well, there you go," Mrs. Blair said cheerfully. "A little patience, and soon you will have settled down here in good order."

Fanny nodded thoughtfully. She had never really thought about what a married woman did all day. Her mother always seemed busy, but Fanny had not a clue what her mother's routine activities involved. She knew the marchioness was a firm believer in lists, and spent many hours a day composing new ones and updating her old ones, but it couldn't be all she did, could it?

"I guess I will have to spend more time with you, Mrs. Blair. My mother always spends time with the housekeeper, and goes through the menu and so on."

"Oh no, dear child. There really is no need for you to go through the menu with me. Our chef is one of the best in England, and he would never let anyone interfere with what he is serving."

Mrs. Blair shook her head with a kind but patronizing smile. It was not hard to tell she found her young mistress's awkward attempt at becoming the matron of the house quite amusing.

Fanny's shoulders slumped. She didn't have to look around her to realize Pendragon was perfectly maintained. There was no need for her to meddle anywhere. Everything was already taken care of.

"I guess I'll talk to Delia. She might have some responsibilities she would be grateful to get rid of."

"Responsibilities?" Mrs. Blair snorted. "That woman never wanted any responsibilities. She has spent over twenty years in this house and never cared about anything. As long as she got food on a plate, and someone took care of her room and her clothes, she was satisfied."

"How ungrateful," Fanny gasped. "Helping out is the least she can do in gratitude for a home for herself and her children."

"I admit I'm quite thrilled over Mrs. Lawrence leaving Pendragon and taking her offspring with her.

She has been a thorn in my side for a longer time than I care to remember."

This was news to Fanny. "Is Delia leaving?"

"She has already left. They left early this morning, while you were still sleeping, Your Grace."

Fanny blushed. So she had slept in a little today. Mrs. Blair would have too, if she had such an attentive husband during the small hours of the night.

She did feel a little sorry for Delia, who had left what she had thought of as a home for the last two decades. But if she could believe Mrs. Blair's gossip, Devlin's aunt wouldn't be missed.

The thought about Devlin led to another thought. Had she just been given the most perfect excuse to seek him out? Devlin must of course be notified about his aunt leaving Pendragon.

She put down her cup, and Mrs. Blair gave her a surprised look as she stood up. "Please excuse me, Mrs. Blair. I must go and tell my husband about his aunt's departure."

"No need for such haste." Mrs. Blair chuckled and forced Fanny to sit down again with a gentle tug on her arm. "His Grace was up and about when they left, and I know he watched them as they got into their carriage, as I brought him his breakfast then."

"Oh."

"Can I offer you a scone?"

Fanny accepted a warm scone and ate it silently as Mrs. Blair continued her gossip about Delia and her shortcomings.

So Devlin had watched them leave. This must mean he knew they were leaving, and if so, he must have been the reason for their departure. And the only reason he would practically throw them out now was because of her.

Poor Delia.

Even for one of the nastiest women she had ever met Fanny still couldn't help but feel a little guilty that the older woman had lost the only home she knew.

Fanny had no memories of the woman's children. Both Amelia and Simon had been unusually bland, and she could only guess the two of them were so used to standing behind their much more colorful mother that they had gotten used to blending into the background.

How easily Devlin had gotten rid of the only living relatives he had. She was both impressed and scared. Impressed at his strength, and scared at how little they meant to him. Was he this cold? What if he ever decided to throw her out?

She couldn't stop a giggle at the mental picture of Devlin throwing her out. Poor man, if he ever would try something like that. Her brothers had taught her how she best could defend herself if attacked. If her husband discarded her, she would use every last trick she had learnt.

Mrs. Blair offered her more tea, but this time Fanny declined. It was time for her to continue her investigation of her new home and leave the housekeeper to her chores.

As Mrs. Blair headed toward the kitchen, carrying the tray, Fanny decided there was no way she would sit in this room the whole day, not when the weather outside was warm and sunny.

When she passed the foyer, she gave a footman her letters for delivery and then headed toward the front door. Jarvis, the butler, frowned at her as he opened the door hesitantly for her.

"Wouldn't you be much more comfortable in your parlor, Your Grace?"

"No, thank you, Jarvis," Fanny smiled, a bit awed at being called Your Grace. "I'd rather go outside, as it seems to be such a lovely day."

"But Your Grace…"

Sending him her most shining smile, she dashed out through the door and ignored his stuttering behind her. She didn't care if she was being rude; she wasn't the kind of person who enjoyed spending day after day in a secluded parlor, as the servants seemed to think she should.

Slowly she strolled in the gardens, enjoying the beautiful summer weather. The castle rose high overhead as she walked through the perfectly kept grounds surrounding it.

Upon her return to the entrance, she found an empty coach parked in front of the stair leading up to the front door.

Fanny hesitated for a second before entering the house in search of the visitor. A part of her wanted to do the impolite thing and avoid the guest, but as her mother probably would kill her if she ever learnt Fanny had eluded a visitor at her new home, she decided not to try.

And besides, she was pathetically desperate for some company.

So when Jarvis informed her that Mrs. Overton had arrived, she merely nodded her head in agreement.

"I've put her into the parlor next the foyer, Your Grace, as we do usually place visitors." With that he showed Fanny into the room where the dame sat in the armchair beside the roaring fire.

Fanny sat on the sofa, facing the elderly lady who looked as fragile as an old parchment. White wispy hair surrounded the delicately lined face where large, somewhat faded blue eyes dominated. Her small frame was dressed in the most vivid pink dress Fanny had ever seen, a dress one would have thought better suited for a much younger woman than Mrs. Overton.

"It's so nice to meet you, Mrs. Overton." Fanny smiled politely and offered a cup of tea from the tray Jarvis brought, with impressive foresight, and set on the small table. "You are the first of my husband's acquaintances I have met since we arrived here yesterday."

"Thank you," Mrs. Overton said graciously in an amazingly strong voice for such a small person. She accepted the cup of tea Fanny held out. "I have always made sure no newcomers arrive in our parish without being properly greeted and introduced to our small corner of east England."

"How nice of you, Mrs. Overton."

"I know," the old lady admitted, and Fanny had to cough to cover her laughter. Mrs. Overton cast a probing gaze upon her, and Fanny forced herself to sit still, trying to look as innocent as possible.

"So where is your new husband?" Mrs. Overton continued. "I haven't seen the young man for quite some time now, as he has been abroad for so many years. I do hope everything fares well with him?"

Fanny smiled inwardly at the lady's transparent attempt to get information from her hostess. This visitor was no different from the ladies of her own home parish in Berkshire. In small communities, gossip was like air, and everyone constantly searched for information about others. No one could do anything without everyone knowing about it.

Living in the countryside had its benefits, but this wasn't one of them. As Fanny didn't know how Devlin felt about the ladies and their wagging tongues, she decided to tell the lady as little as she possibly could without being rude.

"He is just fine. Thank you so much for asking."

Mrs. Overton bent forward and patted Fanny's hand. "You poor little thing. You have to promise to come and see me if you feel lonely, as I know it can't be easy for a young girl to be married to such a busy man as Hereford. And you must miss your family dearly, being such a young girl. This was your debutante year, I understood?"

Fanny nodded, thankful for not having to answer in more detail. Mrs. Overton frowned, a bit vexed with her hostess. She obviously had thought it would be easier than this to obtain the information she wanted.

"It must be hard for you, being so far away from your mother. I have always said a husband is just a husband, a friend is just a friend, but a mother will always be a mother, no matter the distance. You must come to see me if you feel lonely. You are always welcome, my dear child."

"Thank you," Fanny replied politely, silently promising herself to never go there alone. She really didn't like the older woman's gossipy nature, and loathed her probing questions. There were some things about people's private lives you just didn't ask.

She offered Mrs. Overton cakes, which were accepted with a little cry of joy; the lady obviously had a sweet tooth. Just as Mrs. Overton put the last cake in her mouth, Jarvis entered the room, closely followed by a young lady who gazed around her with eyes big as saucers and her mouth open wide.

She had obviously never been to Pendragon before and was now having the time of her life, finally getting to see what was inside this magnificent old castle.

"Your Grace…" Mrs. Overton's carefully modulated tones became a high-pitched squeal in reaction to her excitement. "It is my pleasure to introduce to you my own dear, dear granddaughter, Annabelle."

Mrs. Overton stared pointedly at the young lady, who stepped forward in a superior manner with a simpering smile on her pretty face. Fanny disliked her immediately, as Miss Overton was obviously spoiled rotten and too aware of her own beauty.

Fanny had no doubt this girl must be the incomparable one among the socialites in the parish. It was like seeing Charmaine in the shape of another girl. Yet even though this girl was prettier than most, she was far from the astounding beauty of the incomparable queen of the London *ton*.

For her part, the girl took one look at Fanny and apparently crossed her off the list of rivals for the place as the most popular beauty and instead gawked at the gloriously decorated room, obviously awed by its luxury. Fanny had no doubt the Overton family lacked large funds. Besides the staring, small details about their outfits and the worn old carriage at the steps told Fanny the truth.

"How nice to meet you, Miss Overton," Fanny said with a slight bow of her head, silently putting a distance between her and the guests by being impersonally polite. Unfortunately, Mrs. Overton wasn't a person who listened to others, not what they told her straight out and especially not what lay between the lines. She had already decided her own granddaughter, now that she couldn't become the new duchess, should be Fanny's best friend, and nothing was going to stop her from achieving her goals.

"Oh, you must call each other by your first names, being of the same age as you are. As her friend, you can feel free to call her Belle."

Both Overton ladies looked expectantly at Fanny, waiting for her permission to use her given name in return. She cursed silently, not knowing how to get out of this awful situation.

But, being her special knight in shining armor, Devlin chose just this moment to search for his wife. "Ah, I see we have visitors," he exclaimed as he entered the parlor, unaware he had saved his wife from a fate worse than death, that of becoming Annabelle's friend.

Mrs. Overton cried out with joy and rushed forward to greet the magnificent man who stood before her. Her granddaughter, who obviously had never met Devlin before, looked unusually un-pretty as she stared at the duke, her mouth wide open.

Fanny hid a smile. She knew Devlin was a lot to take in even when one was already acquainted with him, and seeing this splendid-looking man for the first time had to be a shock like no other. Mrs. Overton had to say her granddaughter's name four times before she woke from her stupor and was able to collect the pieces of her dignity enough to perform a stumbling curtsy in greeting.

"We have missed you sorely, Your Grace," Mrs. Overton said as Devlin sat down in the only free armchair, opposite his wife. Fanny kept her gaze on her guests, but she could feel Devlin's eyes on her.

She had no doubt her husband was very nervous about how he would be met by her today, and she could hardly blame him for his insecurity. She had been quite unstable in her behavior toward him these last days, from extremely happy during the wedding to extremely angry in the carriage to extremely passionate in bed. It was no surprise he wasn't sure where he was with her.

She was a little annoyed with him, though, as he had, after all, left her this morning without one word and stayed away nearly the whole day. A part of her wanted to punish him for it, make him suffer a little, so he would know what she had gone through that day, not knowing where he was or who he was with. But her heart was too good, she thought with a wry smile, because her conscience told her not to give him pain.

Instead of ignoring him, she looked directly at him with a sweet, alluring smile. It turned him into stone for a second, before a fire started to burn in those golden eyes.

Poor Mrs. Overton and Miss Overton. They had no idea their host was now in desperate need of them to get lost, so he could hurl himself upon his duchess and kiss her senseless.

The lady chattered on, talking about this and that, who had done what during the years Devlin had stayed away, unaware of how unwanted she actually was. All the while, Annabelle sent Devlin flirty looks more like the ones a common whore would send a prospective client than those an innocent young miss sent a man of her liking, especially when the man's wife sat right beside her.

After finishing three cups of tea and two plates of cake, Mrs. Overton and her granddaughter finally declared themselves ready to leave. But not before they forced a promise from Fanny that she and Devlin would attend an upcoming Overton dinner party.

"You certainly do know how to choose your friends," Devlin said as he and Fanny finally were alone again.

"It's almost impossible to tell the woman no." Fanny laughed. "She won't take no for an answer. Or actually, she won't take an answer at all! Lord, how will I ever be able to get out of her dinner party without hurting any feelings, or ending up on the social black list?"

"You shouldn't worry about black lists, my dear, as you are the Duchess of Hereford and as such the unmovable queen of social life here. Mrs. Overton knows this too, and I would hazard a guess that would be why she rushed here, so she could make sure she would end up on your good list. As your guide to society here and as the one to introduce you to others, she will climb the social ladder, and I dare say her granddaughter will have better hands in marriage to choose from."

"It sounds so shallow." Fanny frowned. "Everybody must know social standings are not important. It is the family who really count."

Devlin gave her an amused smile. "You really don't understand the slippery ladder most other debutantes and their families have to climb, do you?"

She shook her head. "No, I don't.

"So I am important to you, then?" he teased her, and she cursed silently as she felt a blush creep over her cheeks.

"Well, you are my husband, so I guess you should matter," she replied with a wink.

He leaned back in his armchair and, with a sultry grin, beckoned her with a finger to come to him. At first she decided to refuse. She was still a little upset with him, first for dragging her away from her family, and then for leaving her all alone, without caring how her day was.

But again, she did find his kissing most wonderful, and so, before she could change her mind, she went to him. He grabbed her by the waist and hauled her into his lap, as if he liked having her close to him.

She leaned her head against his chest, and he kissed her hair as he put his arms around her. She sighed happily and felt him chuckle in response.

"I must say I find your honesty in speech and reactions most attractive."

"Where have you been today?" Fanny ignored his comment, asked the question uppermost in her mind and, glancing up, saw he smiled with his reply.

"It pleases me more than I thought possible that you care enough to want to know where I've been."

She frowned at him. "Of course I care about where you are. You're my husband."

"So I am."

"I must admit I felt a bit abandoned when I woke up and found myself alone in bed, without any knowledge of your departure or your whereabouts."

"I was making sure my aunt and my cousins got on their way."

"So I heard." Fanny sighed. "Please don't tell me you threw them out of here because of me?"

"Of course I did. I don't want your first time at Pendragon to be colored by that witch and her children."

"Devlin, this is awful. You really shouldn't have done such a thing."

"Oh yes I should, and I did. It should have been done years ago."

"But it's so brutish. Your poor, poor aunt."

Devlin snorted at her misdirected compassion. "Poor aunt? There is nothing poor about Delia. She would have made life terrible for you. It's better this way, with all our relatives a couple of days away."

"There is nothing wrong with my relatives."

"No, they are the best, especially at this distance."

"Devlin!" Fanny gasped, trying to look outraged, but laughter lurked in her throat. He hauled her closer again, and this time he bent down and gave her an earthshaking kiss that made them both breathless and in desperate need of their bedroom.

Without another word, Devlin rose with Fanny in his arms, kicked the door open, and carried his wife up the stairs and into her bedroom, where he threw her onto the bed as the door shut behind them. Fanny immediately started to unbutton her dress, and with a chuckle over her obvious frenzy, he helped her.

Chapter 25

What Devlin didn't know was that her relatives weren't as far away as he thought.

When the bride and groom left the wedding so unexpectedly without any time to say farewell properly, the Darling family was shocked. For a few days they all went around grunting and behaving in a rather unfriendly manner toward each other, until Hannibal had enough.

"For goodness' sake, stop moping about. Go to her instead," he boomed to her parents with a roll of his eyes, and a few days later, after finally overcoming their hesitation to commit such inconsideration toward the newlyweds, Fanny's parents and Rake left in a carriage heading eastwards. Few words were spoken during the long trip; they all had a lot on their minds, and each was worried about what they would find at Pendragon but didn't want to alarm the others.

They had promised each other to not care what Devlin said, or had the right to, if they found Fanny was miserable and unhappy. If she was suffering in any way, they would take her home with them, even if it meant they would have to use force.

"I will kill him," George muttered through his teeth. "If she has shed but one tear, he is mine and only mine."

The last part was directed to Rake, who nodded,

just as seriously determined, and Caroline rolled her eyes over their childish declarations. The men of the Darling family tended to be a little too dramatic sometimes, and she had a feeling this was a time their antics wouldn't be a good thing.

But she knew better than to try talking them out of it, as that would only put more wood into their fire. Instead, she decided on a change of subject, and she looked at Rake, who had a forlorn air about him these last days.

Since the night Penelope had tumbled in through Fanny's bedroom window, Rake had become more and more silent, until he was like a brooding shadow moving through the house. At first he had seemed desperate to know what Penelope had gone through, but when they kept the lid tightly screwed on, he stopped asking questions.

It was not hard to understand there were deeper feelings than friendship between those two, but they both were stubborn as mules about keeping a distance from each other.

Penelope had asked Caroline to let her stay at Chester Park when Fanny's wedding was over, so she wouldn't have to return to London and rejoin the social scene. The Lord Bolton affair had destroyed something inside her, and Caroline had every intention of finding out what lay beneath the surface when she got back from Pendragon.

Rake, on the other hand, had been roaming London with a new beauty on his arm every day, except for the one night when he had a beauty at each arm. He flirted outrageously with every lady he met, leaving piles of broken hearts behind him. Both George and James had tried to talk to him, but their efforts met with such a cold stare they gave up. Solemnly George told his wife that the time for the younger brother to surrender to his heart had not yet arrived.

It had surprised them, though, when Rake had insisted on going with them to Pendragon. The surprise was not because of his non-relationship with Penelope, but that he would leave London and all the ladies currently throwing themselves happily all over him.

Now he sat on the opposite seat in the carriage as they came closer and closer to Fanny, and for the first time since they'd left Chester Park he seemed to actually want to talk.

"Killing him won't be enough," he objected. "Dragging him behind the carriage with a snare tightly around his malicious head might do, as a starter."

"Richard Darling!" Caroline gasped, deeply offended by his crude language, but he didn't even look at her. George, who rather liked the image his brother painted, ignored his wife too, and leaned a bit closer to Rake.

"I can't believe he kidnapped her right out of our home. He took our Fanny, without even asking what she wanted. Or more importantly, he didn't ask if it was all right with us."

Rake nodded sternly, agreeing with his brother over this incredible insult, while Caroline threw out her hands in despair. "Oh, come on, Rouge," she said aghast, using George's old nickname from his libertine days. "She is his wife, and he has all the right in the world to drag her all the way to the colonies if he wants to, and there is nothing we can do about it."

Both men stared at her as if she had lost her mind,

253

and she continued quickly, before they had a chance to say something.

"It's Devlin we are talking about. It is your best friend, Rake. You know in your heart he would never mistreat Fanny in any way, because he has a kind heart, and he does love her."

Rake muttered something inaudible, but in the end he had to give in. Caroline was telling the truth. Devlin wasn't a bad man. He was honest, straightforward, and brave, and would never go berserk on a woman. "But he still stole her away," he objected, not wanting to give up the indignation completely.

"Oh, for goodness' sake," Caroline sighed. "They were newly married, and he must have wanted to have Fanny for himself when he finally could. He just forgot to enlighten us about his plans to leave immediately instead of staying put for another week."

"It wasn't so hard to see that he had forgotten to tell Fanny too," George interjected harshly.

"He still didn't do anything wrong. He only followed his heart and didn't think about how he left the rest of us standing there feeling rather abandoned."

"I hope she has made him as miserable as he made us," Rake said with a grim smile, and George nodded in agreement.

Caroline shook her head. These two Darling men had obviously decided they were upset, and nothing she said would change their mission. They would continue their brooding until they had Fanny in front of them telling them everything was all right.

She leaned her head against the seat and closed her eyes, knowing she had to use the time left before their arrival at her daughter's new home to gain some strength. Strength to hold the stubborn, ridiculously indignant men back, and strength to hold herself from hurting Devlin if Fanny had been in any way mistreated.

She knew what she had said to her husband and brother-in-law about Devlin, but deep in her heart she was too afraid to believe in those words herself.

If Fanny was unhappy, it wasn't the grumpy men Devlin should fear. No, he should fear the mother—the Saxton daughter without a conscience.

Chapter 26

Unaware of the coming storm, Fanny and Devlin had begun their new life as husband and wife by falling into a nice rhythm that suited both. They slept together in her bed, where they thoroughly enjoyed waking up together and making love before breakfast. The morning meal was spent discussing everything they read about in the newspaper, and afterwards Devlin left to spend his day with Pendragon's supervisor while Fanny continued her explorations of her new home and its surroundings. They met at the dinner table again and spent the rest of the evening in the library playing games or in bed making sweet love.

All in all, it was a good life.

Devlin had several times told her how amazed he was at how easy life with a wife was and how he couldn't believe he had feared married life so much before.

Fanny was happy too but couldn't help feeling a bit lonely. She loved her mornings with Devlin and held on to her shiny happy smile until he left her for the supervisor. But she had to spend the rest of the day all alone, counting the long hours until they met again at the dinner table.

One day she was so lonely she had a carriage drive her down to the village, to the small manor where Mrs. Overton and her family resided. She had endured the overjoyed lady's gossip for an hour before she went back to the castle and her loneliness.

Devlin thought it was better she spend her first weeks inside her new home learning how to take care of it as a mistress should rather than running around the countryside visiting the neighbors.

Only one little problem with his idea arose: as Fanny had already learned, Pendragon was a household run in an exemplary manner by the more than competent servants. She had next to nothing to focus on when it came to the housekeeping, and she was more a body in the way than an involved mistress.

She searched through the grand library for books about Pendragon and the Ross family, but there weren't many in that genre, as the former residents of the castle had seemed more interested in the books' covers than in what they contained.

She spent two days embroidering a cushion she then put on her bed with a satisfied smile, only to find it removed and put in a closet by a servant with better decorating skills.

One especially nice day she spent in the herb garden searching for weeds to pick, but like everything else at Pendragon the garden was in perfect shape. No weeds dared to grow under the sharp eyes of the gardeners.

She asked Devlin if she could join him and the supervisor, but Devlin had only chuckled over her request. He told her it was men's work, and sent her away to do something more appropriate for a woman.

When she asked him to tell her exactly what this could be, he simply shrugged and changed the subject.

She was so bored she even started to take naps to

make time go by. But even with all the time alone she still was happier than she ever had been before, because the time she spent with Devlin made up for all the boring hours.

She was madly in love with her husband, and, when he was with her, life was perfect.

The day the Darling carriage stopped in front of Pendragon, Fanny was spending her day in the library, recounting all the books. She might have missed one or two the first time she inventoried them.

Devlin had left for the supervisor's office, and as it was pouring rain outside, she had no choice but to spend her time indoors. As there were no specific responsibilities with her name on them, she had to invent some for herself, like counting books.

She had just climbed up the long ladder to be able to count the awkwardly placed but un-dusty books on the top shelf, when the door opened behind her. As the castle was full of servants who quietly walked in and out of rooms, she didn't look down, not until a very familiar voice cut through her silent counting.

"One would think a man as rich as Devlin could hire someone to dust in the library."

Fanny yelped and turned around too hastily, forgetting she was at the top of a ladder, and fell helplessly backwards. With a small scream, she toppled straight into her father's waiting arms.

He immediately hugged her close to him, and she threw her arms around his shoulders with tears streaming down her face. She dug her nose into the curve of his neck, inhaling his familiar scent.

Caroline was next in line for a hug from Fanny, and they both cried as mother kissed daughter thoroughly on nose, chin, and cheeks.

The last one to take her into his arms was Rake. Fanny sank into his embrace, cherishing the sound of his heart against her cheek.

"What are you all doing here?" she squealed, delighted, as she left Rake's warm embrace.

George arched a perfect eyebrow. "Aren't we allowed to visit our beloved daughter?"

Rake coughed.

"And niece," George continued, with a shake of his head toward his brother.

Rake gave him a toothy smile, which the older brother ignored.

"Of course you are welcome. If I had known you were coming, I could have had the servants preparing rooms for you in advance."

Caroline patted her daughter's soft blushing cheek. "I don't mind waiting. You can show us around your new home in the meantime, although perhaps we should wash off the dust of our trip somewhere."

"Of course." Fanny smiled and rang the bell. Ten minutes later, her relatives had washed up and everyone was making their way slowly through the grand rooms of Pendragon. It was a lovely castle, and every room had been decorated to perfection with lavish fantasy.

"Where is that husband of yours?" Rake asked as they lingered in the enormous ballroom encompassing the whole north side of the first floor.

"He's with the supervisor of Pendragon, who also takes care of Devlin's other business arrangements. They usually spend the day together, so you will meet my husband as he joins us for dinner tonight."

Rake frowned at her.

"He spends all his days with his supervisor?"

"Yes, he does," Fanny answered cheerfully.

Caroline and George shared a look, knowing their only daughter. Had she sounded just a little too cheerful?

"So," Rake continued curiously, "tell me, what do you do when Devlin is busy all day?"

"Oh," Fanny said with a shrug. "This and that. You know. Wifely things."

Caroline stopped and stared at her daughter. "Wifely things?"

Fanny nodded and increased her speed, but for nothing. Her mother wasn't easy to distract when she knew she was onto something, especially when it came to her children. Sebastian had once said he was sure she was clairvoyant, and her children thought that quite logical. No one could know so much without actually being there in some way.

"So," Caroline said, mimicking Rake, "you oversee the household, plan the dinner menus, and visit the farmers and the neighbors?"

"Well, Mrs. Blair takes perfect care of the household, and our excellent chef plans the dinner menus. However, I do admit, he does it really well, because dinner usually is absolute heaven."

Her father harrumphed, and Fanny was afraid he'd finally caught his wife's game. "But you do visit the farmers, don't you? It is your obligation as a landowner, my dear, to take care of the families in your charge."

Fanny sighed. She was really not up for this, not yet anyway, but there was no way out of it. They would continue to ask her their probing questions, and they would not stop until they had all the answers. What was the point of trying to hide her standing in the household? They were only a couple of questions away from the truth.

"Useless," she muttered.

"Excuse me?" Rake hadn't really heard what she'd said under her breath.

Fanny turned and glared at her uncle. "I am useless, that's what I am. Completely useless."

George frowned at his daughter's distressed tone of voice. She knew his loving heart had a really hard time dealing with her when she was troubled. It was more her mother's part of parenthood. He much preferred and enjoyed the cuddling and playing games part.

Thankfully, Caroline knew her part of parenthood too, and she took her daughter's hand and led her to a small sofa.

"Why do you think you are useless?"

"Mama, I have nothing to do, and it drives me crazy. Everything is perfect here—the castle, the servants, Devlin. Everything. I don't fit in, because I'm not as perfect. And I just can't stand going around doing nothing all day."

"Have you told Devlin about this?"

"I have tried, but he never listens enough for me to make him see what I see. He doesn't understand my point of view about how his servants are so well trained they attend to everything perfectly well without me."

She sobbed, and fell into Caroline's waiting arms.

"Why don't you go out for visits?" Rake asked. "There must be lots of suitable friends for you in the county."

"Because Devlin thinks I need time to get used to

my life here before I start socializing with the locals," Fanny said with tears in her eyes. "And I don't want to go against his wish, at least not yet. I went out and visited one lady, who came here to greet me at my arrival, but she is such an awful person, I really can't stand her. And since I haven't met anybody else yet…"

"You won't go against him *yet*?"

Fanny looked up from her mother's embrace, and met Rake's twinkling eyes. "Yes, I'm currently leaving him alone. I want the happiest of marriages, and so I'm trying very hard to compromise."

"As I see it, it takes two persons to make a proper compromise. From what you tell us, it seems only you are doing the compromising here."

Fanny shrugged. "I can wait. And while I wait, I will try to make life as smooth for my husband as possible."

Rake grinned. "The kitten is hiding her claws."

"I would prefer the angel is hiding her horns. But yes, I'm biding my time."

"I must confess, it feels so strange to see you this emotional," Caroline said, thereby closing the subject of compromising.

"I know," Fanny sighed, getting all teary-eyed again. "I don't know what's the matter with me. I'm not this sensitive normally, as you are well aware. But it's like moving away from you all has transformed me into an unstable wreck, and I can't find my way out of it."

"Oh, dear," her mother breathed, her green eyes piercing.

"What?" George asked, curiosity getting the better of him.

"George, why don't you and Rake go to see if you

can find Devlin and let him know we are here."

Fanny saw her father open his mouth, but her mother moved her piercing look to him, and seconds later the door closed behind the escaping men.

Caroline let go of her daughter's hands, folding her own neatly in her lap. Fanny couldn't stop a wave of nervousness. Her mother was up to something, and she had not a clue what it was. And not knowing scared her the most.

"Fanny, can I ask you something?"

"Anything." Fanny swallowed, and hoped her panic wasn't visible.

"It's just something I need to know…"

"Yes?"

"Could there be a possibility that… that…"

"That what?"

"That you could, possibly…be…you know…"

"What?"

To Fanny's surprise, her mother did something she hardly ever did—she blushed. Something was definitely wrong, something that caused Caroline the hardest time getting the words out.

"What?" Fanny repeated impatiently, and Caroline took a shaky breath, as if she tried to find strength.

"Could you be pregnant?" she finally burst out, surprising her daughter with the insight.

"You think?" Fanny gasped, feeling dizzy over the possibility of carrying Devlin's child.

"Yes, I do," Caroline answered slowly. "Well, at least if you were…"

Fanny waited for her mother to continue, while her heart almost burst out of happiness.

Could it be? Could she be carrying a child?

Tears of joy ran down her cheeks, and her mother dried them tenderly away.

"This is so embarrassing for me, but I have to know." Caroline took a deep breath. "Did you and Devlin make love before your wedding?"

"Mother!" This time it was Fanny's turn to blush.

"Oh, dear," her mother breathed, as if Fanny's blush told her everything she needed to know. "You did. Have you had your bleedings lately?"

Fanny frowned. She wasn't too comfortable with the subject, but the possibility of being pregnant somehow made the embarrassment seem less important. "No. Now when you mention it, I haven't for a while. Not since… Well, not since before the Easton Ball."

"Francesca Darling!" Caroline cried out, and Fanny shrank back, bewildered, not understanding what her mother's problem was. What could make her mother stare at her with such an angry look on her face, just because she hadn't had her bleeding?

"Oh, my God."

"When?"

"Oh, my God!"

"Fanny, when?"

"Mother!"

Caroline's patience was gone, and she gave Fanny her strictest if-you-don't-tell-me-what-I-want-to-know-now-you-will-be-dead-in-ten-seconds look, and Fanny paled.

"The day of the proposal," she whispered, knowing her words would hurt her mother.

Caroline closed her eyes and Fanny felt as if the whole world was falling apart. She had never thought her mother would have reason to look at her with such disappointment. Devastated, she didn't know what to say or do. She had done the worst thing possible: she had let a man take her virginity before marriage.

But Caroline had yet another surprise for her daughter. When she opened her eyes again, the disappointment was long gone and a sweet, tender love remained.

"I can't say I'm thrilled over your actions. But what's done is done, and since you are married to the man, I will drop the subject."

"Thank you, Mama," Fanny whispered, and threw herself into her mother's waiting arms.

"Can you believe I am about to become a grandmother?" Caroline shook her head with a little smile. "Such wonderful news you give me, my dearest daughter."

For a long time, they looked deep into each other's eyes as their relationship changed from mother and daughter to that of a grandmother and a mother.

Caroline put her hand against Fanny's belly, and when she pushed the soft flesh, she could feel the hard swelling of the child.

"I would guess you are three to four months pregnant. You should soon feel your baby move…or have you already?"

Fanny frowned. "I don't know. I have had a rather strange feeling in my stomach lately, like when I am nervous about something. Fluttering, you know."

"It's the baby, silly." Caroline laughed. "And it is just how it is supposed to feel in the beginning. Later it will be regal punches."

"Punches don't sound as nice," Fanny grumbled, and Caroline patted her daughter's belly lightly.

"You will soon change your mind," she said dreamily. "It is such bliss to carry a child inside of you, and to feel it move. Men will never understand this part of pregnancy, nor will they ever understand how sacred one feels when you carry a new life under your heart."

"Devlin will be overjoyed," Fanny breathed with a smile that told her mother exactly how hysterically happy she was. "I can hardly wait to tell him."

She grabbed her mother's hand. "Promise you won't say anything to Papa or Uncle Rake. Not until I've had a chance to tell Devlin all about it. Promise!"

"Of course I promise." Caroline smiled. "This is between you and your husband now, and I won't tell anyone, not even your father."

This was going to be the best surprise ever.

Chapter 27

Devlin sat quietly in his chair, listening with a small smile to the gossip flying over the table.

It seemed much had happened in Berkshire during the two short weeks since he and Fanny left for Herefordshire. His wife and her relatives had been chattering constantly for an hour now about everyone in their acquaintance.

The disappointment he'd felt when he first saw Rake and George had quickly disappeared when he saw the joy in Fanny's face. She was so happy over the unannounced visit it was small-minded of him to feel the Darlings could have left them alone for a little while longer. He and Fanny hadn't been married for such a long time, after all, and had a new life to get used to. In his mind, that included privacy and no relatives for, preferably, a couple of months.

However, this family was tightly knit. He had known it before marrying Fanny, so he should not be surprised over the visit. It just felt too soon, and now the calm and functional routine he and Fanny had begun to establish was disturbed. It would take some time to fall into those comfortable steps again.

But, on the other hand, Fanny's laughter was like music to his ears. He did like seeing her happy, and he hadn't for a while, not like this, not since they left the wedding.

"Are you going to sit there and sulk all day, or will you give me a sample of your best port?" Rake drawled, interrupting Devlin's thoughts.

"I'll give you some port, my friend, but not my best one. I'm saving my finest port for more important guests who could come to visit, like the royal Georges, for example."

"So take out your best port, because we are also known as the Royal Family, and therefore, you shall approve of us tasting it!"

Devlin laughed; Rake had a point there. He stood up and led the men out from the dinner room. They took a glass in the library, but soon George excused himself to find his wife and daughter.

Rake, on the other hand, didn't seem in any rush to find Fanny now he was here. Instead, he wiggled his glass encouragingly, and Devlin filled it again.

"So, how's life in London?"

"Dull, as it is the off season." Rake held a cigar to a flickering light. "But I have had the time of my life, as it seems there are more welcoming ladies in town than ever."

Devlin frowned. Rake seemed almost reckless. It was as if he didn't care anymore, and this was not something usual for his cynical yet warmhearted friend.

"What about Penelope?" he asked, to see if the problem lay there.

"What about her?" Rake almost snarled, and Devlin knew without doubt he'd nailed it. For a moment he pondered whether to continue with his probing or choose the easy way out and let the subject go. It was not hard to see Rake had no wish to speak about his niece's friend.

"Is she still residing at Chester Park?"

"Yes."

"Is she still in love with you?"

Rake shrugged, trying very hard to look indifferent—without succeeding. "I don't know. I haven't spoken to her for a while. I've been too busy in London, plowing any possible field, to think about her or her tender feelings."

Devlin frowned. Rake looked ready to kill, and this was obviously not the best time to press him for further information.

"I'm surprised she didn't join you here. I know how much Fanny misses her, and I can only assume Penelope misses her equally."

"She was planning to come, but something got in the way and she had to stay put."

"You knew she was coming?"

"Yes, of course I knew. That's why I wan…" Rake broke off, but too late; Devlin already had his answer. Rake was not finished emotionally with Penelope, no matter how he tried to convince Devlin, or himself, about it.

Instead of continuing with his probing, Devlin suggested they join the others, and Rake immediately agreed, his relief visible.

They found Fanny and her parents in the front parlor, sitting closely together on a sofa. The love the threesome felt for each other was overwhelming. Devlin couldn't stop a little prick of envy; no one had ever loved him so completely.

Fanny gave him a radiant smile that took the edge off his newfound envy. Her love washed over him, and he found himself wishing there were a spot available next to her. He was in desperate need of touching her.

"Devlin, you won't believe what mother just told me," Fanny crowed with a glowing smile. "Nicholas Pembroke has asked the American heiress Lucinda Bell to marry him, and—guess what?—she accepted him! Even though he has no title or vast lands, which one would think someone like Lucinda, or rather her family, would want."

Devlin took Fanny's cup and raised it high into the air. "To Nicholas and Lucinda. A matchmaker's dream comes true."

"Hear, hear," the other men mumbled.

"Oh, come on!" Caroline exclaimed, aghast. "You can't be serious, can you?"

"Why not, my dear?" George asked.

"Oh, George." Caroline snorted. "Do you really think Nicholas and Lucinda make the perfect combination in matrimonial heaven? If so, I have to say you are not the man I thought you were."

Rake, whose thoughts had been elsewhere, woke up and didn't realize how close Caroline was to eruption. "Exactly my opinion," he agreed eagerly. "All the crap about two people being made for each other? It's just fairytales. Crap!"

Just as he finished his monologue, Rake caught the other men's frantic head-shakes as they tried to stop him from putting his foot in his mouth. It was too late.

Caroline, the goddess of love and eternal happiness, stood before him, her hands on her hips, and he shrank back into the armchair, silently hoping for someone or something to save him from her wrath.

"I have just one thing to say to you," she hissed. "If you have decided to turn yourself into some miserable martyr who wants to live his life without love, fine. Just don't try to rub it off on everyone else. You don't want to be happy. You don't want to be content. You don't want to feel complete. So be it, I'll respect your wish. However, if you don't learn to respect me and everyone else who wants love and fulfillment…"

Caroline took a deep, shaky breath, and George grabbed the moment of silence to step in front of Caroline, effectively hiding Rake behind him.

"It has been a long day, my love. What do you say we two retire to our room for the evening, and get a good night's sleep?"

Fanny hid a smile as Caroline glared at her husband. Her mother didn't appreciate George's meddling when she would much prefer a little verbal slashing with Rake. But after a war of the eyes, she nodded, defeated.

Devlin and Fanny called out goodnights as the couple left the room, leaving behind a silent Rake with a strange, bewildered look on his handsome face. He was used to Caroline's sometimes hefty temperament, but this was more than bad temper. This was something personal, and it seemed he was causing it.

Slowly, still looking somewhat dizzy, he rose and mumbled something that sounded like goodnight before he walked out, leaving his hosts alone for the first time since breakfast.

"Come here," Devlin growled, and held out his arms so Fanny could walk into his embrace. She lifted her face to his, inviting him to kiss her.

He gratefully accepted her offer and gave her a kiss that made her heart sing like a nightingale.

"Devlin," Fanny whispered into his mouth, and he

lifted his head so he could see her face. His golden eyes warmed her with their heat, and she forgot what she was about to say, mesmerized by his beauty.

"What, dearest?" Devlin mumbled, as he let his thumbs stroke the soft skin of her chin.

His unusual show of affection made her knees go even weaker, and she couldn't hold back a contented sigh. In this moment, she understood what Caroline had meant about fulfillment through a partner, as she couldn't think of life without him.

She felt his hands and his breath caress her, and she knew in her heart this was it. This was the love of her life. Somehow, by a wonderful twist of fate, she had met the one person who lifted her heart and her soul toward heaven and made her feel complete.

He gave her a smile so filled with love she knew he felt the same way, though she wasn't so sure he was aware of it himself yet.

He had a stubborn streak when it came to feelings, and she guessed she had only two choices. To wait for him to learn what was in his heart, or to tell him.

As she had an impatient streak when it came to feelings, she decided to share what was in her heart.

"I have something to tell you."

Devlin didn't lift his head from her neck. Instead, he started to place small kisses all over her cheekbone, and again she almost lost track of her thoughts.

But only almost.

This was important to her, and she took a step back, so he had to let her go.

"Devlin, please listen to me. This is most important."

"What can be more important than me kissing

you?" Devlin said with a grin, as he reached for her again.

"That I love you," she blurted out, effectively stopping his stride. He stared at her with disbelief written all over his handsome face.

She had surprised him down to his handsome toes. The only problem was she couldn't tell if he thought her loving him was a good idea or a bad one. The man stared, dumbfounded—but still magnificent. It was as if he didn't understand what she had said.

"You do?" he whispered hoarsely.

"Of course I do," she snorted, trying hard not to sound as insecure as she felt.

He blinked. And blinked again.

Fanny sighed. Her impatient streak really didn't like this waiting around. She took the step back to him and put her arms around his waist. He still stared at her, bewildered, and she sighed again. "You can put your arms around me now and proceed with telling me how much you love me."

Slowly, he lifted his arms and put them around her waist, and she put hers around his neck.

"And?" she urged, and his eyes started to twinkle, as he finally woke up from his stupor.

"And what?" he teased.

"Lord, have mercy," Fanny sighed. "How much do you love me?"

Devlin couldn't hold back a chuckle. "How can you be so sure that I love you?"

"How can you not?" She rolled her eyes.

His warm laughter surrounded them, and Fanny knew she would remember this moment forever. Standing in his arms, with his warmth showering all over her, made her feel special, and she knew this was for eternity.

They belonged together, now and forever.

"So?" she probed, and he gave her a look that clearly told her all about the wonderful feelings inside of him.

"I love you."

"I know."

This kiss wasn't as hot as the last one. This lingering kiss wasn't passionate at all. This kiss was all about love, and Fanny cried when he lifted his head again.

"I have something more to tell you," she sobbed, as he gently dried her tears away.

"Oh? What can it be? Are you going to tell me how much I adore making love to you?"

She gave him a serene, almost holy smile, and he frowned back at her, as if he felt something wasn't right. She lifted her hand and stroked his cheek to calm him before she beckoned him closer again.

"We are going to have a little baby," she whispered happily, so sure she was bringing him the best news of his life.

Instead he froze, then ripped himself loose from her arms, glaring. Her happy smile vanished, and she stared at him with shock.

"Devlin, didn't you hear what I just said?" she whispered, not believing he could act in this strange way when she had just shared her wonderful news. He seemed angry, almost overwhelmingly so.

"Are you sure?" he gritted through his teeth, and she saw his knuckles turn all white as he clenched his fists hard. She nodded solemnly, not knowing what to say or what to do.

He, who should be laughing, crying, or just going crazy with happiness, seemed only angry and distraught. He withdrew silently, backing until they had the entire seating area between them, as if he needed a barrier to keep himself from touching her.

"Devlin?" His jaw moved, but he didn't say anything, and he seemed to be strengthening himself against her. "I thought you would be happy." Fanny couldn't stop her voice from trembling with agony, and she saw him close his eyes, as if he hated himself for being the one who hurt her like this.

"Why would I be happy?" he whispered, as he slowly moved toward the door.

"I thought all men with titles wanted an heir. I thought you would want our child."

He ignored the last part, as if it hurt too much to acknowledge her pain. "Of course I want an heir, but not yet. Not so soon."

Anger rose inside her, a twisted, unhealthy anger that consumed all her earlier happiness and left her an empty shell.

"You said you loved me."

"I do."

"Then why are you doing this to me?" she sobbed. "Why are you putting me through this nightmare? If you love me, you want our child."

Once again Devlin ignored her pain and instead walked to the door and put his hand on the knob. For a minute, he stood silent, his back toward her, and she knew this was the last moment she had to persuade him.

Too upset to think straight, to find the right words, she whispered brokenly, "Don't…don't leave."

She saw him take a deep breath, as if he needed to strengthen himself against her, and again that unhealthy anger came over her. "Go then," she screamed. "Leave me!"

And he did.

Chapter 28

Fanny cried all through the night.

For the first time since their wedding, Devlin hadn't joined her in her room. Instead she had spent the rest of the evening on the cold floor of her bedroom, her ear pressed against the door connecting her bedroom with his as she listened to his every movement.

Every time she heard him walk closer to the door, her heart started to beat faster in anticipation, but not once did he step all the way. She heard him talk to his strange valet, Bear, but never did she hear him utter anything that told her he was as devastated as she was.

What had she done wrong?

She didn't know, and he hadn't told her anything significant, nothing to give her the tiniest hint of his reason for treating her this way.

She was carrying his child, for goodness' sake, and in her family, children meant happiness. Her mother had told her so many times how silly her father had been every time they were expecting a child. He had acted like a crazed lunatic, especially the first time, Caroline had said.

Fanny had spent the whole of dinner daydreaming about the different ways she could tell Devlin her news, anticipating how he would react.

She hadn't been close at all.

When the first rays of light came through the large

windows, she still hadn't fallen asleep. She sat in her armchair and watched the sun slowly rise over the horizon, her hands resting on her belly in a protective manner.

During the long hours of the night, she had made a decision, and she wasn't going to let her husband get away without talking to her.

Devlin had to tell her why he didn't want the baby, and explain to her why he insisted on walking all over her heart. He was a good man. She'd instinctively been aware of that from their first meeting. She knew he would never do anything to hurt her without a reason.

She needed to know what his problem was, so she could know what she was fighting against.

She closed her eyes and sat silently, waiting for him to wake up. When she finally heard a noise from his bedroom, she rose and went slowly to the connecting door, taking a few deep breaths for confidence.

"You can do this," she whispered reassuringly to herself before she knocked lightly on the door and opened it before she could change her mind. But instead of her husband, she met the startled eyes of one of the maids making the large bed.

"Oh, I'm sorry," Fanny apologized. "I thought it was Hereford. I hope I didn't scare you?"

The maid shook her head, and curtsied before she scurried away, leaving Fanny all alone in the room.

Everything was in perfect order, not a thing out of place. Not like her bedroom, which was in a terrible mess since she had been moving about the whole night.

With one last lingering look, she went back into her own room and rang for water so she could freshen herself up. When she was appropriately dressed, she rushed down to the breakfast room, only to find it deserted. She continued to the library, and then to his office, but she didn't find her husband anywhere.

Where was Devlin?

He wasn't in any of his usual places, but as this morning wasn't like any of the other mornings of her married life, she guessed she shouldn't be surprised.

She continued her desperate search for her husband until Jarvis finally rescued his mistress from rushing hysterically all over the castle and told her His Grace had left for London earlier this morning, together with his valet. The man helped his shocked mistress to the breakfast room, where he made her sit down in a chair before he sent a maid for her mother, who immediately sent the servants from the room and sat down beside her daughter. As she opened her arms, Fanny slid into them with a devastated moan, crying all over her mother's lovely morning dress. Caroline sat silent as her daughter wept, tenderly caressing her silky hair.

Patiently she waited for Fanny to compose herself enough to be able to talk about whatever was breaking her heart. They sat still for a long time, all alone, until Fanny's tears dried, and she finally managed to sit up and face her mother.

"What is it, my dearest?" Caroline asked softly, and Fanny almost started to cry again. "Did Devlin do something to you he shouldn't have?"

When Fanny shook her head, Caroline put her hands against her daughter's cheeks and forced her to look her in the eyes. "Tell me."

Fanny took one deep, shaky breath and released herself from her mother. She leaned back and closed her eyes, as she didn't want to see her mother's reaction to her words.

She was afraid her mother would be just as outraged as she was, and she wasn't strong enough yet to face her own feelings, no matter where they appeared.

"Yesterday evening, when you all had left us, I told Devlin about the baby."

"And?"

"He doesn't want it, and now he has left for London. He has left me, and he did it without a word or an explanation."

Caroline sat back, her confusion all too obvious.

"This is indeed a strange behavior from a man who should be exhilarated over the prospect of an heir."

Fanny nodded, tears in her eyes. "What makes this even stranger is that I know he has deep feelings for me. Why he would do something this selfish is beyond me."

"I need to talk to your father about this," Caroline admitted gravely. "I need to get his perspective. Please stay here, sweetheart, and I'll be back as soon as possible."

She disappeared through the door, and Fanny heard her ask a passing servant to tell Lord Newbury to come to the breakfast room.

Ten minutes later, both George and Rake sat silently looking at her while Caroline gave them Fanny's brief explanation.

"The bastard!" Rake spat, as he finally broke the silence.

"Indeed, he is," Caroline agreed.

"He really meant it," Rake added as though to

himself.

"Did you think this actually would happen?" George asked, looking just as astonished as he sounded.

"Wait a minute," his lovely wife said, frowning, but the men ignored her.

"No, I thought he would get over it once they were married," Rake answered with a glance toward his niece, who, like her mother, was starting to get a little annoyed with the two men who obviously knew something more about what had caused Devlin to run away.

"I feel responsible, because I knew about it and agreed not to pass it on to Fanny," George admitted thoughtfully.

Rake nodded in agreement. "I feel stupid. Love solves everything... Ha! Bloody hell, I never thought it would come to this. Sorry."

Rake's last word was addressed to Caroline, whose look of rage at Rake's obvious lack of faith in love might have shriveled a turnip. George, who sometimes was as sensitive as a stone, didn't see his wife's reaction to Rake's words. Instead, he agreed heartily, and two seconds later a pillow smacked him in the face.

"What?" He frowned at Fanny, who had thrown the pillow.

"Exactly," she gritted between her teeth. "What?"

This time it was George who looked befuddled, so his younger brother asked the question, "What what?"

Caroline rolled her eyes. Sometimes she wondered why women found these Darling men attractive at all, even though she should know, as she was married to one of them and had been for more than twenty years. Sometimes they were too ignorant for their own good, and they certainly lived their lives without reading between the lines, ever. Men.

Fanny stood and went to her father, not masking her frustration. "What are you two talking about? What is it you knew about?"

"Oh," George said forlornly, finally understanding what his daughter wanted to know. "Nothing special, just something I found out about Devlin, something not known to many."

"Not many know at all," Rake said reassuringly, rushing to his brother's defense. "Just I and George know about it. And Saxton too, of course."

Caroline looked astonished at him. "My father?" she shrilled. "How can he know? I know he knows a lot about many persons, but this kind of information is hardly of any importance to him, if not…"

She turned quiet, and covered her mouth with her hand. "Don't tell me Devlin's a dangerous enemy to the country!"

"For goodness' sake, Caroline," her husband said, aghast. "Don't you have more confidence in your own father than to believe he would have let his beloved granddaughter marry someone he knew—or believed to be—an evil person?"

Caroline blushed prettily, feeling rather stupid. "Of course he wouldn't."

"Devlin is one of Grand-Papa's men, or at least he was before he returned to England," Fanny enlightened her mother. "And as he was one of Basil's Boys, I guess Grand-Papa needed to know as much as possible about him."

Caroline walked over to her husband, and slapped his arm. "Don't you ever make me believe something that vile about my father again."

George stared in astonishment at his wife, who in his eyes was behaving rather ridiculously, but he had clearly learnt his lesson and didn't say a word. Instead, he looked at his daughter's puffy eyes and gave her a loving smile.

"Fanny, my dearest," he said slowly, "you know Devlin had a pretty bad childhood?"

"Yes I do."

"When you grow up with someone who is as wickedly evil as Conan Ross was, you can't help but become somewhat unbelieving in yourself, and in love. Well, Devlin decided a long time ago never to have any children, because he didn't want his bloodline to continue."

"But why did he marry me then? It mustn't be such a big surprise to him, how babies are made."

Rake couldn't hold back his laughter, but a single look from Caroline cut it straight off.

"As Devlin grew older, he became wiser, and he decided he wanted an heir. The dukedom of Hereford is old, and as the dukes before Conan had been great men, he felt he couldn't end their greatness because of one bad seed. So he decided to find a wife who would make a good mother, and who would be well protected by her family. Such a woman could give him an heir and then raise the child, or children, with her family, and thus he would make sure the family bloodline would continue, without Conan's evilness influencing them."

Fanny looked at her father. What was he talking about? "How on earth can a dead man influence the living who never met him?"

"Through Devlin," Caroline filled in softly, as she

began to understand what George was trying to tell them.

"But it is such an insane idea," Fanny objected. "Devlin is not like his father, and he would never behave in such a selfish and destructive way."

"Devlin don't think it's insane," Rake said. "For him, who lived under the rule of his father, it *is* possible. You must understand Conan wasn't a man who abused people physically, because he never laid a hand on Devlin. No, he abused him mentally, always telling him he was no good, that he would never be worth anything. Devlin grew up hearing all about how worthless he was, and how no one wanted him. He admitted to me once that the old man hadn't told him his mother died. Instead, Conan kept telling Devlin his mother left him because she didn't want him."

Tears ran down Fanny's cheeks as she listened. How she wished Devlin were still there, so she could wrap herself around him and tell him how much she loved him, again and again, until he knew she would never leave him.

How could a father do such a thing to his own son?

"So you see, my dear," George said gently, "Devlin has removed himself from you and the child you are carrying so he won't have any effect on the child's upbringing. He wants the child to be happy and strong, and because of his father, he thinks that can only happen if he stays out of the picture."

"How can he do this to me?" Fanny cried. "How can he leave me alone, and think I will be happier when he's not around? I can't believe he is doing this—and what is worse, I can't believe I thought he loved me."

"He does."

Fanny snorted. "No, he doesn't. If he did, he would be here telling me how happy he is over the baby, and how much he loves me. But instead he sneaked away during the night, because he couldn't even face me."

She walked over to the window, turning her back to her family. "You know what he said when I told him about the baby? He only told me it was too soon. As far as I am concerned, this is not what a man tells his wife when he finds out she is carrying his child."

Rake strode to Fanny and grabbed her arms, forcing her to look at him. "Don't you get it, Fanny? He loves you."

She shook her head, unable to speak.

"He said it was too soon, you say. And what do you think he meant?"

When Fanny still didn't speak, he caressed her face softly and gave her a sweet, uplifting smile.

"Think about it from his side. Here you have a man who has decided never to make a child suffer like he did as a youngster. How can he do that, since he must have a child to carry on the title? He promises himself not to influence his child badly in any way. And the best way to accomplish this, he decides, is by staying away. But then he meets you, and you know as well as I he fell head over heels in love with you. He couldn't stay away from you, not even for a single day. He must have thought he'd died and gone to heaven, because he found himself in love with the woman who was the perfect essence of what he had wished for in his future wife. You are such a strong person, and you love with all your heart. And besides this, you have a large and caring family. What he never thought about was that by marrying you he did the dumbest thing he ever had done."

"Now, wait a minute." Fanny frowned. "How can you say he was dumb to marry me? I thought you just said I was his perfect woman?"

"Because marrying a woman who was perfect in every way, but whom he didn't love, would have made much more sense, because such a woman would have been very easy for him to leave and stay away from. But instead he met you, fell madly in love with you, and married you. He probably didn't think about babies at all, being too caught up in his married bliss. And then you threw his whole world around by admitting to him you're pregnant, and what did he tell you?"

"That it was too soon," Fanny repeated slowly, finally understanding what Rake was talking about. Lord, she hadn't thought about it in this way at all. His strange sadness hadn't been over her being with child. No, he had been sad because she had become pregnant so soon. He wanted to spend more time with her, but because he had made this stupid promise to himself he had to leave her.

Caroline stood and clapped her hands, effectively interrupting her daughter's thoughts. "So how do we fight this battle?"

"No, no," George said nervously. "*We* are not going to fight any battle at all. The only thing to happen now is Fanny's decision on what *she* will do about her missing husband."

Caroline shut her mouth and gave him a kill-you-later look.

Fanny turned back to the window and looked at her own reflection in the glass. How much could she take? How far would her love for Devlin survive?

She sighed deeply.

Really far, she guessed, because she felt a great need to go and kick her stupid husband in the butt and never let him go again. But it was such an easy solution, and somehow she didn't want it to be easy.

She wanted him to want her.

She wanted him to come to her and tell her he had been out of his mind believing he could live without her. If she went after him and made him return to her, she would never know if he wanted that or if he stayed only to make her happy.

And nor would he.

She could hear her parents whispering behind her back, and she knew she was lucky to have a family who cared so much for her, who would be there to help her get through this.

She turned back to them and gave them a little smile, and all three of them sighed, relieved.

Her mother came forward and grabbed her hands.

"What do you want to do?"

"Nothing," Fanny said, and felt a sudden urge to giggle when she saw her mother's astonishment. This was clearly not what they had expected her to say.

"Nothing?" Rake breathed.

"You have to forgive me, Fanny, but that sounds like a rather stupid plan for getting your husband back to your side," her father said, a bit patronizing, but she forgave him for it. He wanted to help, and doing nothing wasn't his way. He was a man of action.

"My first thought was to go after him and drag him home with me and live happily ever after."

"Sounds perfect in my ears, so what's the catch?" George said, as he crossed his arms over his chest. It was easy to tell he was trying very hard to be patient with her.

"I want him to want me."

"But he does want you." Rake frowned.

"I know now he wants me, but I want him to want to live with me." She put her hands on her belly. "With us. And I want him to know that it's by his own will."

Caroline nodded slowly. "I see. But how will we make this happen?"

"Well, not from here. I must go to London and let him yearn for me a little first."

"Ah," Rake said, and nodded with a wicked smile. "This is a very good plan, sweet pea, and one that will work. I don't think Devlin ever thought about how it would be to meet with you in the social swirl and have to watch you being admired by other men, without being able to interfere. I almost feel sorry for him."

"Almost," Fanny echoed.

Chapter 29

"I have never seen the tongues of the *ton* wagging as quickly as they are now."

Devlin looked up from his lonely glass of brandy and met Bear's probing gaze.

"Finally speaking to me again, are we? And here I was getting used to this wonderful solitude you put me into during these last couple of weeks."

Bear shrugged. "I obviously can't change your mind, so why bother to be mad at you for being a bloody stubborn fool?"

Devlin decided not to answer that. He was too relieved Bear was finally acknowledging him again.

After Fanny told him about the baby, Devlin had immediately ordered his things to be packed. Bear had been outraged to hear they were heading for London without Devlin's wife, all because of, as he put it, his boss's partial stupidity. He was so outraged he had spent the whole journey telling Devlin about it.

Devlin had endured his friend's ranting until they reached Hereford House at Grosvenor Square, where he finally had lost his patience and told Bear to shut up. Bear had stared at him with disbelief at the harsh cut and had since not said a word.

"Please do tell me what the tongues are wagging so excitedly about now," Devlin urged, even though he was well aware of the answer.

"Your missing duchess, of course. Or did you honestly think they wouldn't notice how you returned to town by yourself? Your marriage was *the* happening of the Season, and everyone knew it was something as unfashionable as a marriage of love. And here you are alone, only a few weeks later, flirting wildly with every female you meet. Of course they wonder."

Devlin frowned at his glass, not at all pleased to hear he was the subject of gossip. But what had he expected? Bear was right. His and Fanny's love story had been the talk of the *ton* when it happened, as neither of them had bothered to hide their feelings.

Everyone had thought it would last forever, and, in the end, forever had turned out to be a mere fortnight.

He sighed, as the now familiar heartache burnt through his body. It had been weeks since he'd seen Fanny, and he was practically drowning in his own loneliness.

He missed her more than he had thought possible, but he would have to live with his misery, as he was just as determined as ever to continue with his mission of changing his father's legacy.

"The rumors about you and your wife are actually quite amusing," Bear continued. "Everyone wonders where your wife is, especially as not one of the Darling family has been seen anywhere."

"Amusing? Really?"

"Oh, put that ironic face away," Bear sneered. "They are amusing, as they are mostly about what you have done with your wife."

Devlin arched an eyebrow, interested against his will. "So, what am I supposed to have done to her?"

"Well, one rumor says you killed her."

"Oh, my God." Devlin coughed. "Killed her? Are they out of their bloody minds?"

Bear chuckled. "It is said you have buried her somewhere at the grounds of Pendragon, and now her poor relatives are searching desperately for her body."

"Oh, my God," Devlin repeated outraged.

"I wouldn't get too upset if I were you, as it is only a rumor. Furthermore, there are few who believe in that specific rumor."

"There are more rumors?"

"There is the one that says Fanny eloped from you and now hides somewhere whilst her family, again, are searching desperately for her."

"Why on earth would Fanny elope from me?"

"Yes indeed, why would a spouse run away from her, or his, loved one?"

Devlin ignored Bear's stab. "And how many believe in this one?"

"This rumor has more believers, although only men. It seems no woman believes Fanny willingly would leave you."

Devlin couldn't stop a smug smile. "Good news, indeed."

Bear frowned at him again but didn't remark upon the smugness as he continued, "The rumor with the most believers is the one about how you have come to London out of boredom, while your wife has gone to her family to try to mend her broken, abandoned heart."

"So no one guessed the truth?"

"As no one would do anything so stupid as to leave his spouse because he is too happy, they don't even consider this a possibility."

"I didn't leave her because we were too happy."

Bear snorted. "Yes, you did."

Devlin shook his head. He knew there was no point trying to change Bear's opinion; his friend happened to be even more stubborn than he was.

But at least he was speaking to him again.

"What is your plan now?"

"Survive, I guess."

Bear snorted. "And here I thought you were out there hunting for a mistress, since you have been flirting wildly with every last woman you meet."

"I have to move on, Bear. I can't continue to live in this puddle of misery I have hurled myself into. Meeting someone else will make the days pass by faster and easier. I'm not looking for love. I just want someone I can feel a little close to for a couple of hours."

"So who is your choice?"

"I don't know. I haven't decided yet."

"How hard can it be?" Bear grinned. "It's not like you are out of options. To me, it seems every available woman has made it known she is yours if you want her."

Devlin closed his eyes in frustration.

Why had he been relieved that Bear finally talked to him? Now he would have preferred his friend and valet to be quiet and leave him sitting in his own misery. But Bear obviously disagreed with him about this, too, as he continued the conversation without acknowledging Devlin's frustration.

"Do you want me to write you a list? I could narrow it down to the most attractive ones, and it might be easier for you to make your choice."

Devlin shook his head. He knew there were dozens

of women in London who would give anything to be his mistress. All he had to do was to choose one of them.

But no matter how beautiful, witty, or interesting they were, he still found too many faults with each one. Maria was too blonde, Sarah too skinny, Emmeline too busy…

He knew he was acting stupidly. He'd never before had any problem with wandering from one woman to another. However, since meeting Fanny, something in him said, "Stop, don't go any further."

Staying celibate forever wasn't his plan, but maybe it was too early to bed another lady, with Fanny so vibrantly clear in his mind. So instead he flirted with every available woman and made sure he had a chance once he was ready to move on.

"Have you heard anything about her?"

Bear understood it was Fanny whom Devlin meant, and he shook his head. "No, I haven't. I tried to get some of the Darling servants to tell me what they knew, but unfortunately they are quite angry with you, and it affects me. That butler of theirs even shut the door in my face. Nasty man."

Devlin sighed, defeated.

How hard was it to get information about his wife's whereabouts? He had thought someone of her family, probably Rake, would come after him to demand an answer, but no one did. He couldn't find any of them in London at all, not even Lord Saxton.

He had written a letter to his supervisor at Pendragon, hoping the man would give him some answers without Devlin having to ask, but the man didn't catch on; he was all business in his reply.

When two weeks had passed by without any news

of Fanny, Devlin sent a footman to Pendragon with the mission to find out what his wife was doing.

Or rather *how* she was doing.

However, upon his return, the footman could only inform him that Her Grace had left the same day Devlin had. She had gone with her family without saying where she was going or when she would return.

He guessed she had gone back to Chester Park to lick her wounds, his intention from the beginning.

So why was it bothering him?

He should be relieved.

She was where he had wanted her, in the loving arms of her family. But instead he felt alone and, strangely enough, rejected.

"I need to know that she is all right. I need to know how she is holding up. As long as I don't know anything about her, I can't go on with my life. If I know she has a good life without me, I can let her go."

In the chair across from Devlin, Bear stretched his long muscular legs. "You want me to break into Berkeley House? I could snoop around and see if I could find some information for you. Hell, I can even hide in Lady Francesca's bedroom, if she's in town."

Devlin sat straight up. "No, you won't. For goodness' sake, Bear, we have to tread carefully with this. I don't want it to be commonly known why I left her, and you being thrown out or collected by an officer from Berkeley House would fire those wagging tongues even more."

Bear made a disappointed face. "All right. I won't break into Berkeley House, even though I still think it is the best idea we have so far."

"I could go back to White's," Devlin said

thoughtfully. "I could wait around for one of the Darlings to go there. If we meet in public, they would have to greet me."

"Maybe," Bear agreed. "But lurking in White's sounds most boring."

Devlin grinned. Bear had a deep aversion to anything having to do with the *ton*. He was probably the only gentleman, although currently a pretend-valet, who would rather go out for a ride than gossip with his peers.

"You have a point there. And besides the boring part, sitting at White's would only make me available for my friends to ask questions I'm not ready to answer yet."

Devlin felt Bear's probing eyes upon him, and he wished he knew what to say to ease his friend's angst. But as he didn't even know how to soothe his own feelings, how could he soothe Bear's?

Maybe he was doing it the wrong way.

Devlin frowned. He would continue with his life, even though he wasn't over Fanny yet. The distraction of another woman could be just the little thing that would make him feel better.

Without a word to Bear, he walked straight to his office, where he scribbled down a short letter he gave to a footman to deliver.

It was time he went on with his plan.

He had to leave Fanny behind him, and the one thing to really send him over the edge of that cliff should be bedding another woman.

He *had* to get a mistress.

The footman delivered the letter to Lady Maria Ashton, who squealed with joy and sent back a note replying she would love to join him this evening. Meanwhile, Devlin took a long bath, preparing for the night to come.

And the new bed he would spend it in.

He dressed all in black, making sure he looked as dark as he felt, although he only succeeded in looking more magnificent than ever.

Without meeting Bear's disapproving gaze, he took the steps downstairs three at a time. As he sat in the carriage, headed for the Ashton townhouse, he felt like a large stone had fallen off his shoulders.

He was finally going to get rid of Fanny.

****

The whispers about the arrival together of Hereford and Lady Ashton at Vauxhall Gardens immediately traveled from ear to ear. When the whispers reached Rake, who stood listening to the orchestra playing softly, he cursed silently. How could Devlin do such a stupid thing as walking into the midst of society with another woman at his arm?

He looked down at Fanny, beside him. The dreamy look in her face told him she was far away in her mind, and he wished he could get out of being the one giving her the bad news.

What should he do?

The best idea was probably to whisk Fanny out of there, so she wouldn't have to face her husband and the utter humiliation she would feel as she met his new mistress.

Maria Ashton was a lady who knew what she wanted, and as a wife to a high officer who spent most of his time abroad, she had the full opportunity to get it. She was an intelligent woman with too much wit and too sharp a tongue, one that could easily slash Fanny's poor suffering heart into shreds if given the chance.

Nevertheless, maybe a meeting was what needed to happen. Fanny wanted her husband back and had spent three weeks preparing for this, but was she really ready? He didn't know, and for a short second he thought about taking Fanny and leaving the gardens, thus making sure she would get more time to harden her stance before putting it to the test.

But before he had a chance to make up his mind, Sin joined them and made the decision for him. "He's here," Sin told his sister, with a grave voice.

Rake felt a tremor pass through Fanny's body, but she didn't show a thing outwardly, and an overwhelming wave of pride in his stoic niece washed over him. She was there to get her husband back, and she seemed ready for the fight.

"Where is he?" Rake asked, and Sin nodded toward the entrance, where a large crowd had gathered. They could see the glances people were already sending their way, and they knew they couldn't escape facing Devlin even if they tried. The crowd loved a good showdown; they wouldn't let them sneak out.

"Can you do this?" Sin asked his sister, distressed, and she nodded.

"I need to do this," she answered harshly, and only Rake knew how this pained her, as her fingers were digging into his arm. "I must meet him. It's all I have wished for since the day we left Pendragon. I need to see him, to know he is what I want, and to be sure he is worthy of all our plans. And besides my needs, he needs to know I'm in town."

"He's not alone," Rake said quietly, and by the

stricken look in her face, he knew she got the message.

She took a deep shaky breath and closed her eyes for a short second before she nodded and let her uncle lead her onto the dance floor to join the other dancers.

Another man soon cut in, and Rake left Fanny in her admirer's arms and walked back to Sin's side to watch the drama unfold.

Chapter 30

She wasn't supposed to be dancing.

Devlin had walked into Vauxhall Gardens, the lovely Lady Maria Ashton on his arm, feeling better by the moment, thanks to the stir they created. He knew it was silly, but he desperately needed something other than Fanny to focus on, and the vultures' happiness over seeing him with someone else, and so openly, made him laugh and flirt with Maria and the other ladies they met.

It wasn't until they came to the dance floor that he understood why everyone he'd met seemed almost giddy, as he spotted his wife in another man's arms.

Jealousy hit him full force and nearly sent him flying through the dancing couples to tear his smiling wife away from the bastard, but only almost. What made him stop was something he never had thought to see again.

His wife was smiling.

Something cold took hold of his heart. How could his wife be smiling? She had just been left by her husband, and she was supposed to be in love with him. Therefore, she should be at home crying her eyes out, mourning as her heart broke into just as many pieces as his heart had.

But not Fanny. She was dancing.

And not just dancing, she was waltzing, for

goodness' sake. He started to walk toward the dance floor, dragging Maria Ashton behind him.

When she too saw the reason why they so suddenly joined the dancers, she tried to move the other way, but it was too late. All she could do was try to hang on to Devlin as he twirled her around with almost hysterical frenzy, until they crashed into his prey and her beau.

"Excuse me," Devlin drawled when Fanny looked at their attacker, and he felt ridiculously happy to see a blush discolor her face when she recognized him.

"Well, hello, what a surprise to meet you here," he continued, behaving like the scoundrel and libertine he tried to be as he looked into Fanny's gray eyes.

He loathed himself for such behavior, but at the same time he couldn't help rejoicing that she was no longer smiling.

"Hereford," her partner greeted, but Devlin only nodded without letting his eyes leave hers. She looked good, as alluring as ever, and it took all his willpower to keep from bending down and tasting those lush lips that shivered before him.

"If you don't mind," he told Fanny's beau, and before anyone had a chance to react, he had thrown Maria into the other man's arms and grabbed his wife.

Without another word, he started to dance to the gentle music the orchestra played. Fanny was stiff as a board, and the mere thought of her reacting to him in a bad manner made him feel strangely good.

He had behaved so badly toward her, even though it was for her own best, that he needed her to feel as bad as he did. And smiling to another man wasn't a part of feeling bad.

"Fancy meeting you here in London," he drawled,

trying to break the uncomfortable silence.

She snorted in a very Fanny-like way, and he almost smiled at the familiarity of it. Lord, how he had missed her.

"And here I thought you would be at Chester Park. I never imagined you would be in London, enjoying yourself in another man's arms."

His jealousy was showing, and he forced himself to be quiet. The problem was that having her in his arms made him realize how lonely he had been and how fast he had grown used to having her around.

Ever since their first kiss at Almack's, they had been together every day up until he left her at Pendragon, and it wasn't until now he felt whole again. A large piece of him had been missing, out of place.

He knew he would have to leave her again, because his decision was made, and he had no intention of altering it. But now he could part with her, because he knew she was all right.

Furthermore, now he would have a chance to say goodbye to her.

It had been a mistake to leave her in the middle of the night without getting a chance to hold her one last time. Unconsciously he dragged her a bit closer to himself, and she stiffened as their bodies touched. A jolt of need made him hard in an instant, and he pressed his abdomen against hers and groaned as she shivered in response.

Without a word he took her hand and walked out into the gardens, heading for the darker section. As soon as he found a deeply dark corner where they could be alone, he stopped and turned to face her in the darkness. Before she had a chance to speak, his lips were on hers, kissing her like a thirsty man drank water.

The darkness surrounded them and hid them from everyone else's eyes, and Devlin took full advantage of the situation.

His hands dove inside her dress and fondled her soft breasts until she moaned. His mouth and tongue followed, and he kissed the hard nipples while he let his pants down and at the same time lifted her skirt, so he could thrust inside her so harshly she cried out with surprise.

For once his need for her was larger than his need for her to enjoy it too, and he thrust over and over again, until he climaxed with a roar. His fulfillment was extreme, and he hardly noticed the salty tears on her cheeks.

He took a step back in the darkness, bumped into a bench, and sat, his legs shaking so badly he could barely stand. As his head started to work again, he heard his wife's quiet sobbing, and he became dead still. Not once had he thought about her. And as if that wasn't bad enough, she was pregnant.

"Oh, God, Fanny, I'm sorry," he blurted, full of remorse.

He heard her snort again, a tear-filled snort, and this time he wasn't as amused by her response as he had been earlier. He reached out into the darkness and found her waist, but when he tried to drag her toward him, she took a step away, effectively ripping herself out of his grip.

"Fanny, I said I was sorry," he urged as he stood up, trying to make out the outline of her in the thick darkness.

"Sorry?" she asked with a voice high-pitched

enough to tell him how upset she really was. "Is sorry all you can say to me? Sorry…"

Her voice broke, and he could hear she was crying again. Once more he tried to reach out for her, and again she avoided his embrace.

"Fanny, my dear, please listen to me," he begged. "I'm so sorry. I never meant to do this, but it overwhelmed me, and I just couldn't stop. Did… Did I hurt you?"

He waited breathlessly until she whispered, "No," and then he took a ragged breath, full of relief.

He guessed he could forgive himself for many things, but hurting her was something he couldn't live with.

He buttoned his pants, and when he was as respectable as the darkness could allow him to believe, he took hold of her hand again and held it tightly as she tried to pull it loose.

He walked briskly onto one of the walks, lit with hundreds of lights over their heads.

As he turned and looked down on his wife, his gaze didn't miss a thing as it roamed her person. Her hair was tousled, but not more than one could think it was supposed to look like. Her dress had been torn slightly, and a dirty smudge was seen on her sleeve, but you had to look at her as closely as he did to see it.

All in all, she was in good shape, and no one could tell her husband had just selfishly embraced her.

She kept her head bent forward, as if she hadn't the strength to hold herself upright and look him straight in the eye. She was trying to avoid him, and he felt bad enough to let her have her way.

They strolled along the dimly lit walk until they

were almost to the dance floor and meeting other couples enjoying the evening in the gardens.

They stopped, and Devlin put his finger under Fanny's chin, forcing her to lift her head up so he could look into her beloved face one last time. Her lovely eyes were the same color as rain clouds as they looked into his with a sadness that almost made him drag her into his arms again, to hold her close and never let her go.

But he couldn't do it to her. He wanted her to be happy. Furthermore, he wanted the child she carried to be happy.

"I'm so sorry, my darling," he said softly, his fingers stroking her peachy cheek. "I never meant to hurt you as I did."

She bent her head and leaned closer to his hand until her cheek rested in the palm of his hand. She closed her eyes, and a single tear ran down her cheek and landed on the tip of his finger.

He withdrew his hand and gave her a sad smile before he slowly planted a soft kiss on her lips.

"How are you doing?" he asked, as his warm eyes melted the last of her resistance.

"Not fine," she whispered. "My husband left me."

"What a bastard," he replied with a wry smile.

"He's not a bastard. He's just a bit simpleminded."

"Simpleminded? What if all he wants is for his wife to be happy?"

"By staying away?"

"Sometimes staying away is better than staying put."

She snorted, this time accompanied with a roll of her eyes, and he had no doubts about her having another opinion. Not that it mattered to him. He knew what his father had been like, and she didn't. There was no way she ever could understand his point of view, especially as she was surrounded by her large, loving family.

He looked down at her, absorbing every piece of her for the last time, to keep it deep inside of his heart forever. "I'll try to stay out of your way," he whispered hoarsely. "Meeting like this isn't good for any of us, and I thank the Lord the Season is almost over."

Fanny grabbed his arm. "Devlin, don't," she cried openly, with her face again covered with tears.

He tensed and felt a pain in his chest he'd never felt before. Before he could change his mind, he gently removed her hands and, with a small bow, turned and left her standing there alone.

"Please…"

Her deep sobs cut through his heart, and for a last time he hesitated, but the image of his father flashed before his eyes, and he took one ragged breath before he continued on his way. Dazed, he walked through the big-eyed crowd, not stopping for the angry voices of Rake and Sin, or the pleading voice of Maria Ashton.

He didn't stop until he reached his carriage, where he sat on the velvety cushions and was whisked away. Not until he had left Vauxhall Gardens far behind him did he hide his face in his hands with a groan. His large shoulders shook with every gut-wrenching sob that went through his body.

Chapter 31

Fanny stood motionless, staring at the back of her disappearing husband.

He had left her.

Again.

But this time she wasn't mortified. No, this time she was furious. She harshly wiped away the tears from her cheeks, breathing deeply as she tried to soothe the wrath rising inside of her.

The fool!

The stupid, irrational, simpleminded fool!

So he was going to play the part of a martyr, was he? Well, he could forget it, because she wasn't going to let him.

When Devlin was out of sight, she grabbed her skirts and hurried away. Rake and Sin were arguing in lowered voices about who was going to follow Devlin and who was going to take her home.

As she joined them, they stopped their bantering and looked at her with so much pity she nearly started to cry again. But she squared her shoulders and took a deep breath so she wouldn't make a fool of herself in front of everyone.

She could feel the eyes of the crowd taking in her person. Some were gloating, some pitied her, and there were some who were simply bored. She knew she was the talk of the *ton*, and it was something she could use.

She was going to make her husband suffer harshly before she let him come crawling back to her and beg her for mercy.

"Fanny, please tell me you're all right," Sin said. "I'll kill the man if he hurt you."

"I'm fine," she replied, giving her brother a tight smile to ease the frown on his handsome face. Unfortunately she succeeded only in making it deeper.

Rake took her hand, forcing her to look at him. "You don't look fine, sweet pea. You look like he dragged you through the bushes. If he did anything to you, harmed you in any way, you have to tell us immediately, and we will avenge you."

Well, she wasn't about to tell them about Devlin's selfish act toward her, so instead she asked if they could leave the gardens for the night, and before she knew it she sat in their carriage, heading homeward.

"I have thought about it," Rake said, as they crossed the Thames. "And I think we will have to kidnap him."

"What?" Sin and Fanny replied in unison.

"Are you crazy?" Sin followed up.

Rake shook his head. "No, I'm not, because it is the only way he can't ignore us, or Fanny."

"I still don't like it," Sin grumbled. "Hereford would be furious, and a furious man doesn't listen to his wife. He beats her."

"He wouldn't beat me," Fanny interrupted harshly.

"How can you be so sure he wouldn't?" Sin asked, and gave her a very brotherly look of impatience.

"He isn't the wife-beating type." Rake agreed with his niece before she could hurl herself at her brother.

"I still think kidnapping is a stupid idea," Sin

muttered.

"So tell me, mister-against-everything, what *your* big plan is?" Rake asked patronizingly, leaning back with his arms crossed before his chest.

Sin bestowed on his uncle an ugly face and turned to his sister. "I think you will have to seduce him."

"No," Rake said matter-of-factly.

"Why not?"

"Because it would be too easy for her, as he's desperately in love with her, and he would probably let himself forget all about his troubled past so he could spend more time in her arms. Then he would just shake it off and tell her goodbye again."

"How silly," Sin snarled.

"Maybe, but it's still the truth. We do need a better plan, something to make him understand he don't want to spend the rest of his life without Fanny. I'm sorry to say this, but he can get his bodily needs seen to by any woman. It is the heart we need to touch."

Rake could see Fanny agreed with him, as she was too aware of how Devlin would have no problems finding a mistress, or any woman who would gladly spend a night with him. He was, after all, the very handsome and magnificent Duke of Hereford, and even though he was off the marriage market he still would be a trophy for any woman to take to bed.

"I see your point," Sin admitted. "But I'm still not up for the kidnapping, as I think it is not the way to catch this bird."

"I guess you're right," Rake gave in, and both men sat silent, ransacking their heads for any good ideas, until the carriage stopped in front of their townhouse at Berkeley Square.

As the hour was late, the house lay empty and silent, and only Butler was still awake. He immediately understood the need of some privacy for the three of them and ushered them into the library, where a roaring fire warmed the chill out of them. A large tray with tea was brought to them before Butler closed the door behind him.

Sin and Fanny sat down in the cozy armchairs in front of the fire and sipped their hot tea. Rake grabbed a sandwich and walked over to the large bay window to gaze at the quiet square outside.

"What do you want to do, Fanny?" he asked, breaking the silence.

She looked up at him and shrugged lightly as he turned to glance at her, waiting for her answer. "Not kidnap or seduce him," she acknowledged with a small smile, and Rake grinned back, relieved she was still able to make a joke.

Sin obviously felt the same way and gave his sister a reluctant grin. "So, sister dear, if you're still up to it, how shall we approach the moron?"

"Oh, I'm up to it. Believe me, I'm more than up to it," Fanny said, her determination shining through.

"Really?" Rake was astonished. "You sound like you are ready to fight for this."

"Yes I am ready, and I'm ready to fight in quite as ugly a manner as necessary to gain what I want, which is my husband back at my side."

"Really?" Sin echoed, just as astonished as Rake.

This was a part of his sister he'd never met before, as she was usually all soft and sweet. Now she seemed made of steel.

Fanny leaned forward until her nose almost

touched Sin's. "I mean war," she growled.

"Yes!"

"Sin, she's serious." Rake frowned.

"And so? I sure want to go to war. I'm sick and tired of staying here, drying up all the shed tears. I must admit I much prefer to do something rather than just sit around and wait for the bloody fool to have a change of heart."

"Thank you," Fanny murmured lovingly to her brother.

"Fanny, are you sure?" her doubting uncle asked, still frowning all over his handsome face.

"Yes, Uncle Rake, I couldn't be more sure," she reassured him, trying to put all the determination she felt into her words. "I can't sit around here and let him go on with his life. Sooner or later we both will get used to our different kind of life, and then it will be too late. I have to act now, before he gets over me."

"He will never get over you."

"But he will learn how to live without me."

She had a point there, Rake had to admit. Misery always seemed endless when you were deep in it, but it would fade as time went by. Eventually it would only be a sour taste now and then.

Devlin obviously had done a great job of putting his father behind him, and it would be no problem for him to put Fanny and the baby in some vast corner of his heart and close that door forever, too.

"Do you have a plan?" Sin asked.

"Yes."

"What?"

"I'm going to beat him at his own game. I am going to live my life as if he's not a part of it."

"It won't hurt him. You are only doing exactly what he wants you to do, continuing without him."

"I know."

Rake and Sin looked at each other, not grasping her game.

"Come on, don't you get it?"

"No."

"Devlin told me something when we were dancing that made me think a little further. He said he was surprised to find me in London, as he thought I would be at Chester Park."

The men still looked like two question marks.

"Obviously he wasn't prepared for meeting me," she continued, "And so I am going to make sure he will be fully aware of my presence in London."

"Ah," Rake breathed, as he thought he finally got her plan. "We just have to find out where he will be spending his days and evenings and make sure you will be there."

"No, Uncle Rake. I'm not going to follow him around. It would just make him more determined to stay out of my way. No, I am going to stay out of his way, but at the same time make sure he knows all about what I'm up to."

"You are going to use the gossips," Sin said with a slow smile.

"Oh, yes." Fanny smiled in return.

"I don't see how this would be so much better. Staying out of his way would just be fulfilling his wish not to see you again," Rake mused, as he started to walk to and fro in front of the fire. "I don't think the gossipers have the spine to tell him directly all about you doing this or that. No, he will attend these last

311

weeks of the Season without hearing a word about you dancing with a beau."

Fanny laughed. "Did I once say I intended to go back to my life pre-Devlin? No, I'm going to start my new life as the abandoned Duchess of Hereford."

"This is so good," Sin chuckled, and rubbed his hands together.

Now Rake finally understood what she was up to, and a slow, wicked grin grew, as he stopped in front of her. "We are going to behave a little badly, aren't we?"

"What shall a poor, abandoned duchess do?"

Rake laughed and sat down in the empty chair. "You only have two weeks left of the Season, you know, so you'd better have a rather good idea how to get started immediately."

"I know. There really is no time to waste. Luckily, I have a hidden card Devlin doesn't know about."

"You do?"

"Yes, I do. You see, during those months he was courting me I got to know much about him, but he never once asked me about anything, and so he still doesn't know about Uncle Gorgeous."

Rake went perfectly still. "And Uncle Gorgeous wasn't able to attend the wedding," he mused.

"No, he had other things he had to do, and you know how sad he was about missing my wedding."

"He kept nagging your father about moving your wedding, so he could attend, and in the end George finally sent my father to shut him up."

Sin wiggled his eyebrows. "I think we need to go for a little visit tomorrow."

"Yes, indeed we do." Fanny smiled, so relieved she would get some help in making her plan work. "And as he won't be up until late, I'll spend the morning ordering a few new dresses, ones that will better suit a decadent married woman. All I have is debutante dresses, all innocent and white."

"Don't go too far."

Fanny rolled her eyes at her brother. "How shall I be able to be gossiped about if I don't have dresses that are more alluring and inviting than my high-necked virginal gowns?"

Rake grinned at Sin's obvious discomfort regarding his sister turning into a scandalous socialite, even if in name only. It was lucky she was used to being surrounded by libertines, as she wouldn't be overwhelmed by the sensual flirting that took place between men and women in search of a little fun.

"I still don't like you dressing the part," Sin muttered. "But I will let you do it, but only if you will let me have the last say about what you wear."

"Sin!"

The look Sin gave her made it clear there was no way she would get out of him having the last word, so she gave in to his demand. As he let her have her way with the rest, she guessed she couldn't be too annoyed with him.

When Fanny couldn't stop yawning, they decided to part for the evening and all get a good night's sleep. They would need it for their upcoming quest.

They were going to war.

Chapter 32

It took five days for the rumor to reach Devlin, but when it finally did, it nearly crushed him.

His wife, whom he had thought gone from London and safely tucked away at Chester Park, had stayed put and now spent her days socializing. He had been convinced she was in her grandfather's caring hands. How wrong he had been.

Fanny had been quite busy creating a minor scandal by having an affair with Tristan Knightley, the Earl of Graywood, a man known for his many love affairs.

Devlin knew Graywood, as he was a close friend of Rake's, and he had always liked him immensely.

Until now.

Now it all had changed, as the image of his wife in Graywood's muscular arms turned the friendship and respect into pure hatred. The agony Devlin felt was consuming, and the worst part of it was that he couldn't do anything about it.

He knew he had practically thrown Fanny into the arms of the awaiting wolves.

When he thought about it, it wasn't so strange she had decided to stay in town. Most members of her family had remained in London for the last part of the Season.

It made perfect sense for her to wait until they all

could travel together to Chester Park. It was the most logical and practical choice, and he hated it.

She was supposed to be elsewhere, and not here. Not where he could bump into her occasionally, even though he hadn't in the week since they met at Vauxhall Gardens.

He had bumped into Rake and some of his brothers at different assemblies during the last days, and even though they hadn't been friendly they had at least been polite.

He had tried to talk to Rake in private, but the friend had ignored his request, and instead walked away. It hurt, being ignored like this, and especially by the man he considered to be his best friend, but he had no choice but to endure. There was nothing he could do about the situation, as it all was his own fault.

He had left Fanny pregnant in the hands of her family, and even though he had given her his name and would declare the child as his, she was still abandoned. He had nursed a small hope of Rake staying his friend, as he knew all about Devlin's childhood, but the friend—or ex-friend—firmly took his niece's side.

If he hadn't met his Cousin Simon, he probably still would have had no idea what was going on. But his cousin had been too filled with malicious delight to not tease Devlin viciously about it.

Simon was born envious, and to be able to take his perfect cousin down a notch or two was something he was unable to resist. He had started the conversation nicely enough, thanking Devlin for the house and money.

"I hope you don't gamble this money away too," Devlin had pointed out, using maybe a slightly more superior tone than necessary, but Simon had a way of getting him annoyed. "It is supposed to cover all your family's expenses, including food."

"No problem," Simon had said, with an ugly leer. "I have made a bet, though, one I am not going to lose, because I have someone who can give me inside information on the matter."

"Nothing illegal, I presume?"

"Oh, no, of course not. I might be a gambler, but it doesn't mean I'm dishonest."

"I don't know why I don't believe you," Devlin had drawled, and Simon had given him another disgusted sneer.

"You have always thought you are so much better than I am, just because you were born the heir and I am a mere Mister. But you see, things have changed, and now I am the one who will be rich and famous, while you will remain alone and infamous."

"What makes you think I ever will end up alone and infamous?" Devlin had frowned, knowing deep inside his heart he didn't want to hear the answer to his question, but at the same time, he felt he had to know what his cousin meant.

"As I said earlier, I need inside information that you, my dear cousin, are the man to give me."

Now Devlin was befuddled. "About what?"

"About Fanny."

"Fanny?" Devlin had echoed hoarsely, suddenly too afraid to hear what his cousin had to say. Images of what could have happened to his wife flared before his eyes, making him sick with concern.

"Yes, Fanny. I need to know what you will do about the Graywood situation, because if I know, I can set my bet right in the Book of Bets at White's and will make a fortune."

"What Graywood situation?" Devlin had asked, unwillingly walking straight into Simon's trap.

"Don't you know?" Simon had feigned surprise.

"Know what? Is there something wrong with Fanny?"

"I wouldn't exactly call it wrong with her. I bet she thinks it's all right. Otherwise she wouldn't have made such an open thing of it."

Devlin glared at his cousin. His patience was running out fast, and he was close to hitting the man just to get him to talk.

What had happened to Fanny?

Had she had a miscarriage? Had she had an accident? Was she dead? And what was this about Graywood… Did he mean Lord Graywood?

"So what will you do?"

"Simon, please. I don't know what you're talking about."

"One would think you, as her husband, should know if there was something wrong with your wife. How is your marriage doing? Not too well, I presume, as your lovely wife has got herself a lover."

Lover!

It was amazing how such a nice word could turn into the worst he'd ever heard. Simon, of course, had not been able to stop himself from rubbing it in as much as he could.

"She has good taste, one must say. Graywood is the most eligible bachelor of the *ton*, now that you are married. Amelia is terrible envious of your wife, who steals all the best men."

Devlin hadn't said another word as Simon chatted away, instead he had rudely turned his back to his cousin and walked away. He had been stabbed in the heart and was slowly and painfully bleeding to death.

How could she?

The treachery she had done almost blew him away, because she wasn't supposed to do something like this. She was his wife, his pregnant wife. And she was his.

So what if he had left her to live her own life without him? She still had no right to continue to the next man, at least not with the baby on the way. How she decided to live her life, once the child was born, was something he didn't want to think about.

He knew he had been a bit naïve about her life before his arrival in London at the beginning of the Season, but he hadn't in his wildest imagination thought she would go out and find herself some company immediately when he left her.

As he thought about it, he realized she probably had walked straight from their lovemaking in Vauxhall Gardens to the open arms of Graywood, while he had been sitting in his carriage crying his eyes out.

Crying, for goodness' sake.

He was pathetic. She had turned him into a woman, full of self-pity. He turned the corner, and walked on into Grosvenor Square.

When he stepped through his front door, a footman came forward and handed over a thick envelope emblazoned with the royal crest. Devlin opened it immediately. A letter from the Prince Regent, Prinny as he was called by his friends, was not something to save for later.

The envelope contained an invitation to a dinner

party the same night, and Devlin quickly scribbled down an acceptance and sent it over to Charlton House.

You didn't refuse Prinny if you were in town, not if you wanted to stay in the close circle of friends who surrounded the heir to the throne.

As Devlin lay in his bath, he remembered another bath a month earlier, at Pendragon, that had led to him showing his wife how to make love in a bed. It had been the first night of the happiest time of his life, and he wished he could go back to relive those few weeks of fulfillment and happiness.

For the first time he actually pondered how life would be if he collected his wife and went back to being married. Maybe it wouldn't be so bad.

He knew he was good with the husband part. Fanny's radiant smile through those weeks had told him. So maybe he wouldn't be such a bad father, either?

He tried to picture a small boy with his golden eyes and his black hair, but he failed completely. Instead, a little girl came twirling, with brown hair, sparkling gray eyes, and a smile that sent shivers of delight through his body. The mischievous little girl's knees were full of bruises, and her dress torn from some fantastic adventure in the garden.

The memory of Fanny as a child made him smile with melancholy, as more memories popped up and took him back thirteen years, back to the only time of his childhood where he had found himself feeling secure and at ease outside of school.

She had been a little nuisance, for sure, and Rake had been furious with her for destroying their quest to become men. But he had enjoyed her feistiness and her stubborn pursuit of him.

George and Caroline had thought she was a bit embarrassing with her harassment, but he had enjoyed it. Her parents had repeatedly told him how much they admired his patience, and that he would make an excellent father someday.

He opened his eyes, as the memory of their words rang in his ears. An excellent father.

What if they were right?

What if being a husband and father was something he actually would be really good at? His own father had insisted on telling him how worthless and unwanted he was, but with Fanny he wasn't worthless. Instead, he had been admirably good at keeping her happy and content, and proved his father wrong.

Maybe Rake had been the one who had been right all along, declaring Devlin stupid in his commitment to turn wrong to right by avoiding family life. Could staying away mean Devlin simply continued Conan's legacy of misery?

He tried to picture himself as a caring father to a little girl who resembled Fanny a lot, and to his surprise it felt good, a wonderful contented feeling that grabbed his heart. Maybe being present as a father, and not only in the making, wouldn't be so bad.

But what if the Conan part of him emerged?

What if he mistreated his children in the same way his father had done to him?

He tried to picture himself doing some of the least ugly things his father had found pleasure in, and his own immediate revulsion and complete rejection of the idea made him sit straight up in the tub.

My God, how stupid was he?

He would never behave like his father. Not in this lifetime or any other, and finally it dawned on him that Rake had been right all along.

By forcing himself out of his wife's life, he was only completing the circle of Conan's madness and keeping himself—and Fanny—miserable for the rest of his life.

Oh, Lord, what had he done?

Chapter 33

Charlton House was a palace of divine beauty, a monument full of good art work. Too bad the wonderful art pieces from all corners of the world didn't look so well together; there was simply too much of everything in Prinny's stately home.

Devlin walked through the grand gallery, where paintings from every artist imaginable hung side by side, each looking as though it was trying to outshine its neighbors. In Prinny's private salon, larger than the hallway of Pendragon, the host presided in a throne-like chair, entertaining his eight guests, all close friends to him.

And among them, to Devlin's horror, sat a man whom he earlier had claimed as a friend but now was the worst sight imaginable—Lord Graywood.

Devlin went cold, and for a moment he panicked and wanted nothing but to turn around and run from the room. But another part of him wanted to stay and perhaps be able to find a reason, or at least a chance, to throttle the laughing lord who sat in a cozy armchair, chatting away with Rake.

"Ah, Hereford! How nice to see you again," Prinny said with a delighted smile. Graywood stiffened, which satisfied Devlin immensely, and turned to look at the newcomer as he heard Prinny's greeting.

"Your Royal Highness," Devlin murmured, as he

bowed politely.

It was an awkward situation, but it was most uncomfortable for Graywood, presumably, as he was the one handling someone else's wife.

Rake looked silently from one friend to another, and a small frown marred his forehead. The other six guests were standing silent, looking as though they would prefer to leave the room—an impossibility, as it would only infuriate Prinny.

"I heard it was time to congratulate you on your marriage," Prinny continued, obviously not aware of the tension in the room.

"Thank you," Devlin said sternly, and before he could stop himself, he continued, "I am the luckiest of men, married to a good woman."

In the corner of his eye, he could see Graywood shift position, and Devlin had a hard time not to grin wickedly.

"Good, good," Prinny beamed, before he turned and waved his hand toward the other men sitting around him. "You know the rest? Rake you know, of course, being an old chap of yours."

Prinny introduced the others to Devlin, who knew them all by name but not personally. They were all laughing too heartily, and he guessed the tension between himself and Graywood was the reason for it.

Rake seemed a little warmer toward him this time, and even rolled his eyes toward the merry men, and Devlin nodded with a faint smile, as he almost felt like getting all merry and joking himself so he wouldn't have to look into the eyes of the man who had bedded Fanny.

Prinny didn't introduce Graywood, and Devlin

guessed he too knew about the problem between the two former friends and was for once rather subtle about it.

"Why don't we sit down for dinner?" Prinny ushered, playing the perfect host, as he loved to do during his more private sessions.

Arriving to a dining room just as overly decorated as the gallery and salon, the guests sat down around the massive table. Soon well-functioning servants served the first course, and without any accidents.

"I brought these sausages with me from Germany, and I tell you, friends, they are simply divine. I must have eaten hundreds during my journey, and I am still not tired of them."

Devlin looked at the large sausage lying on a nest of cabbage on the plate in front of him, and he couldn't stop the image of what it looked like. He cast an eye at Rake, whose laughing eyes told him his friend saw the likeness too.

"I have come to like these wonderful creations so much, I may even consider starting a traditional national holiday by the name of the sausage."

All the men laughed politely at Prinny's joke, and as their host started to eat his sausage, the others also tasted the odd-looking food and, to their surprise and to Prinny's delight, they all found the sausages very tasty.

The chatter continued as course after course was served, and by the time they finally came to the port and cigars, Devlin thought he would die from restraining himself.

It took all his concentration not to look at Graywood. If ever he did, he wouldn't be able to stop himself from jumping over the table and hitting the man as hard as he could with his fist. Rake, who sat beside Devlin, probably knew exactly what was going on in Devlin's mind, because he kept up a steady conversation with the men closest to him and refused to let his friend out of it even once.

Not until the dinner was over did Devlin start to relax. Prinny led the way down the gallery to their carriages, as they would continue the evening at the last grand ball of the Season, and Devlin lingered to allow Graywood a chance to get out of there first.

But he'd relaxed too soon, he realized as he came to the end of the gallery and suddenly found himself alone with Graywood and Prinny. All the others had already gone on, unaware of what was happening behind their backs.

"My friends," Prinny said gravely, "you two have an issue, and I want you to resolve it."

Devlin dug his nails into his palms, hoping to keep his head cool. "Why?" he asked, trying to keep this interview short. But unfortunately it seemed Prinny had other ideas, as he turned to Graywood instead of answering Devlin's question.

"You have been friends with Rake Darling for ages, and as I understood it, have been practically an uncle for the younger ones of the family."

Graywood must have nodded his agreement, because Prinny continued without waiting for an answer. "You should have kept your distance from them, especially the young woman who also is the wife of a friend of yours."

"I have kept my distance," Graywood said solemnly, and for the first time that evening, Devlin looked straight at him.

"Oh, really?" he drawled.

"Yes, really."

"That's not what I heard," Devlin snarled, and Prinny took a step forward.

"There, there," he soothed, with a nervous laugh. "It's only a wife. You don't have to be so aggressive about it."

"Only a wife?" Devlin shouted, not believing his ears. What an unintelligent thing to say, even for Prinny. "My wife is not 'only a wife.' She is *my* wife, and I love her more than anything. She is the one thing in the world that matters to me, so to call her only a wife is a huge understatement."

Prinny started to look a bit cornered, and Devlin took a step back, so he wouldn't stand there hovering over the poor royal prince who just wanted to soothe his friend's feelings.

He opened and closed his mouth, as if he wanted to say something but didn't know how to say it.

In the end it was Graywood who ended the uncomfortable silence.

"So why did you leave her?"

Devlin's gaze left Prinny for Graywood so quickly he almost snapped his neck. "For private reasons, and none of your business, so just leave it."

"Well, if you listen to the rumors, I would say it is my business."

"You don't love her."

"How do you know I don't?"

"If you did, you wouldn't have waited this long to make your move, as you have known her during her entire life. You must have had hundreds of chances to fall in love with her, flirt with her, court her."

"Maybe I'm not the marrying kind, and this suits me better."

Devlin growled, a deep guttural sound from some medieval part of him deep inside his fashionable outside, and this time Prinny grabbed his arm and, with one surprisingly strong pull, dragged him back so he wouldn't stand so close to Graywood.

"Besides," Graywood continued, "I have another young lady in mind for becoming Lady Graywood, as she's got a certain part of England in her dowry that I want and the only way for me to get my hands on it is by marrying her."

"You do?" Prinny asked, interested. "Where might this be?"

"Yorkshire. There is a small slip of land between my estate and the small lake abounding with fish, and I want it, just as my father and grandfather wanted it, and now I finally have it in my power to get it."

"Why don't you just buy it?" Prinny asked, without letting go of Devlin's arm.

"The owners have always refused to sell to us, because of an old family rivalry thing. But now there is only a daughter of the late owner left, and as she is of marriageable age and a widow, I have finally found a way to get the land."

"Poor girl," Devlin gritted through his teeth, wanting to hurt Graywood in any way possible, but the other man just shrugged indifferently.

"So?" he said uncaring. "She'll have to learn to live with it, just as your wife had to find a way to cope with you abandoning her."

The last insult was too much for Devlin's restraint, and with a growl of war, he ripped his arm free from

Prinny's grasp and hurled himself at Graywood, punching the poor man hard on the chin.

Prinny shouted for help as he tried to wrench the two fighters apart, but it was a lost cause. This fight was bound to happen sooner or later. Servants and watchmen came running and succeeded in splitting the two combatants, but not before Devlin had a chance to send his fist deep into Graywood's midriff.

"Put them in my office," Prinny ordered the servants, and led the way through the hallway, where more servants stood staring, wondering what the commotion was all about.

Rake, who was the only other dinner guest who remained at Charlton House, followed the procession into the spacious room that functioned as the personal office of the Prince Regent.

Devlin and Graywood were placed in armchairs on opposite sides of the room, and the four men were left alone again as the butler closed the large doors. Rake walked over to Graywood and looked at his chin, which was already starting to bruise.

"My, my." Rake grinned as he looked at the bruised chin. "I have to admit that was one good punch."

"Enough is enough," Prinny pleaded. "Now I want you to promise me to behave the next time you two meet each other. This is not the way two gentlemen act when it comes to an argument. If you want to settle this in a more gentlemanly way, you should do what we all do when someone does us wrong. You have to duel."

"What?" the three gentlemen in the office gasped.

"You have to duel," Prinny repeated cheerfully.

"You want us dead?" Devlin asked, astounded, as

both he and Graywood were excellent shots, and he knew Prinny was aware of it.

"But it's illegal," Rake objected.

"I don't think this can go on without them making up somehow, and I don't think Hereford ever will forgive Graywood for flirting with his wife, even though it's such an innocent occurrence, and happens all the time."

"Innocent occurrence?" Devlin repeated, aghast, staring at his royal friend with disdain. This wasn't leading to anything good, and Rake changed the subject.

"So where shall the duel take place?"

"I think Green Park will do just fine," Prinny mused. "My guards will make sure no one comes close enough to see who the contestants are."

Graywood nodded solemnly, rubbing his sore chin. He seemed to think a duel was a good idea, and Devlin wanted to laugh out loud; he was getting a chance to put a bullet in the bastard's black heart, and he was going to make his best of it.

It was like the good Lord in the sky had listened to his heart's prayers and sent him a way to fulfill them.

"Shall we say at dawn?" Rake asked, and Prinny nodded.

"We shall," he agreed, and turned to each man and bade him a good night before leaving them alone.

Rake immediately ushered Devlin out of the office and into an awaiting carriage that started to roll as soon as they sat down.

The last thing Devlin saw, as the carriage rocked away from Charlton House, was Graywood standing alone on the steps, looking as resolute as Devlin felt.

It dawned on him that he was about to kill a friend. Someone who up until this point had always been a person he relied on, someone he would have turned to in an hour of need.

Graywood should have been with him, not against him, and the darkness of the situation grew on him. Graywood was a good person and not meant to be killed before he had a chance to accomplish anything.

He had goals with his life, a marriage in the future, and maybe one day he too would father his own children.

How easily things had degenerated!

Devlin didn't want to kill the man, but he couldn't stand down now. Graywood was, after all, having an affair with his wife, and it wasn't something Devlin ever could, or would, forgive.

The duel would be carried out, but Devlin knew in his heart he had no choice.

The loser would have to be him.

He would never be able to live with himself if he killed Graywood, and he didn't think Fanny would forgive him for it, either. And when one honestly thought about it, what did he have left to live for?

Nothing.

He had failed in every part of his life, and the pain in his chest was so profound he had trouble breathing.

His father had won the battle.

Devlin would leave the world as he had entered it, alone and unwanted. He closed his eyes and saw immediately the picture of Fanny before him. He had wanted so much to do the right thing, and all he had ended up with was making everyone miserable.

He was worthless.

He felt Rake's probing eyes and kept his head turned away so his friend wouldn't see the grief that welled up inside him.

He knew what he had to do, and the only regret he had was that he wouldn't be able to tell Fanny how much he loved her once more before he died.

Chapter 33

Fanny let her partner lead her across the dance floor, but her heart wasn't in it.

Something was wrong; she could feel it in every cell of her body. As she looked around, everything seemed just as it should, but subconsciously she knew something awful was about to happen.

She scanned the crowd, as her partner twirled her in the soft waltz, and had no trouble finding her husband standing in the far corner, surrounded by women flirting outrageously with him. He looked dark and brooding, and even from this distance, she felt her heart skip a beat, and she knew she hadn't a chance when it came to feeling indifferent toward him.

Rake had looked a little worried earlier when she got him alone after he and Devlin had arrived at the grand ball, but he had told her not to worry, as he had everything under control.

Graywood stood at the other end of the ballroom, and he too was surrounded by unmarried women of all ages. He too looked jaded, and his chin had the same deep blue color as his evening jacket.

Something was wrong, and she knew she had only one way of finding out what. When the dance was over, she excused herself from her partner and left him standing alone on the dance floor with his mouth open. She hurried over to her parents and, telling her mother quietly she had a bit of a headache, asked if it would be all right if she went home ahead of them.

Her mother immediately wanted to go with her, but Fanny knew how much she loved these balls and quickly made sure Caroline stayed put.

Instead she asked Penelope to go with her.

Penelope, who had been, in effect, dragged to the assembly, agreed thankfully, and in a minute the two were on their way. Fanny sat considering her silent friend, who stared through the dark window without noticing the carriage was heading the wrong direction.

Penelope had had to suffer through a great shock when they arrived at the ball earlier and found both her father and sister were attending the ball, and she had requested to be taken home immediately. But the Darlings had insisted she stay for a short while, as they knew they might never be able to convince her to go out with them again if they let her escape immediately.

Charmaine had, to Fanny's surprise, given her a letter for her sister, and now she took it out from her reticule and handed it over to her friend. Penelope looked at it like it was a poisonous snake before she finally took it and ripped it open. Fanny waited until Penelope had read it all, then broke the silence.

"What did it say?"

Penelope bent her head, a tear falling onto the paper in her hands. "She misses me."

"How nice."

Penelope nodded, folded the letter neatly, and put it in her pocket. "She says mother is sick, but father won't let her meet me."

"Oh, Penelope," Fanny said compassionately, and one small sob became a torrent of tears from Penelope.

She fell into her friend's arms, crying her heart out. Her mother's illness had finally broken the barrier, and even though it was an awful situation for Penelope, she still needed to get her grief into the open and not keep it closed inside her heart as she had until now.

The raw sobs shook Penelope's petite body, and Fanny soothingly stroked and patted her back until her friend only hiccupped slightly. When Penelope finally managed to compose herself enough to sit up, Fanny gave her a warm hug and was rewarded with a shaky smile.

Her friend would come through this, maybe not immediately, but somewhere in the future.

"Feeling better?" she asked, and Penelope nodded.

"It's just that it hurts so much," she whispered. "I never knew how much I cared for them until I lost them. And now Mother is sick, and there is nothing I can do about it."

"We'll find a way," Fanny said resolutely.

"We will?" Penelope smiled. "Well, I know you are resourceful enough to make it happen."

Fanny laughed at her friend's teary-eyed banter. "I cannot deny the truth," she replied with a dainty shrug, and the two friends smiled at each other, feeling the warmth of their love drying up the last tears.

The carriage stopped, and when the door was opened by the driver, the two ladies climbed out. Penelope looked up at the imposing house before them and stopped dead. "This is not home," she said slowly.

"No."

"This is Charlton House."

"Yes."

"What are we doing here?"

"We are going for a little visit."

"At Charlton House?" Penelope questioned her friend, as if she thought Fanny had completely lost her mind.

Fanny didn't answer but gave her friend a smile meant to soothe her worries and took Penelope's arm. They climbed the stairs up to the front door, where two watchmen looked down on them.

"Would you please tell His Royal Highness that the Duchess of Hereford is here, with a friend, to see him?"

One of the watchmen opened the door and talked quietly with someone inside, closed it again, and faced them. "One minute," he said gravely, before he looked over their heads, ignoring them very effectively.

They had to wait for ten minutes before the door opened again. A butler ushered the two ladies inside and showed them into a small parlor, where they sat to wait for the Prince Regent.

"Do you really think he will come?" Penelope whispered.

"Of course he will," Fanny said with assurance.

"How can you be sure of it?"

"Have you forgotten he is my godfather?" Fanny asked, smiling, just as the door opened and Prinny walked into the room.

"Fanny, my darling," he greeted, obviously happy to see her.

"Uncle Gorgeous," Fanny squealed, and leaped into his open arms. They hugged closely for a long time before he held her away from himself and looked at her with loving eyes.

"You look good, my love," he said.

"I am good."

"Are you sure?" he asked sincerely, and she nodded.

"Yes I am, because I know this will all end well when the stubborn goat finally gives in and comes back to me, to let me love him for the rest of his life."

Prinny smiled at her youthful cheerfulness, and gave her a peck on her forehead. "Oh, I'm so happy to see you, and I'm so sorry I missed your wedding, but I had to go to Germany, as I had promised my wife this a long time ago, and her family aren't as forgiving as you are."

He looked at Penelope, who stood behind Fanny unaware she looked rather stupid with her mouth hanging open.

"And you must be the de Vere girl Fanny always talks about. The best friend ever."

Penelope closed her mouth and nodded before she remembered her manners and gave him a deep curtsy. He accepted courteously. Then he rang the bell, told the butler to get them a tray with tea and cakes, and ushered the two ladies to comfortable seats.

"So why do you grant me the pleasure of your company at one o'clock in the middle of the bloody night?"

"I want to know what they are up to."

Prinny looked confused at first, before comprehension dawned, and his guilt-stricken face told her she had made the right decision coming here.

"Fanny, I can't tell you."

"Yes, you can. It's my husband we are talking about."

"But they are my friends, and I promised Rake…"

"I don't care," she interrupted. "You promised me

first, when you accepted becoming my godfather."

Prinny gave her a dark look. "This is blackmail."

"I know."

Prinny sighed, and she knew she'd won, as she had known she would from the beginning. Her dear godfather had never been able to tell her no. She felt a little ashamed for using him like this, but Devlin was too important to her.

"You must love him."

"I do."

"And he loves you, you know."

"Yes, I know."

"Poor man, he's suffering a lot about Graywood and you."

"I know."

"You are an evil woman."

Fanny just smiled wickedly, and Prinny couldn't help but grin back.

"Well, well." He sighed. "I guess I'll have to tell you the truth."

"Yes, you must."

He stood up and walked over to the bay window, clasping his hands behind his back.

Penelope turned to Fanny with her eyes as big as plates; this was all a bit much for a depressed young lady to take in, although she didn't look much depressed at the moment.

Just as Prinny turned, apparently having decided what to say, the door opened and the butler entered with a large tray filled with tea and cakes. He placed it on the table next to the sofa before silently leaving the room, and the door closed tightly behind him.

Prinny squealed with delight and clapped his hands

together as he seated himself on the sofa. Fanny served him and Penelope a cup of tea each before she sat in an armchair with one of her own. She kicked off her shoes and curled her legs and aching feet up in the chair beneath her, and Prinny couldn't help but grin at her; she looked too much like an innocent little girl, not a duchess married to one of England's most powerful nobles.

"So?" Fanny probed, and Prinny sighed.

"Can't I at least finish my lovely cup of tea?"

"No."

Another sigh. "Well, well."

"What happened tonight? Rake told me you invited my husband and Graywood here to get Devlin to take a stand and question the situation and stop ignoring it with his head deep in the sand. Graywood, who is the dearest friend a woman ever could have, has done a great job helping me create the scandal, although Devlin has been rather slow with his actions."

"He certainly has," Penelope agreed. "One would think he would have gotten rather upset by now, not just grinding his teeth to dust and keeping silent."

"He'll soon be out of teeth to grind." Fanny giggled.

Prinny shook his head with a superior, manly grin, and offered them more of the delicious cakes before he helped himself to another large one.

"So my question still remains: what happened earlier tonight?"

"Devlin finally snapped."

"Yes!" Fanny jumped up and shouted, and the other two laughed at her obvious delight.

"Please settle down, my dear, before the watchmen

come barging in here to save me."

Fanny blushed prettily and sat down again as requested. "I was simply declaring my satisfaction with the situation."

"Indeed, and most clearly, too. I don't think anyone in this room misunderstood your feelings regarding your husband having a breakdown."

"Putting it like that, it sounds like I'm a terrible person." Fanny laughed.

"Immphheed," Prinny answered, his mouth full of cake.

"Devlin snapped, you say?" Fanny probed to get her godfather to continue his story.

"Ah, yes," Prinny said, trying to remember what had been said and done. "He got very angry and hit Graywood on the chin, and just when we thought we had him under control he hit him in the stomach. Poor Graywood, he was quite taken, even though he assured us he didn't mind, because a little pain was nothing if you two would live the rest of your life in heavenly bliss."

"Poor Graywood," Fanny said, feeling guilty even though he had been more than keen on acting the bad part.

"And as we agreed upon, I declared a duel to be the only way out."

"So?"

"Devlin accepted."

Penelope gasped with horror and Fanny became pale in an instant. "He did what?"

"He accepted the duel, and we will all meet in Green Park at dawn to watch them execute it."

"Oh, my goodness!" Fanny sat dumbfounded.

Their plan had been to get Devlin to snap and go after Graywood, so they would finally be able to get through to him, to be able to tell him what they thought about him putting himself on the outside of the happiness window looking in. As he and Graywood were good friends, they had been so sure he would refuse and realize how stupidly he was behaving. And he would come for her, and she would tell him the truth, how he was and always would be the only man for her.

She didn't mind the *ton* continuing their gossip about her supposed affair with Graywood, as long as Devlin knew there was no truth in the rumors.

"But tell him he is stupid, and how this was all a prank to get to him."

"Doesn't work, I'm afraid. Rake says he has closed himself completely, like a clam, and won't open up. We can't get through to him."

"Oh, my goodness," Fanny repeated, and clutched her hands in a grip that made her knuckles go white.

Penelope put her hand on her friend's and gave her a sympathetic smile.

But Fanny was devastated.

She had been so sure she would finally have an end to this stupidity of Devlin's, but instead it seemed she had only made things worse.

Devlin would never behave like this if he didn't think he had no choice. He was a good, good man, and what scared her most was that the fool probably was thinking of getting himself killed. She had no other explanation to his extremely ridiculous behavior.

"We have to stop them," she whispered. "Before someone gets hurt."

"We will."

She looked at Prinny with surprise, as he did sound a little smug. "How?" she asked.

"We are not going to put bullets in the guns, only gunpowder, and so maybe Devlin finally will understand how dumb the idea of killing his friend is."

Fanny opened her mouth to tell her godfather what she really thought about Devlin's plan for the outcome, but she closed it again.

This whole scheme had come to a horrible end, and maybe it would have been better if she had done what she'd thought in the first place—get Devlin alone and sit on him until he listened to what she had to say.

But her family had kept showering her with their grand ideas and intriguing schemes. They thought Devlin should realize his faults by himself, so that he would be the one to come to her and apologize, not the other way around. She had liked that thought, but now doubt was slowly wheezing its way in.

She loved her family with all her heart, but she loved Devlin too, and the one thing she wanted most in the world was to have Devlin back, to continue with their lives at Pendragon, and to give birth to so many children Mrs. Blair would faint with sheer happiness.

As if on cue, the baby moved perceptibly inside her for the first time, and tears filled her eyes. Had she been so eager to listen to her relatives that she had forgotten all about Devlin?

Her parents and Rake had been there when Devlin left her at Pendragon, and they had immediately taken over, rushing her down to Chester Park, figuring out what to do.

She had lived in a daze until she met Devlin at

Vauxhall Gardens and all the small pieces of her life had come together again in his arms. She felt complete with him, and without him she was a mess in the hands of her overprotective family, who would do anything for her, especially anything they thought was best for her.

She was a grown woman and a married one, and she should know by herself what to do. What if she had been alone with Devlin at Pendragon when she realized she was pregnant? Well, to begin with, she wouldn't have realized it until some time later, but if Devlin had left her then, she would have followed him and told him exactly what she thought of him and his plans.

She would never have gone to London, would never have made the whole *ton* think she was a loose woman. No, she more than likely would have locked herself in a room with Devlin, refusing to open the door until he told her he loved her more than anything and would never leave her again.

She had let her relatives undo the thing that was *her* new family, the family she now had with Devlin, and the small baby inside her. Those two were everything she needed and everything she wanted.

She closed her eyes and decided that from this day forward she would take care of this family by herself. No more helping relatives, best friends, or godfathers.

She was going to go to her husband and beg him to take her back. She would beg him on her bare knees if she had to, as long as he held her once more and told her he would love her forever and would never, ever let her go.

Chapter 34

Devlin stood silently in the darkness of Green Park, waiting for the others to arrive.

He felt numb, like nothing mattered anymore.

All he wanted was to get it all done with, to end his life so the misery that had been his constant companion lately would be over, and thus make sure Fanny could go on with her life.

He closed his eyes and took a deep breath. He was ready to die.

"Please don't."

It was amazing; he could actually hear her voice. It was so real, almost as if she were there with him on the dewy lawn.

"Devlin?"

This time her voice was closer, as though she was standing beside him, and he opened his eyes and looked at his wife, who did indeed stand there, nervously wringing her hands, looking tired and worn.

He smiled at her with genuine delight at first, but when she just looked at him seriously with tear-filled eyes, the smile faded away, and he realized she wasn't something from his imagination— she was real and she was there.

With him.

In the park.

In the middle of the night.

"What on earth are you doing here in the middle of the night? My God, Fanny, are you out of your mind? Don't you know how many villains roam the streets of London during the nightly hours?"

He took the few steps to her and grabbed her wringing hands in his. He could feel her shiver, and he glared at her. "You're freezing," he said accusingly, and she frowned at him.

"My freezing is not important," she objected in a shaky, angry voice. "You are what is important, and I won't have it."

He looked at her, confused. "What are you talking about?"

"You wanting to get yourself killed is important, not my freezing."

"Ho-how did you…"

"I'm your bloody wife," she said between her teeth. "I'm supposed to know what you are up to."

He let go of her hands and took a step back to clear his mind.

How could she know?

Who could have told her about his plans?

Nobody—he answered his own question—because nobody knew about his plan to not shoot Graywood. She had figured it out all by herself, and for a second love and pride swelled his heart. But it passed quickly, and the numbness took over again.

"You should be happy," he snarled. "Graywood will still be alive."

"I don't care about Graywood," she cried out, obviously running out of patience with him.

"But I do. Graywood is the one you chose, the one you spread your legs for. He is the one who will have everything I ever wanted, as soon as I am no longer around."

"So stay and take it for yourself."

"It's too late for that," he whispered. "I already accepted the duel, and I can't kill him, as he's my friend and, furthermore, the man you want to spend your life with. I'm doing this for you, Fanny. Can't you just accept it?"

Instead of looking thankful, she stared at him with a strange mix of astonishment, laughter, outrage, and pity. "Do you think I want you dead?" she gasped.

"Of course not, you're not that kind of person, but this way you will get a happy life, and I don't have to live watching you from the side."

"So don't."

He looked at her bewildered, not understanding what she meant.

"Don't watch me from afar. Live with me, instead. Spend the rest of your life with me. Let me make you happy."

"I can't," he whispered. "I have to face Graywood."

"Why?"

"Why?!" he bellowed. "Because he has had you. He has made love to you. Kissed you…"

His voice broke, and he turned around again, trying to hide his tears from her. He felt her hand on his back, and he took another step to get away from her, but she followed, and this time she quickly scooted around him and found her way into his arms, where she hugged him closely so he couldn't get away.

At first he was stiff, as welcoming as a plank, trying to force himself to mentally ignore her, but her touch and her scent sent shivers through his body, and with a deep sigh he gave in and folded his arms around her. He pressed her even closer to him before he buried his face in her hair, smelling the wonderful familiar scent of her.

"I love you," she whispered into his chest.

"I know," he admitted, while kissing her forehead.

"Do you?"

"Why, yes… At least, I think you do. Don't you?"

"I just said I did."

"Ah, yes, then I believe you do."

He thought she mumbled something about him being stupid, but he wasn't sure, and he wasn't going to ask her. They stood silently hugging each other tightly for a while, enjoying the familiarity of it.

"So the duel with Graywood is just because of me?" Fanny asked quietly, breaking the comfortable silence, but she felt the need to hurry on a bit, because soon the others would join them and she wouldn't have Devlin and his attention all to herself anymore.

"Yes," Devlin answered stiffly.

"Then you don't have to."

"Of course I have to. I have to defend your honor."

She bent backwards, without letting go of him, so she could meet his eyes. "My bloody honor doesn't mean anything," she said disrespectfully, and he glared at her.

"Your honor is important to me."

"Not to me," she snapped, and he frowned at her.

"How can it not be? When everything else is gone, your honor is all you have left."

"No, it isn't. If you don't duel, I will still have you."

He snorted over her illogical arguments, and she had to hide her face for a second, just so he wouldn't see the smile she couldn't stop. He was such a wonderful, intelligent, beautiful man, and yet sometimes he was just plain stupid.

"But if I go through with the duel, you will have Graywood," he pointed out.

"I don't want Graywood."

"But why…"

"I just don't."

"So why have an affair with him?"

"Have you thought of marriage to all the women you have been with?"

"No, only with you."

"So, there you have it! Graywood is just a fling. You are forever."

"But my affairs have been before our marriage. Yours has been during it."

"So Lady Ashton means nothing to you?"

He actually blushed, and she leaned forward and kissed his lips before he had a chance to stop her. The feeling of his lips against hers was divine, and she had to force herself to end it much sooner than she wanted to. She was starving for his touch, but this wasn't the time.

"I never bedded Maria," he said in defense.

"I never bedded Graywood."

Her confession caught him off guard. "You didn't?"

"No."

"B-but…"

She wagged her finger at him, and gave him her best governess look. "You should be ashamed of

347

yourself, Your Grace, for thinking so low of me. I am your wife, and if you had thought about it, you would have known I would never disrespect you or our marriage, and never ever with a friend of yours."

He had to give her this one.

He had been so full of hate for himself for leaving her he had almost welcomed the rumor when it came, because he could focus on her doing something wrong instead of on his own faults.

He looked down into her face and followed lovingly the lines of it with his eyes. She was so perfect in every little way. Maybe she would never be the beauty queen of the *ton*, but to him she was the most beautiful woman in the world.

"I love you," he said tenderly, and tears filled her eyes.

"Don't say it like that!"

"Like how?"

"Like you are telling me goodbye, because you aren't. You are going to tell Graywood and the other men you won't be doing any duels tonight, or any other night."

"Fanny…" Devlin started but was immediately interrupted by his wife.

"There is nothing to argue about. I said 'no,' and 'no' it is."

"All right."

"Really?"

"Mm-hmm," he said as he bent forward and put his lips against hers, and when he felt her response, he gave her a kiss that curled her toes.

They were so thoroughly distracted by their kiss they never noticed the men who joined them. Not until a very familiar voice interrupted it.

"Well, well, what do we have here?"

Devlin looked up and met the unreadable eyes of Prinny, who stood there together with Rake and Graywood.

He cursed under his breath. What a good spy he was, who didn't even notice three men walking up to him in the middle of the night in an empty park.

Fanny turned to see what was causing her husband to stop ravishing her mouth so delightfully and then took a step back so she stood beside Devlin instead of in front of him.

She could tell by the faces of her two uncles they were not going to let Devlin get away too easily. He had hurt her and so he should be punished, and she guessed all she had to do was to try to soothe it slightly for him by standing by his side.

"Your Royal Highness." Devlin bowed politely before nodding sternly toward the two other men.

"Hereford."

"Enjoying the moonlight?" Rake drawled, and crossed his arms before his chest. Fanny couldn't help smiling at the mere look of him. He was the perfect dandy, dressed in spotless eveningwear and looking like he should be in a ballroom, not in Green Park in the wee hours of the morning. He, of course, didn't miss her smile and arched his eyebrow in a ridiculously high manner, making himself look even more a libertine than before.

"It certainly is a lovely evening," Devlin answered.

"Rather late for an evening, wouldn't you say?"

"Then I have to say you are up uncommonly early, Darling."

"As are you, Hereford."

"There, there," Prinny said with a jolly laugh that effectively ended the highly intelligent conversation. "Why don't we all go down to my carriage to discuss this evening, er, morning's happenings? Oh, not you; you go home."

The last sentence was directed to Fanny, who had plastered herself to Devlin as he started in the direction Prinny pointed. She stopped and gave her godfather a look that made it clear she was not planning to obey him.

"I will not."

Devlin stiffened, knowing how easily offended Prinny was, and neither he nor Fanny had good things coming if he got upset with them.

"You will too."

"You can't force me!"

"Oh, yes, I can."

"Oh, come on," Rake interrupted. "She's never going to give in, so why not just let her come with us?"

Prinny looked at Rake and sighed, defeated. "I know. I just thought it was worth a try."

Devlin frowned at them.

There was too much familiarity between the three of them, and the way Fanny and Prinny had been arguing reminded him of her bantering with her brothers and uncles. "Are you related?" he asked, confused.

"Why, yes." Prinny laughed. "Haven't you heard? We are all members of the royal family."

They all laughed at his joke, everyone except Devlin, who frowned even harder.

"No, really, are you?"

Fanny went to Prinny and put her arms around his waist, leaning her head against his shoulder while his arms surrounded her in a loving embrace.

"He's my Uncle Gorgeous."

"Your what?"

"He's her godfather, you fool," Rake spat, as his patience with his nephew-in-law and best friend ran out. "And a rather interfering one, for sure."

"I am not," Prinny defended himself.

"Oh, yes, you are." Fanny laughed, and gave his cheek a kiss before she released herself from his embrace and returned to her husband's side. "But you have never heard me complain about it."

Devlin closed his eyes and groaned.

This was just getting better and better. Not only did she have the most attentive family, now he would have the Prince Regent of England on his back, too.

"So the duel?" Rake probed.

Devlin looked at Graywood, who stood silent beside Prinny and glared at him. "It's over, but I tell you one thing, though," he said sternly. "If you ever, ever do anything to me like this again, I *will* duel with you, and I will actually try to shoot you."

Graywood snorted, but Devlin could see he got the apology, and his relief that the truth was in the open was clear to them all.

Prinny clapped his hands together. "What a wonderful outcome to this horrible event. I must admit, Devlin, that I was against the whole thing when Rake and Fanny approached me. But look how well it all turned out. Wonderful, indeed."

Devlin looked from the Prince Regent to Rake and then to Fanny. "Do I even…"

"No." Fanny shook her head. "I promise to tell you one day, but not now. Not yet. Let's just put this aside for now and go home."

"I still have a lot of things to say," Rake puffed, but the married couple happily ignored him, Devlin instead grabbing Fanny's hand.

"If you don't mind, Rake, I would rather enjoy the company of my wife, if it's all right with you?"

Prinny grinned and dragged the muttering Rake into the carriage. The driver closed the door, jumped to his seat, and in a minute the Duke and Duchess of Hereford stood alone in Green Park, looking lovingly into each other's eyes.

Devlin lifted his hand and caressed her soft cheek with so much love in his eyes his wife burst into tears and threw herself into his waiting arms.

She cried and laughed, and cried a little more before she calmed down. "I'm sorry," she whispered, feeling a bit embarrassed over her emotional behavior.

"It's okay," he said softly. "I guess it's been a little much for you lately."

She laughed, teary-eyed, and took a step back so she could see his face in the moonlight, without releasing his hands. "Is everything fine between us again?" she asked, her eyes telling him how serious she was.

"It is."

"And you won't leave me again?"

"Never."

"And you will love all our babies, and be the most wonderful father ever to them?"

He felt something wet run down his cheek, and he knew he was crying openly, but he didn't try to hide it.

He wanted her to know how much he cared about her, and how much she meant to him.

He had hurt her so badly, and he guessed it would take some time before she trusted him completely again. But it was a price he was willing to pay because nothing in the world mattered more to him than her.

"I will start with the little girl you're carrying now, and continue with the rest of them."

She tried to make sense of what he'd just said. "A little girl?"

"Mm-hmm."

"Why do you think it's a little girl? It might be a little boy."

"I know it's a little girl, the first of many."

She couldn't help but laugh. "You can't know it's a girl, and besides, you keep forgetting I come from a family that has been breeding only boys for generations, so I would rather say it will only be boys."

"No, it will be girls. Many girls."

"You are a silly man."

He started to walk faster, hauling her with him.

"Why are you in such a hurry?" she gasped, trying to breathe as they left the park and hurried up Park Lane, rushing past house after house.

"I want you in my bed. Now."

"Oh." Well, she had nothing against his plans, so she walked faster, and soon they were running hand in hand toward their home in Grosvenor Square.

Epilogue

Devlin stood in the corner of the Easton House ballroom and glared at the young beaus who kept staring toward his family with eagerness and determination. He had thought to subdue them by mere looks, but the puppies didn't notice him at all.

No, they were all too busy drooling over the three pretty young ladies in white who stood between him and Fanny.

When Rake strolled up to him and winked wickedly, Devlin cursed between his teeth. He really didn't need his friend's bantering right now, but he knew he had no choice, as Rake wasn't known for being subtle.

"You know, it's rather hilarious?"

"It's not fun at all," Devlin growled, sending one especially killing look toward a dandy who happened to come too close.

"Oh, yes, man, it is. Here you are, one of the biggest libertines of your time, trying to keep this year's libertines away from your daughters."

Devlin sent him a look that would have killed a man with less toughened skin, but Rake only laughed.

"Seven daughters, Devlin, seven! Why?"

"I don't know why. Maybe it is God's way of making a joke. He does work in mysterious ways, you know."

A Family Affair

Rake looked at the threesome of girls, who couldn't hide their obvious excitement over their first ball. "And triplets. You sure don't know how to make an easy start."

Rake whacked Devlin in the back before continuing on his quest to harass all his friends, and Devlin looked down at his three oldest girls with his heart almost bursting with love and pride.

It hadn't been an easy start, Rake was right about that, but he would never want to change a minute of it. They were so lovely, his flowers, and he knew he was silly for wanting to grab them and take them home and force them to stay children forever.

He guessed most parents felt the same way, with a certain amount of grief as the children grew up and turned into young adults. Soon they would be married, all three of them, and have children of their own, and he had to swallow the lump that came into his throat at the mere thought.

Could anything be of bigger moment than his children's children? Thank God he still had more children at home to love and cherish, although eventually it would be only him and Fanny left, and the children and their families would come to visit and be gone again.

He lifted his eyes and met Fanny's adoring ones over the heads of their daughters, and he sent her all the love in his heart. She gave him a smile that told him he would have something really nice to look forward to when they returned home, but he guessed, listening to his daughters' excited voices, it would not be as soon as he'd like.

It was incredible how much love was daily

355

bestowed on him from his wife and children, and he knew they had transformed him into the man he was today.

A man not afraid of love or trust.

A man who gladly opened his heart to let sunshine and laughter in.

He sent a thought to his father, the man who had tried so hard to destroy his son's every chance of happiness and almost succeeded, and he felt only pity for him.

The orchestra played its first dance, and in a second they were surrounded by eligible bachelors asking their daughters to dance. Fanny agreed before Devlin had a chance to deny them all, and soon the two stood there alone, watching their offspring twirling on the dance floor.

"How fast times fly," Fanny said, with a sad smile.

"I just thought the same. Soon they will be married and have children of their own."

"Soon it will be only you and me left in our big old drafty house." Fanny winked, and he laughed before shocking the people close to them by putting a kiss on his wife's pretty nose.

Her scent filled his head, and he felt a contentment he knew would last forever. "I love you so much, my darling," he whispered into her ear.

"And I love you."

Life was good.

A word about the author...

Jennifer Wenn has been a great lover of romantic books since she read her first Barbara Cartland at a tender age. When not enjoying life with her husband and their children, she spends every last precious minute tapping away on her laptop.

You can read more about Jennifer at:
www.jenniferwenn.com